LOVE IN EVERY BITE

LOST CREEK, TEXAS HILL COUNTRY
BOOK FOUR

ALEXA ASTON

PROLOGUE

MARCH—AUSTIN

*E*merson Frost glanced at the clock, knowing her friend Finley Farrow would arrive at any moment. She began wiping down the counter, eager to leave the bakery.

And hopefully land a teaching position in Lost Creek, Texas.

Her companion, a high schooler who was the niece of the owner, leaned against the wall, scrolling through her phone. The girl hated having to work here and did as little as she could.

The bell above the door chimed, and she glanced up, seeing Finley breeze in. Her roommate from their freshman year in college was a natural beauty, an inch taller than Emerson's own five feet and three inches, with blonde hair and startling aquamarine eyes. Although they had only roomed together that first year, Emerson knew she and Finley would be lifelong friends.

"You ready?" Finley asked, smiling.

"Let me get my things," she said, heading to the back, where she told Joe, the bakery's owner, that she was clocking out.

His wife, who was icing a cake, said, "Good luck with your interview, Emerson."

Emerson removed her apron, hanging it on the peg with her name above it. She picked up the sturdy brown paper sack with handles, which contained her interview outfit, PJs for tonight, and a few toiletries. Returning to the front of the bakery, she saw Finley buying cookies.

"I'll also need some kolaches," her friend said, picking out some in apple, pear, and cherry.

Finley paid for her purchases and then turned to Emerson. "I also got two bottles of water for us. Let's hit the road."

The pair went to Finley's new car, an early graduation gift from her parents, and got in. They drove through Austin, talking about the upcoming interview they both had tomorrow at Lost Creek Elementary, where Finley had gone to school.

Once they were on the highway, Emerson said, "I can't thank you enough for driving back to Austin to get me, Finley, and letting me stay at your house tonight. Your friendship means the world to me." Her voice wavered as her eyes misted over.

Her friend reached out and took Emerson's hand, squeezing it.

"I'm happy to do so, Em. Besides, we can be nervous about tomorrow's interview together."

She thought Finley had the job in the bag. Her friend's family owned a Montessori preschool in Lost Creek, and Finley had talked over the past few years about what a tight-knit community her hometown was. She would be certain to land one of the two open positions. Emerson only hoped she could be hired for the other one.

Already, she'd had two interviews this week, one with Austin ISD and another with a charter school in the area. She had presented herself as best she could, but both times, the person interviewing her seemed disinterested, as if they were merely going through the motions and had already decided upon another candidate for the teaching position.

"So, how have you been spending spring break?" she asked.

"I've read a couple of books. For fun. I haven't had time to do that since last summer. I also helped Ches and Sally with some inventory."

Finley's brother and wife owned Hill Country Water Sports, which was located on Lost Creek Lake. They rented equipment such as kayaks and jet skis.

"Other than that, I finished writing that final paper that's due for our Ed Leadership class. Have you finished yours yet?"

"I wrote it last weekend."

"Of course, you did," Finley said, laughing. "You always get every assignment done before anyone else."

Emerson had to. Working two part-time jobs while taking a full load of classes at UT meant she had to use her time extremely wisely.

"You'd be proud of me," Finley told her. "I've completed the rest of my lesson plans for the last month of student teaching and already submitted them to my cooperating teacher for approval. I'll be glad when we're done with student teaching. I'm itching to have my own students and do things the way I want and not how The Dragon wants them done. You are so lucky you did your student teaching in the fall and had a great mentor."

Finley called her cooperating teacher The Dragon with good cause. Emerson had completed her student teaching at the same elementary school and had been relieved not to be under The Dragon's supervision. Finley was a bright light and eager to teach, full of creative ideas, but The Dragon had tried her best to snuff out that light.

"How are things between you and Jeb going?" she asked.

As Finley talked, Emerson wanted to tell her friend she didn't think Jeb was good enough for her. The couple had been dating for the past three years, and Emerson had never warmed to Jeb. She thought the frat boy was a self-centered asshole who took his girlfriend for granted and would eventually break Finley's heart. When he did— and she was certain this was a given —Emerson would never say *I told you so*. She'd simply help Finley pick up the pieces and start again.

They arrived in Lost Creek, a place Emerson had visited once before during their freshman year. The town was as picturesque as its name, and the people she had met during that weekend were warm and friendly. It was one of the reasons she had applied for one of the openings at Lost Creek Elementary. She wanted to be a part of a community. Have a school family.

And maybe a family of her own someday.

Finley pulled up in front of the large ranch house her parents owned, and Emerson claimed her purse and sack from the back.

"I'll need to iron my dress," she told her friend.

They went inside the house, where Mrs. Farrow hugged her, saying, "I'm so glad you could come and stay with us, Emerson. It's so good to see you again. I only wish you could stay longer."

"I've got work, Mrs. F. If I didn't, you wouldn't be able to get rid of me. I'm just grateful Finley came back to Austin to pick me up for this interview since I don't have a car. Don't worry. I'll pay her for the gas."

Dianne Farrow pulled Emerson to her again, hugging her tightly. "Don't worry about that, honey. Let's get you set up in the guestroom. I'm making lasagna for dinner. Hope that sounds good."

"A home-cooked meal sounds wonderful," she replied, not recalling the last time she'd eaten one.

Even though she lived in the dorm, Emerson was not on one of the UT meal plans. She found she could eat more cheaply on her own. Joe was kind enough to let her have whatever she wanted from the bakery. The sports bar where she worked on weekends let her buy meals at half price. Between that and the small fridge and microwave she had in her dorm room, she got by.

She took her things from her sack, lamenting the fact that she'd never owned a suitcase. Once she landed a teaching job, a suitcase was on her wish list of items to buy. She would also need to buy a car. For the last four years, she'd gotten around Austin on a second-hand bicycle, but she would need more reliable transportation. She couldn't arrive at school looking like a drenched rat on rainy days, which had happened numerous times over the years as she'd ridden her bike to classes and various jobs.

Mr. Farrow joined them for dinner, asking both Finley and her all kinds of questions, trying to help prepare them for tomorrow's interview.

"You both gave very thoughtful answers," Mr. F told them. "Mary Miller would be a fool not to hire each of you on the spot."

"I know you're friends with Mary, Dad," Finley said. "Do you have any idea how many other candidates there are?"

"We haven't discussed it," he said. "Mary knows you're applying for the job. We've kept everything aboveboard."

Still, Emerson could see in Mr. F's eyes that he believed his daughter would be hired by the elementary school principal.

They finished dinner, and Emerson offered to do the dishes.

"No, you're a guest," Mrs. F said. "You need to relax tonight."

She and Finley decided to watch a romcom on Netflix, and Emerson ironed her dress as they did so. She had already polished her only pair of dress pumps.

The movie ended, and Finley said, "That was cute. I wish real life could be more happily ever after like that."

"Is something wrong, Fin?" she asked.

"I have a bad feeling about Jeb going to Wharton," her friend admitted, worry in her eyes. "I thought we would be engaged by now, Em. I assumed we'd get married this summer, and we'd both be moving to Pennsylvania. I'd teach while Jeb earned his master's degree. The fact that he's leaving Texas and I don't have a ring on my finger makes me feel that he isn't as committed to our relationship as I am."

"Has he told you he wants to break up?"

"No, but my gut is telling me it's going to happen." Finley wiped away a falling tear.

"Then you should break up with him," she advised.

Finley's eyes widened. "Why would I do that? I love him."

She could tell no matter what she said, Finley was going to have to figure things out on her own.

"It was just a suggestion. Maybe absence will make the heart grow fonder. There has to be something to those old sayings, or they still wouldn't be around."

They went to their separate rooms, and Emerson fell asleep immediately. She usually ran on empty, getting only three or four hours of sleep a night, so anytime she fell into bed, she slept like the dead.

She awoke early the next morning and showered, using the wonderfully scented shampoo and body gel in the guest bathroom. She dressed and then applied a bit of makeup, something she usually went without because it cost money she didn't have. This interview was a special occasion, though, so she swept on two coats of mascara.

She would put on lipstick after she ate breakfast and brushed her teeth.

In the kitchen she found a note for each of them from Mrs. F, wishing them good luck today. The Farrows would already be at the school they operated.

Emerson helped herself to a bowl of cereal and made a cup of coffee. Finley joined her, also drinking coffee, but said she was too nervous to eat.

They drove to the school, the place deserted except for two cars in the front parking lot. Most school districts in the Hill Country took the same spring break UT did, and so staff and students were gone this week.

They entered the building, and Finley directed them to the office, where one lone worker was tapping away at her computer. She glanced up and came around from behind the counter, hugging Finley.

"Oh, it's so good to see you again, Finley. I was thrilled to see your name on Mary's calendar."

The woman turned to Emerson. "Hello. I'm Sheila, the school secretary. Are you Emerson Frost?"

"I am. It's nice to meet you, Sheila."

"Emerson and I were roommates our freshman year," Finley told the secretary. "Before I left the dorms and moved to the sorority house."

"Well, I'm happy you both are here. If you'll have a seat, I'll let Mary know you've arrived."

Minutes later, Sheila escorted Finley in for her interview. Emerson sat, her mouth growing dry, butterflies raging in her stomach. She took out her phone and checked her email and then jumped around various sites, trying to keep her mind calm.

Forty-five minutes later, she heard voices and knew Finley had emerged from her interview. Moments later, her friend appeared in the office, accompanied by an older woman in her early fifties. The two shook hands.

"HR will be in touch about your contract, Finley," the principal said.

"Thank you, Mrs. Miller. I'm so happy I'll be a Lost Creek Lion again."

Mrs. Miller's attention now turned to Emerson. "And you must be Emerson Frost."

She shot to her feet, approaching the principal. Offering her hand, she said, "It's so nice to meet you, Mrs. Miller."

The administrator shook her hand and said, "Come back to the conference room. Let's get to know one another."

Her heart pounding, she followed the older woman down a hallway and into a room.

"Have a seat, Emerson," the principal said, indicating a chair at the conference table and taking one at the head. "Usually, I interview with teachers from the team our applicant would be a part of. With this being spring break, however, I didn't want to ask any of them to give up their much-needed time off."

"I understand, Mrs. Miller. Thank you for coming in during your break to interview me."

The gray-haired woman gazed at Emerson thoughtfully. She was used to being scrutinized and looked back steadily.

"Your grades are excellent, both in your education courses and your specializations of math and science. But you have no extracurriculars on your resumé, Emerson. That concerns me. No campus organizations. No community service. We here at Lost Creek Elementary are looking for well-rounded individuals to educate our students. Yes, mastery in content areas is important, but we are molding global citizens here. I'm only seeing you today at Finley's request. She insisted when I contacted her for an interview that you be granted one, as well."

Her heart sank, knowing she had only gotten her foot in the door because of her friend.

"I appreciate Finley championing me," Emerson said. "If you wish, we can end the interview now since you don't believe I'm what you're looking for in a Lost Creek Lion."

Mrs. Miller pursed her lips and studied Emerson. "Hmm. I didn't take you for a quitter."

"I'm not," she said quickly. "However, I don't want to waste your time, ma'am."

Again, the principal looked at Emerson, as if she saw through her. "Finley has always been a loyal little thing. I recall one field day when she was probably in first or second grade. She was winning her race and stopped right in the middle of it. Looked over her shoulder for her friend, who had fallen. Finley let the other runners pass by her as she trotted back and took her friend's hand. Pulled the girl to her feet. They crossed the finish line together, holding hands, the other girl no longer crying but beaming."

The principal smiled. "They acted as if they'd actually won that race."

"They did," Emerson said. "Friendship— and loyalty — won that day."

Mrs. Miller nodded approvingly. "Tell me about yourself, Emerson. Help me to see what Finley does."

She took a deep breath and decided full disclosure was the best policy.

"My dad went to prison for killing a man when I was nine years old. I never saw him again. He was stabbed by his cellmate when I was fourteen. My mom suffered from depression once he was incarcerated. She turned to drugs as an escape and died from an overdose when I was eighteen."

Emerson paused, gauging Mrs. Miller's reaction. The principal appeared unruffled, but she could see sympathy in her hazel eyes.

"Miss Kent was my third-grade teacher. She mentored me. Taught me how to navigate the world. Miss Kent believed in me. Long after my mother relinquished her parental rights and I was placed in foster care, Miss Kent was there for me. She took me to the school's clothes closet so that I had a few different shirts and a pair of jeans. A third-hand coat that kept me warm. She encouraged me to read, telling me I could see the world through books. And she urged me to pursue math and science, telling me I could be anything I wanted to be."

"Your Miss Kent was a wonderful role model for you," Miss Miller remarked.

"She married and her husband took a job in Fort Worth, so they left Austin. Still, she stayed in touch with me and continued advising me. Miss Kent was a Texas Longhorn, so I wanted to go to UT and follow in her footsteps. She guided me through the Texas Advance Commitment."

"Which is?" Mrs. Miller asked, clearly curious.

"I was valedictorian of my high school, which guaranteed my tuition would be paid for during my freshman year of college. It's only tuition, though. Not books or fees. Not room and board. The Texas Advance Commitment is a program which aids low-income students. In my case, I had no family income. In addition to paying for my tuition each semester while I pursued my teaching degree, I was eligible for additional grants and scholarships, which I took advantage of.."

"What about work-study programs or loans?"

"I didn't want to leave college awash in debt," she said frankly. "Loans were never an option to me. I also knew I could make far more money working off-campus though I did accept an on-campus housing scholarship." She paused. "That's why I have none of the extras you're looking for, Miss Miller. I've worked two jobs and carried a full load my four years at UT."

"That's impressive, Emerson. What jobs have you held?"

"The last two years, I've worked three mornings a week at a local bakery. I'm there by three those mornings, baking everything from donuts to cakes to pastries. Out the door by nine so I can bike to campus for my classes. Weekends, I tend bar on Sixth Street. I started as a server, but I subbed one night when a bartender was out and found the tips were way better. It's also close enough for me to bike to."

She sighed. "I don't even own a car, ma'am. When I land a teaching job, I want to buy a used vehicle, so I don't turn up to school looking like a drowned rat on rainy days. But I am a hard worker. Yes, academically I know my stuff, but I also have a deep love for children and know, especially at the elementary level, how much influence a teacher can have on her students. I want to teach life, Mrs. Miller, not just how to divide fractions and what the life cycle of a plant is. I want to be a role model. Help students to become life-long learners while they come to understand how important integrity and gratitude are."

Emerson paused. "I may not be your ideal candidate on paper, but I will work harder, longer, and more efficiently than anyone else on your staff. I want to be the Miss Kent to all of my students. I could have majored in anything— and Miss Kent often told me I should go into medicine or accounting. I wanted to make a difference every day, though, in a direct way, guiding young minds."

The principal placed folded hands upon the table, her gaze direct. "You are very forthright, Emerson. Your passion is obvious. I can see why Finley befriended you."

"I love Finley to pieces, ma'am, but don't consider me for this teaching position because of Finley. If I win it, I want it to be on my own merits."

Finally, the older woman smiled. Extending her hand, she said, "I would be honored to have you as a faculty member of Lost Creek Elementary School, Emerson. Finley has already accepted a position for fifth grade ELA and Social Studies. My other opening is third grade math and science."

A warm glow filled her. "That's what Miss Kent taught." She beamed at the principal. "Yes. I would be happy to teach little Lions in third grade."

Mrs. Miller rose, and Emerson sprang to her feet. Surprisingly, the older woman embraced her.

"Welcome to Lost Creek, Emerson. We are lucky to have you. I'll forward your information to HR. They'll send an electronic contract for you to sign. Once you're officially employed, I'll be in touch."

She left the conference room in a daze.

Finley shot to her feet when Emerson appeared.

"Well?"

Her gaze met her friend's. "I got it. I got it!"

Finley crushed her in a bear hug. "We'll be at the same school. And we can be roommates again. This is the best news ever. I love you, Em."

Emerson smiled at her friend. "I love you, too, Fin."

1

LOST CREEK—SIX YEARS LATER...

*E*merson bustled about the kitchen in her rental house. It seemed odd not to be making coffee for two. Last night, she had watched Finley marry Holden Scott, and she couldn't have been happier for her best friend. Not only had Finley gotten married, she had also turned in her resignation to Mary Miller and would now be pursuing a full-time career in photography.

She buttered the piece of toast that popped up in the toaster and took it and her coffee mug to the table. She wondered if she should get another roommate to split the house payment and bills. Finley had lived with her the past six years, but Emerson thought maybe it would be nice to have the house to herself, at least for the summer.

Reaching for her planner on the table, she flipped it open, looking at the various weddings coming up and the cakes she would be baking for Weddings with Hart as its exclusive baker. Her friend Harper Hart had opened the business last fall, erecting an event center at her family's winery. Harper had even designed the huge kitchen in the facility with Emerson's needs in mind, putting in two commercial-sized ovens so that cakes could be baked and decorated directly on the property without having to be transported.

Business was booming, with many brides drawn to the winery as a backdrop for their indoor or outdoor weddings. Emerson believed she had found her calling when she'd been drawn to teaching years ago, but baking cakes for weddings, as well as other occasions, was quickly becoming her passion. She still felt a bit guilty for having stepped away from her part-time job at The Bake House, Ethel Frederick's bakery in Lost Creek, but the diminutive owner had encouraged Emerson to operate her own business. Maybe since it was now summer, she might check with Ethel to see if the bakery owner needed any part-time help. Emerson only had a few teacher workshops to attend this summer, and she wouldn't mind staying a little busier, working for Ethel, as well as Harper. The additional income would also be nice. She decided to stop by The Bake House and visit her former employer in person.

Emerson showered and dressed for the day, sweeping her long, raven hair into a high ponytail and dabbing on a smidgeon of lip gloss. She picked up her phone and saw she had missed a text from Harper.

. . .

Friday Bridezilla wants to change the frosting back to buttercream. Told her cake was already baked and this was her last chance to alter something for the wedding. Does that work for you?

She texted Harper back, saying she was heading to the events center now to put the finishing touches on tomorrow night's cakes and would also be baking the wedding and groom's for Saturday night's wedding.

Harper replied with three heart emojis, and Emerson laughed, grabbing her purse and driving straight to the winery. She used her set of keys to enter the event center and mixed the batter for the five-tiered wedding cake for Saturday's uncomplicated bride.

Pouring the batter into the various pans, she slipped them into the oven. While those were baking, she mixed up the groom's cake batter and also put it in the additional oven. She then consulted her notes to make certain she had the right icing and shade for Bridezilla's wedding cake and iced it.

Her timer went off, and she removed the wedding cake pans, placing the cakes on wire racks to cool. She did the same for the groom's cake and returned to Bridezilla's cake, piping delicate rosettes and writing in script atop it. When she finished decorating the wedding cake, she stepped back and congratulated herself. It was truly one of her best efforts.

While she was icing and decorating the groom's cake, Harper stopped in.

"Whoa!" her friend exclaimed, stopping in her tracks. "Emerson, you've outdone yourself. Even Bridezilla won't find anything wrong with this cake."

She indicated the cake in front of her. "I'm putting the finishing touches on her groom's cake. I hope he'll be pleased."

The groom had played football at Texas A&M and had requested that his cake look like a football field. In the center of it was the A&M logo, and she completed it now.

"What do you think?"

Harper turned her attention to the other cake and moved closer, nodding approvingly. "He'll love it. You've added some great details. Obviously, Bridezilla won't like it one bit. She will complain it's not classy enough."

"It's his cake," Emerson said. "He should get some say since she's made every other decision. Numerous times," she added, and both women laughed, because this particular bride had changed her mind about everything, multiple times.

"Are you doing Sunday afternoon's cakes tomorrow?" Harper asked.

"Yes. Those won't take me long since the Sunday wedding is a much smaller affair."

"Sunday Bride has been easy to please," Harper said. "I had to convince her to make some of the decisions and not leave everything up to me."

"She's a little younger than most first-time brides," Emerson noted. "I think she'll be fine. Her groom seems like a really nice guy. I think they'll be happy together."

Harper glanced back at the completed wedding cake. "Why do I feel as though Bridezilla will be back here in two years with another groom?"

"Maybe you should start offering premarital counseling as a service of Weddings with Hart," Emerson teased.

"That's on them. Not me. I just make certain the wedding and reception turn out beautifully. See you later, Em."

After Harper left, Emerson stored the wedding cakes for tomorrow, as well as the two she had baked today. Those would be decorated tomorrow. She locked up and went to her car, propping her cell in the cup holder, seeing another text had come in. It surprised her because this one was from Ethel. She brought up the text.

Ned too see you. ASAP. Come upstairs when get here.

Right away, Emerson was concerned. Ethel was very meticulous, and the misspellings in her short text were unlike her. Another thing was that Ethel was always found in the bakery during business hours, and it was only a little after one o'clock now. The fact that she'd asked Emerson to come upstairs to the apartment located over the bakery worried her. Several weeks ago, when she'd gone into the bakery to buy cookies for her students, Ethel had been even thinner than usual, her color not good. Ethel was a very private person, though, and Emerson didn't ask her any questions about her health.

As she left the winery and drove the short distance into Lost Creek, she tried to recall if she'd seen Ethel since then. She also remembered how Dax had been concerned about The Bake Shop's owner and had asked Emerson to make certain things were all right with Ethel. When Emerson had gathered the courage to ask about her health, Ethel had told her nothing was wrong. That she was just getting older and her doctor had told her to stop tasting so many of her sweet concoctions. That was the reason she'd lost a little weight and stayed in a bad mood.

Emerson had let it go, not wanting to pry further, and soon she had left her part-time job at The Bake House because of Ethel's encouragement. Now, a nagging doubt filled her, and she wished she would have pressed the older woman harder about her health.

She parked behind the bakery, which was on the town square, seeing other cars also parked in back of the various businesses. A back staircase led up to Ethel's apartment. Ethel had told Emerson once that she had been born not in a hospital but in this apartment— and she expected to die here, as well.

Knocking on the door, she waited, listening to hear any movement inside. Then her cell chimed, and she glanced down at the message.

OPEN. COM IN.

· · ·

AGAIN, CONCERN FILLED HER AS EMERSON TURNED THE knob and pushed the door open. She glanced about the tidy room, seeing no sign of Ethel, so she called out her name.

"Ethel? Ethel? It's Emerson."

She went to the kitchen and found Ethel sitting at the table, still dressed in pajamas with a tattered robe covering them. Dark circles were under her eyes, but it was the overall air of sadness which permeated Ethel's posture.

Emerson placed a hand on the baker's shoulder, feeling how bony it was.

"Ethel, you're sick. Let me take you to the doctor. No, the hospital in Boerne."

"Sit, child," Ethel commanded, her voice faint but crisp.

She did so, her gaze meeting the old woman's.

"I asked you to come... because I need to tell you something." Ethel coughed weakly. "I'm dying. Stage 4 cancer. No more doctors."

Emerson reached for Ethel's hand, afraid to squeeze it. "What's wrong with you?" she asked.

"Glioblastoma. It's spread through my brain and spine." Ethel winced. "Given me terrible headaches. Made me forgetful as hell. I've pushed through and pretended nothing was wrong, but today it all caught up to me. I sent Frank and Jill home and closed the bakery."

Ethel coughed again, and Emerson asked, "Can I get you some water?"

The old woman nodded, and Emerson filled a glass as

Ethel watched her. She noticed Ethel's hand shake as she tried to bring the glass to her lips. Emerson leaned over and put her hands around Ethel's, steadying the glass, allowing her to drink from it.

She set down the glass on the table and took a seat again.

"What have the doctors said? What kind of treatment are you undergoing?"

"None," Ethel said flatly. "I have no insurance beyond Medicare. The survival rate for this is low. It grows fast and has eaten me up inside. There's no cure. Chemo and radiation just prolong your agony and costs money I don't have. I chose to keep living my life for as long as I could. Until I couldn't live it any longer."

Ethel paused, her gaze meeting Emerson's. "That's why I called you today, honey."

"What can I do for you?" she asked. "I can move in with you and take care of you, Ethel. It's summer, so I'm not bound to school hours. Yes, I have a ton of cakes to bake for weddings, but I can do those early in the morning or late at night. Do you need me to run The Bake House for you?"

A groan of pain sounded from the old woman, followed by a long sigh. It tore Emerson's heart.

"Let me help, Ethel. Please."

Tears welled in Ethel's eyes. "I've put on a brave face, Emerson. It's just been me all these years. Me. The bakery. This town." She swallowed, grimacing. "I do want you to run The Bake House. I've left it to you in my will."

Shock rippled through her. "What?"

"Merilee Swan has it all lined up. She drew up all the paperwork months ago, just after I got the diagnosis. Wanted to… make sure all T's were crossed. While I was still in my right mind. Not that anyone would challenge it. I have no one, Emerson. That bakery has been my life."

Ethel looked up, her tears now falling down her cheeks. "You're the closest thing to a relative I have. I'm leaving The Bake House to you."

Guilt flooded her, having walked away from her job with Ethel to strike out on her own.

"I see that in your eyes. I know what you're thinking, Girl. I *wanted* you to do your own thing. Work with Harper. Spread your wings. Get ready for what the future would hold for you. I know this means… stepping away from teaching, but I hope you'll take over the place and not… sell it to anyone else."

"I would never do that," Emerson said fiercely.

"Good," Ethel said softly, seemingly all talked out. "I need to… lie down. Can you help me to the bedroom?"

She lifted Ethel from her chair, wrapping her arm about the older woman's waist, and shuffling along beside her. They reached the bedroom, and she got Ethel in bed.

"I'll stay with you while you sleep. And then when you awake, we'll call your doctor together and see what can be done."

Ethel smiled and closed her eyes.

Emerson knew there were programs that could help Ethel. She could go on hospice and have workers come in each day to help care for her. As bad a shape as Ethel was in, Emerson didn't think the baker had long to live.

And that meant she would be inheriting The Bake House.

She would keep her promise to Ethel and never sell it. It made sense for her to take it over. But that would mean giving up her position at Lost Creek Elementary. Emerson decided she needed to let Mary Miller know now and dialed the school's number.

Sheila, the secretary answered, "Good morning. Lost Creek Elementary, where the Lions roar every day."

"Hi, Sheila. It's Emerson. Is Mary available?"

"She is. Let me put you through to her."

Moments later, her principal said, "Hello, Emerson. You're supposed to be enjoying summer vacation and baking a few cakes along the way." Mary chuckled. "Or more than a few. I hear Harper's event center is hopping these days."

Emerson swallowed. "Mary, I have something I need to share with you," she said quietly.

"Go on," the administrator urged. "Take your time, Emerson."

"I'm with Ethel Frederick now. She is in Stage 4 of a nasty cancer and doesn't have much time."

"Ethel's going to give you The Bake House, isn't she?" Mary asked.

"Yes. She just told me," Emerson confirmed. "I promised her I wouldn't sell it to anyone else. That I would run it."

"That means I'll need to look for a new third grade math and science teacher," the principal said.

"I know I'm throwing this at you out of left field, but—"

"No, Emerson," the principal said firmly. "You gave me six wonderful years and gave of yourself to your students. Now, you'll simply have a bigger mission. You'll be touching the lives of many of the residents here in Lost Creek. I appreciate the heads up, though. It's going to be very hard to replace Miss Frost."

Her throat swelled with emotion. "I know I'll have papers to sign. A resignation letter to write. An exit interview."

"We can worry about all that later. You take care of Ethel and let me know if you need anything."

"Thank you, Mary. You've been a wonderful mentor to me— and an even better friend."

Emerson ended the call, staring at Ethel in the bed, looking so small and frail. Obviously, her friend had pushed herself beyond her limits, trying to keep The Bake House running. Now, the cancer had caught up to her.

"It's so unfair," she said softly.

Ethel Frederick was one of the kindest people Emerson had ever met. Brusque but goodhearted. She wanted to fault Ethel for not undergoing chemo and radiation, but since this cancer was uncurable, Emerson understood why Ethel had chosen to do things her own way.

Taking her friend's hand, she held it, tears coursing

down her cheeks as she moved to sit on the bed. Ethel's breathing grew more labored, and Emerson realized these were the older woman's last few minutes. She watched Ethel struggle, fighting to stay alive, and then silence sounded.

Ethel Frederick was gone.

And Emerson Frost's life would now move in a very different direction.

2

THREE WEEKS LATER—SAN ANTONIO

*R*yland Blackwood glanced at his watch, knowing his plane would be landing in about twenty minutes.

He would finally be home...

Though he had regularly called and emailed his parents— even writing a handful of letters because he knew that would mean a lot to his mom —he hadn't set foot in his home state in over a dozen years. He and Todd Hart had joined the military fresh out of high school, reporting two weeks after graduation. They'd completed their basic combat training and advanced individual training together. After those weeks of instruction, they had received their TOD deployment orders to the DMZ along the North Korean/South Korean border.

Ry had joined the army as a culinary specialist because of his background. Being the only son of a dad who owned the best BBQ joint in the Texas Hill Country, along with a mom who owned a diner on the Lost Creek town square, cooking was embedded in his DNA. He'd breezed through the extra training he'd received and during his first tour had prepared high quality meals, first as a line cook and then a chef, training other soldiers. An army was only as good as the food it put in its soldiers' bellies, and Ry had cooked and serviced meals at home stations and in the field. As he'd become more experienced with army ways, he had been given additional responsibilities of ordering and inspecting food supplies, as well as keeping the kitchens clean.

He'd joined Todd, his best friend since they were in diapers, in South Korea for three years. They had both been smart but admittedly lazy students when it came to school, doing just enough to get by. Todd's family owned a winery a few miles outside of town, and one day he was destined to be the chief winemaker for Lost Creek Vineyards. Ry figured he would work with his dad at Blackwood BBQ. Because their career plans were set, ones which didn't need a college degree, they'd mutually decided to see the world via the army before settling down into their respective jobs.

During their first TOD, they took their five-day R&Rs to places such as Thailand and Vietnam. The break was too short to fly all the way home to Texas and back, and they enjoyed going to new countries and experiencing the cuisine and culture. Todd's duties were light since it was the rare occasion someone from North Korea tried to cross the DMZ. Only one nut job had crossed from South

Korea into the communist side of the fence in the last several years. Ry had a blast cooking not only traditional American dishes for soldiers and officers, but he also learned Asian cooking techniques and practiced these dishes regularly on others.

They had decided to re-up their enlistment and serve another hitch, hoping to be reassigned to another part of the world in order to explore new places.

Then tragedy struck.

Todd was killed in a training exercise. A freak accident that only happened once in a blue moon.

And Ry blamed himself for having talked his best friend into joining him in the army.

He'd seen off Todd's body, walking the flag-draped casket to the plane, his hand resting atop it. His commanding officer had offered to grant him compassionate leave in order to accompany the body home, but Ry's guilt kept him in South Korea. He didn't think he could face Todd's family. Todd's parents had treated Ry as their bonus kid, and Todd's sisters were like Ry's own.

Instead, he'd signed up for another TOD. And another. And yet another. He'd done time in Turkey. The Middle East. Germany. But he couldn't run forever. He'd been gone long enough. It was time to return home and step up, helping both his mom and dad in their two businesses.

Ry stretched his arms over his head, hearing the bells sound, knowing it was a signal they were about ten minutes from landing. It was hard to believe his time in the military had come to an end. He'd jumped through all the hoops to separate from the army. Filled out his

DD2648, noting the many resources he would have access to as a veteran. He'd also checked his VMET, verifying his military experience and training, finding one mistake on it and having it corrected. As so often was in the army, that had taken several months to sort out.

Most of the paperwork hadn't applied to him. He wouldn't be taking advantage of the GI Bill and doing additional schooling. He had nothing to be packed and shipped. He had attended the mandatory transition session, but he didn't need to write a resumé or network for a job. He did take advantage of a final physical exam and had chosen a temporary healthcare option. One thing his mom would be pleased about was he'd taken part in a photo session, dressing in his various uniforms. He had the digitals of it now and would have a couple printed and framed for his parents to display.

As for where he would live, he would stay home for a couple of weeks, just to please them. While he wasn't ready yet by any means to take advantage of a VA loan and buy a house, he would definitely need to rent something. He'd just turned thirty-one last week, and no man in his thirties needed to still be living at home.

"We'll be landing in San Antonio shortly," the captain said over the P.A. "Being Texas at the end of June, you'll be getting a balmy ninety-four degrees. Hope your visit to San Antonio includes a trip to a water park— or at least a cold margarita while you sit along the Riverwalk."

Ry heard the chuckles around him. While he liked San Antonio, he was more than ready to get home to Lost Creek. He was surprising his parents, though. They knew of his decision to leave the army, and he'd given them an approximate date of his arrival, but they had no idea he would be turning up in Lost Creek today. He'd reached out to Harper Hart about bumming a ride home. He, Harper and Ivy Hart had sporadically texted over the years, and Ry knew Harper and Ivy had returned to their hometown this past year and that both had married. It would be good to see the Hart girls.

He only hoped they had finally forgiven him.

The plane landed on the tarmac. A sense of peace washed over him. He was back on Texas soil. Ready to start the next chapter in his life. He wondered if it would include anything besides working in the family BBQ business. For now, though, that would be enough. Simply to be home and not living on the edge. His last TOD had been in Germany, so he was far from a war zone. Yet he still was jumpy when he heard a loud noise. Had nightmares from his years in the Middle East. He had seen things he could never talk about to others.

As the plane reached the gate, Ry promised himself to put thoughts of war and the enemy behind him.

He helped two elderly women retrieve their carryon bags from the overhead bin and slung his backpack over his shoulder before heading to baggage claim. All that awaited him was one long duffel bag with all his worldly belongings— and hopefully, a life filled with peace.

Passing through the doors to get to the baggage claim area, he spotted Harper. Ivy was also with her, which was a nice bonus.

Ivy spied him first, her face lighting up. Of the pair, Ivy

had always been the dreamer, while Harper was the organized, practical one. Ivy touched Harper's shoulder, and she also saw Ry. Both women came running toward him, slamming into Ry, their arms tightening about him.

"Ry, it's so good to see you!" Ivy exclaimed, kissing his cheek.

"You left Lost Creek as the best-looking guy in your graduating class," Harper told him. "You've come back even better looking, Ry."

He laughed. "I was thinking the same about you two," he said. "The last time I saw either of you, you were rising seniors in high school. Now, you're grown women— and damn beautiful ones, at that."

It was true. Harper's auburn hair and blue eyes had always stood out in a crowd, but she had a maturity about her now. She also had a glow that told him she was pregnant. Ivy, a brunette with hazel eyes and few inches shorter than her sister, had also matured into quite the beauty.

"You've been gone a long time," Harper noted. "Over a dozen years. A lot has happened to us in those years. Let's grab your luggage, and we'll catch you up on everything."

He glanced toward the carousel and saw his green duffel bag coming down the conveyor belt. "Be right back."

Ry strode toward it and lifted it up, placing the strap on his shoulder. As he walked back toward the Hart sisters, a lump formed in his throat. He hadn't known he would be so emotional seeing them. Tears stung his eyes, and he blinked rapidly several times.

"Is that all?" Ivy asked as he reached them. Then concern filled her face, and she touched his forearm. "Are you all right, Ry?"

He shook his head. "No. I need to say something to the two of you. Your parents, too, when I see them." He drew in a long breath and released it slowly. "I can't tell you how sorry I am about Todd." His eyes welled with tears. "I feel it's my fault that—"

"Stop right there," Harper said, taking charge of the situation. "None of us ever blamed you, Ry. Not for one minute. Get that through your thick skull. Todd made his own decisions. What happened was weird and awful, but we never held you responsible for his death." She paused. "If that's what kept you away all these years, I'm sorry."

Ivy spontaneously hugged him again. "We love you, Ry. You're the only brother we have left. Nothing was your fault."

He grimaced. "I can't help but think if I hadn't talked Todd into joining the military with me, he'd be at Lost Creek Vineyards, making damn fine wines."

Harper took his hand, squeezing it reassuringly. "Todd had the most fun of his entire life during his army years with you. Do we miss him? Absolutely. But shake it off, Ry. That's an order."

He couldn't help but laugh. "Coming from The General, I guess I should salute."

Harper had always ordered everyone about as a small girl, and Ry and Todd had taken to calling her The General from the time they were young.

"This general better see you smiling and happy to be back in Lost Creek," Harper told him.

His gaze met hers. "I'm glad to be back. I'm just hoping I can fit in again."

She looked at the duffel bag he carried. "If that's all you brought back, then you'll need to go shopping for some civilian clothes if you really want to fit in."

Ry laughed heartily. "I left my favorite pair of boots at home. I don't think they'll fit me now, though. I grew two inches after I enlisted. Even my feet grew."

"You do look a little taller," Ivy pointed out.

"I'm six-two now. My body also filled out, thanks to all those calisthenics. Uncle Sam made me do."

"Let's go home," Harper said, linking her arm through his, as Ivy did the same on his other side.

In the car, he asked about what brought them back to Lost Creek, knowing both had gone to college and taken jobs in cities much larger than their hometown.

"I was working for an event planning company in Austin," Harper began. "Engaged to a guy who was a jerk. He cheated on me in the most spectacular way."

"Don't make her go into details," Ivy warned. "They're pretty sordid and will only rile her up."

"Okay. Jerk fiancé," he said. "We'll leave it at that. If I know more, I might just have to kick his ass."

"It was the kick in the pants I needed," Harper admitted. "He came from a political family, one whose politics I really didn't agree with. I would've been miserable, having to keep my mouth shut and toe the line. So, I decided to leave Austin and start my own business in Lost Creek.

Weddings with Hart. We've built an event center on the winery grounds."

"That's a smart idea," Ry said. "How is it going?"

"Business is booming," she shared, a wide smile on her face. "More and more brides want to move beyond the traditional scope of what a wedding has been in the past. I have outdoor space if they want to wed outside. The event center can be split so that a wedding ceremony can be held on one side, while the reception can take place on the other."

"It's more than weddings," Ivy added. "Some people host big birthday parties there. Quinceaneras. Anniversary parties."

"In fact, that's where we'll be surprising your parents tonight with you," Harper said. "I decided to tell them we were catering a small party of less than twenty. Shy provides the barbeque for many of the receptions we hold at the center, so he won't think anything of it. I told him he and Shelly could handle it since it was such a small group. Your mom still closes the diner at three every day, and she often accompanies him and helps set up the catering for receptions and parties."

He beamed. "To see Mom and Dad *and* have barbeque as my first meal in Texas will be amazing. Thanks for setting this up, Harper."

"I know you're a beer drinker," she said. "Even if you and Todd weren't old enough to be doing so before you left Lost Creek. But we'll be serving some of our wines tonight." Her face softened. "My husband Braden is the head winemaker now."

"And soon to be a dad, I see," Ry said.

Harper grinned. "Yup. I'm due in mid-November. Just starting to show now. We've bought a house and everything. I can't wait for you to meet Braden. He'll be there tonight. Pretty much all your friends have moved away from Lost Creek, so I hope the two of you will hit it off. He's a Californian. Tall, rangy, and tan, with dark blond hair and beautiful sky-blue eyes, which I'm hoping our kids will inherit."

"You sound happy, Harper," he said. "I'm glad you've moved on from the jerk and found love." He glanced to Ivy. "I know you're married now, too. Give me the scoop on your man."

"I decided to come home when Harper did," Ivy said. "We took a girls' trip together and did a lot of serious talking about our futures. I was working as the assistant manager of an art gallery in Houston. By working, I mean I had no life. I did everything the manager was supposed to do, as well as my job, while he got the big pay and all the credit."

"You were always a talented artist. I thought you'd do something with your art."

"I wanted to, Ry, but I never had time," Ivy shared. "I came home to Lost Creek just as our tasting manager retired, and I've assumed his duties at the tasting room. It gives me a lot of satisfaction, being able to share about wines with others, and I also have plenty of time to paint."

"Tell him about your show," her sister prompted.

Ivy smiled. "I've been asked by a big name in the New York art world to hold an exhibition at his Soho gallery this coming fall. I've taken to painting landscapes of the Hill Country. You know how this place is in our DNA, Ry. My roots are here, and so is my heart. I feel I'm painting better than ever these days."

"She has a studio over the mayor's hardware store. You need to stop by and see what Ivy has painted," Harper encouraged.

"If Ivy doesn't mind, I'd be happy to. I'd also like to come do a tasting. See what Lost Creek Vineyards wines are about." He paused. "Tell me about your husband, Ivy."

The look on her face told Ry all he needed to know. Ivy was one happy wife.

"Dax is a couple of years older than you. He was an accountant in Dallas before his divorce and decided he wanted a different life for himself. He drove around until he came to Lost Creek, and it just felt like home to him. He's opened a coffeehouse— Java Junction —on the square. He also writes music and plays guitar. He DJ's events for Harper or his band, the Lone Star Rebels, plays live music."

"Two artists coming together," Ry mused. "I like it."

"He's a lot of fun. Laid back and smart and funny," Ivy continued. "He's a runner and runs every morning."

"And thinks of new love songs to write about his wife," Harper teased, causing her sister to blush.

"Dax will also be coming tonight," Harper informed him. "He'll provide some music. I think the two of you will hit it off."

"The army turned me into a runner," he admitted.

"Maybe I can run with him some mornings. I'm pretty addicted to running now."

"Our parents are also coming," Harper said. "Mom and Dad can't wait to see you. I've also asked a couple of friends of ours to come, as well. Do you remember Finley Farrow?"

"Vaguely," he said. "The name sounds familiar. "Blonde? Younger than you?"

"Yes," Harper confirmed. "Finley was a year behind Ivy and me in school. She also went to UT and pledged my sorority. I was her big sis. She came home to teach, but she just turned in her resignation because she's going to pursue photography full-time. Finley photographs most of my weddings and receptions and other special events."

"And she just got married," Ivy said. "Her husband's famous although you probably wouldn't know him. He's a writer. And he's just finished working on a screenplay for one of his books which is being filmed around here. Holden is your age. You'll like him. We have dinners every Wednesday night and get together to try new foods Braden and Finley cook."

"Don't forget Emerson's desserts," Harper said.

"Who's that?" Ry asked.

"She's the last of our friend group since we've been back in Lost Creek," Ivy said. "She and Finley taught school together and were roommates. At least they were until Finley and Holden bought their house. They got married at the end of May, so they're newlyweds."

"Emerson is the official cake baker for Weddings with Hart," Harper told him. "She's also turned in her resignation because Ethel Frederick left her The Bake House. Ethel passed away from cancer three weeks ago. Em's just taken over the bakery. I had her make you a chocolate cake tonight, knowing how much you like chocolate."

"You'll have to come to dinner on Wednesdays," Ivy insisted. "Harper takes Wednesdays off since she works every weekend. We really enjoy getting together."

"I'll be happy to come. I can even bring the barbeque."

"Are you going to work for your dad?" Harper asked. "I know that was in the cards all those years ago."

"It still is," Ry confirmed. "We'll need to talk things out. Decide who'll do what. I'll have to ease back into things. I don't know who Dad has working for him now. I don't want to usurp anyone."

"He's got his hands full," Harper said. "I opened the event center last fall, and Blackwood BBQ has been my go-to caterer, so Shy is working non-stop. He'll appreciate the relief."

"Maybe I can take over the bridal catering then," he mused. "I'm sure Dad and I will work it all out."

"You will," Ivy said. "You'll figure out your place, Ry."

"I hope so," he said, knowing he had a lot of new ideas to bring to the table and worried how his dad would react.

They reached Lost Creek, and Harper said, "I know it was a long flight. I'm going to drop you at my house so you can shower and relax a little. If that's okay."

"Sure. What time is the surprise dinner?" he asked.

"Six," Ivy informed him. "Dax and I will stop by about five-thirty and pick you up. He's already got his DJ equipment at the event center, so we can grab you and waltz in."

They dropped Ivy at her studio, and Harper drove to her house, coming inside with him and showing him the guest room and bath.

"I think everything you need is out. There's food in the fridge if you'd like a snack. Wi-Fi password is Hartto-Clark. I need to get back to work."

She hugged him tightly. "We're so glad to have you back in Lost Creek, Ry."

"It's good to be home," he agreed. "Thanks for picking me up and arranging everything tonight."

"Happy to do so. See you later."

After she left, Ry stripped off the clothes he'd worn for the last thirty-six hours as he'd changed planes a few times before arriving in San Antonio. He showered and shaved, dressing in one of the few shirts and pairs of pants he owned. Harper was right. He'd need to shop and begin building a new wardrobe, starting with jeans and boots.

He made himself a sandwich and poured a tall glass of iced tea from the pitcher in the fridge. The first drink of the sweet tea let him know he was truly back in Texas.

As Ry sat enjoying the solitude, he thought about what his role at Blackwood BBQ might be. Shy Blackwood was a man set in his ways. While it had made him a master at barbequing, Ry doubted his dad would be open to some of the Asian-inspired barbeque dishes Ry wanted to place on the menu. Still, he drew up a list of those dishes, starring the ones he'd like to implement first, wondering if it might be better to open his own BBQ joint. Then again, he didn't want to compete with his family's business. He wanted to be a part of it.

The doorbell rang, and he glanced at his watch. Five-thirty on the dot. Ivy was right on time.

When he answered the door, however, Ivy was nowhere to be seen. Instead, a curvy woman with raven hair and gray eyes stood on the porch.

"Hi, I'm Emerson. Ivy asked if I could stop by and pick you up and bring you to the winery."

3

Emerson hoped today would be the turning point in her already chaotic summer. Ethel's death—and the unexpected inheritance of The Bake House —had thrown a curve into Emerson's orderly world.

She had given up teaching in order to take over the bakery. The trouble was, she had absolutely no experience in running a business. While she technically was in business herself, she was her sole employee, baking cakes for Harper's clients. She didn't have to pay anyone else or worry about health insurance and taxes and a thousand other headaches that she now had. Ethel had not only been a talented baker. Her friend had also run her bakery with ease, treating her employees as family. Emerson wanted to continue that.

Thanks to Dax, she was well on her way to figuring out things. He had given her a crash course in bookkeeping, helping to interpret Ethel's spreadsheets. As a former accountant, he had an affinity with numbers she would never feel comfortable with. Dax had taken her under his wing, explaining things in layman's terms. When Emerson had still struggled with many of the details, he had asked if he could simply become her accountant—for free. She had protested, telling him she didn't want to take advantage of their friendship. He had assured her that The Bake House business wasn't terribly complicated and wouldn't cost him much time. They had come to an arrangement, where she would pay him a flat monthly fee, one she believed was far below what she should be paying him but was the number he had pushed for when she insisted upon paying him for his time and effort. Dax would handle payroll, taxes, and health insurance for her. At least until she could find a manager to do so.

Emerson didn't want to devote all of her time to The Bake House. While she enjoyed baking and would continue to do so at the bakery she had inherited, she really thrived when creating the wedding and groom's cakes needed for Weddings with Hart. Because of that, she needed a full-time presence at the bakery, someone she trusted.

And that was why Rhiannon Temple was coming to Lost Creek today.

They had worked together at an Austin bakery while Emerson attended college. Rhiannon was a few years younger, a high school dropout who'd earned her GED. She was by far one of the most intelligent people Emerson had ever known, someone bored by school and conventionality. If anyone could be trusted to take over the day-to-day management of The Bake House, it would be Rhiannon.

She turned to Frank, a bald, short, stout man who'd worked for Ethel the past five years. Frank was dyslexic and couldn't really read, but he was one hell of a baker. His specialties were pies, cookies, and breads.

"My friend will be here soon, Frank. Why don't you take a break and let me finish up on those macaroons for you?"

"Nah. I don't need a break, Emerson. When I used to smoke, I woulda jumped at the chance to squeeze in another cigarette. Since I quit, I just like doing what I'm doing. And ya know what? I can taste things better now. And I don't go home and stink of smoke all the time."

She knew many in the restaurant field smoked and had never understood it, knowing the habit dulled the palate.

"Okay, then. Finish up and then head home. I'll see you tomorrow."

"I may stick around and meet this friend of yours," he said. "Check her out. See if she's good enough to work here."

"That's fine with me," she said, hoping Frank— and Jill —wouldn't be put off by Rhiannon's appearance.

Emerson went to the front of the store, where Jill was ringing up a customer. She waited until the clerk finished the transaction and the customer exited the store.

"It's close to three," she said. "My friend Rhiannon will be here soon."

"Good. We could use the extra help," Jill said.

She couldn't help but like the mother of two. Jill was in

her mid-forties, her brown hair threaded with gray. She was an empty nester, with both her kids in college. Jill was always friendly and willing to go the extra mile and was good with the two teenagers who came in and worked the Saturday and Sunday shifts, when the bakery was at its busiest.

"Guess I'll sweep up," Jill said as the bell above the door jingled.

Emerson turned, spying Rhiannon. "You haven't changed a bit," she said, going to greet her old friend with a hug.

"Maybe a few more tats," Rhiannon said, holding up her right arm, covered in a sleeve of tattoos. "Other than that, I'm still me."

"As thin as ever. I don't see how you can be the baker you are and not like sweets."

Rhiannon shrugged. "Sweets don't like me. They do funny things to my gut health."

"Come meet Jill and Frank," she urged, taking the flame-haired woman over to Jill.

She introduced the pair, and they began talking animatedly, so Emerson slipped away and fetched Frank, bringing him to the front to also talk with Rhiannon. Soon, the three chatted as old friends, and Emerson knew the pair had accepted her friend.

"Come to the back and let me show you our equipment," Emerson said.

"I'll sweep up and mop," Jill said.

"I'll help with that," Frank added. "Good to meet ya, Rhiannon."

Her friend flashed a smile. "Same."

They went to the rear of the bakery, and Emerson proudly showed off the various ovens and other equipment.

"Your Ethel didn't skimp, did she?" Rhiannon said, clearly impressed with the setup.

"No," she said. "Ethel did everything first class. She spent her entire life here. Born in the upstairs apartment. Started helping her parents when she was young. Baking was in her blood. She wasn't shy about investing in the latest technology in a kitchen. Ethel was friendly with the entire town."

"But she left her bakery to you," Rhiannon pointed out. "That speaks volumes, Em."

She frowned. "We were friendly, but we weren't really friends," she admitted. "I was shocked when I found out she'd bequeathed all this to me."

"Ethel recognized you would be a good steward of her legacy," her friend said. "A bakery in a small town on the town square? That's an integral part of a place. I know you worked for her some."

"Yes, I was here part-time for a couple of years. I worked weekends and summers when I had breaks from teaching. Then I had an opportunity to work for my friend Harper as her exclusive baker of cakes for the events she plans, mostly weddings. I do the wedding and groom's cakes, several of each every week."

"You always had a flair for that when we worked together in Austin."

She nodded. "I'm happiest when I'm designing cakes

for weddings," she admitted. "I like the creative challenge. Making every cake different from other ones. Incorporating the bride and groom's ideas into their special day." She sighed. "I just can't keep doing that and run The Bake House full-time. There aren't enough hours in the day. That's why I asked you here to talk about offering you that job."

"What exactly do you have in mind?" Rhiannon asked.

"I'd remain the owner and would come in and assist Frank in the early morning baking, but you'd be the manager. You'd bake. Run the store. Handle ordering supplies. Keep the books if you'd like, or I have someone who can do that for me. I know you're savvy when it comes to graphics. You'd also be in charge of the website." She hesitated. "I know Lost Creek might not quite have the appeal that Austin does, though. I'm not exactly sure what Patch would do here."

Patch and Rhiannon had dated off and on since eighth grade. While Emerson thought Rhiannon could do better, she had to accept they had been a package deal for more than a dozen years.

Rhiannon laughed. "Honey, you couldn't have hit me up at a better time. I just broke up with Patch. Again. And yes, this time it's permanent."

"Are you sure? Seems as if I've heard this before."

Her friend nodded. "I mean it this time. Patch is never going to make anything of himself. He'd rather get high all day than do any kind of meaningful work. He can't hold a job. I'm tired of him sponging off me and told him so."

Rhiannon hesitated. "Frankly, I'm also tired of putting

up with the cheating. Patch is nice to look at, but his eyes stray more often than not. I've taken him back time and time again. Coming to Lost Creek is a chance for me to move up, in both money and responsibility. And to cut ties with him. He'd never fit into a small town like this. He'd never follow me here. I know that. He needed a reason to tell me we're done. I needed the same." She paused. "If you'll give me this chance, Em, you won't regret it. You know I'm a hard worker. I'm a whiz in the kitchen. I get along with people. I'm also great with numbers."

Relief swept through her. "Oh, you're my dream hire, Rhiannon. I had just worried about the Patch piece of things."

"That piece has been tossed in the trash. It was too worn out to repair," Rhiannon assured her. "When can I start? And where's a good place to live?"

While Emerson liked Rhiannon, she had enjoyed the past month of living on her own and didn't want a new roommate anytime soon.

Instead, she said, "I can offer you the apartment above the bakery. Ethel lived there all her life. It's furnished." She chuckled. "Not to your taste, necessary, but you wouldn't have to buy anything right away."

Rhiannon's smile lit up her face. "Let's go see it."

They went upstairs and walked through the place. It was a two-bedroom apartment, and Ethel had used one bedroom for herself and the other as an office. It also had a living room, kitchen, and full bath and laundry room.

Rhiannon spun in a circle. "Wow. This is perfect. I'd

want it for that giant claw foot tub alone. How much do you want in rent?'

They discussed a fair price and agreed upon a figure, with Emerson saying the rent could come directly out of Rhiannon's salary.

"I like that. I like Frank and Jill. This is the fresh start I've needed, Em." Tears filled Rhiannon's eyes. "I feel so lucky that this opportunity came along when it did."

They chatted a bit more about the employees' schedule and decided that Emerson would come in three days a week to bake cakes for the bakery, mostly special orders for birthdays and other occasions, along with a couple for display each day, which she usually sold by the slice. She would devote the rest of the time to her own cake baking business.

"Maybe we can cut your days back to two a week once I get a handle on things," Rhiannon told her.

"We can work it out," she agreed. "Nothing is set in stone as far as I'm concerned. I'm just grateful you want to take on this role at The Bake House. It'll allow me to concentrate on my side business, which brings me joy. So, when can you start?"

Rhiannon laughed. "Girl, I can start tomorrow. Or today if you need me."

She frowned. "What about giving your old boss a week's notice?

"I told you that you'd called at the perfect time, Em. I meant that. When I decided to end things with Patch, that meant I was done with Austin, too, and our life there. I knew if I stayed, I'd give in. Again. And I'd never escape the circle. I left my bakery job a week ago. Got rid of some things. Sold a few others. Packed my car and drove here. If this didn't work out between us, I was simply gonna drive until I found a place I thought I might like. I think Lost Creek will be a great new home."

Emerson hugged Rhiannon. "That's wonderful. Thanks so much."

Rhiannon looked at her steadily. "No, thank you. You're giving me a terrific opportunity. It'll let me cut the cord with the past and get a new start in a different place. Even if Patch gets bored, he won't have the inclination to pursue me to Lost Creek. Not that I even told him I was leaving Austin."

"I cleaned the apartment after Ethel's death. It's a little dusty now. I've already gotten rid of everything in her closets but kept the linens and towels and all the kitchen things. It's up to you to keep what you want and toss out the rest."

Rhiannon threw her arms about Emerson. "You are the best boss ever."

They walked downstairs again, and she showed her friend where she could park in back and the separate entrance she could come and go from without always having to cut through the bakery. Emerson also gave Rhiannon keys to the bakery and the apartment.

As they went to Rhiannon's battered sedan, Emerson said, "I want you to realize you'll be in charge. Once you've been here a while, if you want to change anything — the bakery's hours, add things to the menu, whatever — I want you to feel free to do so."

"Thanks for giving me that freedom. I really appreciate it." Rhiannon gave her a hug. "And living on the square, I can walk to several places. I saw a coffeehouse when I drove in. That'll be nice and convenient. You know how I love my coffee."

"Dax Tennyson runs Java Junction. He and his wife Ivy are good friends of mine. I'll have to introduce you to them."

Rhiannon said she would move her things in now, waving away Emerson's offer to help. "I can handle everything. To be honest, I don't have much. Go and do what you've got to do. I'll see you in the morning. Right now, I want to get my stuff in and then roll up my sleeves and see all the bakery has to offer."

Emerson felt a burden slip from her shoulders. With Rhiannon's head for figures, maybe Dax could teach her enough so that Rhiannon could totally take over management of The Bake House. She wouldn't rush things, though. She wanted to give her friend time to settle in and take the reins slowly. Rhiannon's skill was in her baking. The Bake House wouldn't lack for quality.

She decided to head home and shower before heading to the winery. Harper had invited her to attend a small dinner for a friend who was returning from military service. He was the son of Shelly, owner of the Lone Star Diner on the square, and Shy, who owned and operated Blackwood BBQ on Main Street a few blocks away. Emerson had baked a molten mocha chocolate cake for tonight's dessert, having learned the guest of honor was a chocoholic.

After she got out of the shower, she dressed and spritzed on a bit of perfume and a bit of lip gloss. Emerson had never been into makeup because she'd never been able to afford it growing up in foster care. By the time she was on her own, she thought of makeup as a luxury and not a necessity, unlike most every female student at UT. Then as an elementary school teacher, she hadn't thought she needed to wear it, teaching eight-year-olds all day. Still, she liked how she looked when she wore lip gloss and didn't mind applying it for tonight.

Her cell rang, and Ivy's picture popped up.

Answering, she said, "Hey, Ivy. What's up?"

"Could you do me a huge favor and pick up Ry? He's at Harper's house. She stashed him there so his parents wouldn't see him. I was supposed to pick him up and take him to the winery at five-thirty."

"Sure, I can do that for you. Is everything okay?"

"It's fine. I just need to take a call from Clive about my show. I didn't want to be yacking with him and leave Ry twiddling his thumbs in the car."

"Will do," she assured her friend. Glancing at the clock, she said, "In fact, I'll leave now."

"Thanks, Em. You're a lifesaver," Ivy told her.

Emerson went to her ancient Mini Cooper, which was on its last legs. Since Ethel had left her almost sixty thousand dollars, in addition to The Bake House, she'd felt like a Mega Millions winner. Her goal was to purchase a new, reliable car as soon as she could find the time to do so.

She reached Harper and Braden's house and pulled into the driveway, going to the front door and ringing the bell, hoping it wouldn't be awkward, talking to a stranger as they drove to Lost Creek Winery. She'd never been good at throwing herself out there and told herself it took less than ten minutes to reach the winery. Even she could survive that long.

The door opened— and suddenly she couldn't breathe.

The man standing in front of her was devastatingly handsome. Probably six-two, almost a foot taller than she was. He had black hair, laughing blue eyes, and a killer body.

Swallowing— and trying to be as nonchalant as possible —she said, "Hi, I'm Emerson. Ivy asked if I could stop by and pick you up and bring you to the winery for the surprise party."

His voice was low as he rumbled, "I can't think of a better welcoming committee." He thrust a hand in her direction. "I'm Ry Blackwood."

She took it, a surge of electricity zipping through her. This had never happened before. Never. Ever. She looked at him wordlessly.

Something told her things had taken an interesting turn— and that Ry Blackwood might become someone important in her life.

4

Ry's natural instinct was to smile at the woman standing on the porch, so he did so. She smiled in return, looking a little shy.

He liked shy.

He liked her.

She wasn't a classic beauty, but all the pieces came together, making her very appealing. Someone who interested him a great deal. It struck him that by coming back to Lost Creek, the next chapter in his life would not only include a return to working in his family's restaurant. It would also involve what he personally wanted in his life.

More than anything, Ry knew he wanted kids. Definitely more than one, since he'd been an only child. Each summer when his cousin Tucker came to stay during the school holidays, it felt right having him there. They'd shared a bedroom and talked long into the night. Their days had been full of riding their bikes, playing basketball, and swimming at Lost Creek Lake, usually with Todd Hart in tow. The three had been like brothers— eating ice cream and pizza, reading comic books, and playing video games.

Now, Todd was gone— and Tucker might as well be.

Two years ago, a drunk driver had struck the car Tucker drove. His cousin had been severely injured, but his pregnant wife had been killed. Ry only knew about the accident from his parents. Tucker had never picked up the phone when Ry had called. Never answered any texts or emails. It was if he'd dropped off the face of the earth. Ry only hoped now that he was stateside again that he might find Tucker and reconnect with him.

He pushed aside those thoughts and turned his full attention to Emerson now, saying, "I appreciate you giving me a ride to the winery."

Ry picked up his duffel bag and backpack to take to her car.

Laughter bubbled from her. "You may not be so grateful once you see what you'll be riding in." She glanced up and down his frame and added, "Those long legs may not work in my Mini Cooper." She grinned. "Or you'll be riding with your knees next to your ears."

He glanced over her shoulder and saw a dilapidated Mini-Cooper sitting in the driveway.

Shrugging, he told her, "It's better than walking."

He closed the door to Harper's house and accompanied Emerson to her car. It was a tight squeeze fitting his gear inside the miniscule trunk. He did open the driver's door for her. She flushed a pretty pink, making her even more appealing.

"Thank you," she said.

"The army— and Shelly Blackwood —drilled good manners into me."

Ry closed her door and went around to the passenger's seat, seeing it would be fairly challenging. He climbed in, situating himself, and gave her a thumbs up, despite feeling like a sardine crammed into a tin can with a hundred fellow fish.

"Fortunately, Lost Creek Winery isn't that far from here," she said brightly, inserting the key into the ignition and starting the car. "But I guess you know that since you're from here."

Curious about her, he said, "Tell me about yourself, Emerson. How did you wind up in Lost Creek?"

He saw a guarded expression cross her face as she replied. "I roomed with Finley Farrow our freshman year in college. She really wanted to come home to Lost Creek to teach, and the elementary school she'd attended actually had two positions open. She interviewed for one, and I interviewed for the other. We were both hired, and I've spent six very happy years here."

She paused, licking her lips a moment, causing a spark of desire to flare within him.

"We both are actually leaving our teaching careers behind us, though. Finley is a photographer and will be pursuing that full-time. She just recently got married. I, on the other hand, am committed to being a baker in my new career. Do you remember The Bake House?"

"Best cakes, donuts, and kolaches in the Hill Country," he said. "I rode my bike plenty of times to The Bake House for a sausage kolache."

"I used to work part-time on the weekends and full-time during the summers for Ethel Frederick, the owner." She cleared her throat. "Ethel recently passed away, and she left The Bake House to me. I'm going to be baking there three days a week, while a friend of mine from my days in Austin will manage the bakery for me. A lot of my time is devoted to baking cakes for Weddings with Hart. I know Harper and Ivy picked you up from the airport, so I'm assuming Harper shared all about her business with you."

"She did. I'm looking forward to seeing the event center on the property. Harper really praised your baking skills. You must be some kind of culinary genius."

"I taught science and math. Baking utilizes science. You really have to be precise in your measurements for things to turn out well. What I really enjoy, however, is flexing my creative muscles when I design and decorate those cakes. There have been several innovations in the baking industry in recent years, and Harper put in a first-class kitchen for me to bake on-site so that I wouldn't have to transport cakes." She chuckled. "Trying to move a five-tiered wedding cake can be a nightmare."

"Especially in a Mini Cooper," he quipped.

Emerson laughed— and he wanted to hear more of that.

"Sounds like we're both starting new chapters in our lives," Ry noted. "You, stepping away from teaching and devoting yourself to baking. I'll be going into the family barbeque business. At least, that's what I'm planning. We'll see what Dad thinks."

Emerson put on her blinker and turned into Lost Creek Winery.

"When I heard you were coming home, I wondered if you would be working with your mom or dad."

"Definitely Dad, although I'm happy to help out Mom, too. I have barbeque sauce running through my veins," he joked. "I've been smoking meats since I was in kindergarten. I was actually a cook in the army."

"You were? I guess you didn't have to shoot anyone."

He paused a moment and then said, "A soldier is a soldier, Emerson. I was trained exactly as all other soldiers who enlist. I went through boot camp, where I received my basic combat training. Then I did specific culinary training to be a cook in the army. Periodically, I still had to undergo various training exercises when I was stationed around the world. Cooking was ninety-nine percent of my time in the army during my first TOD. Tour of Duty," he explained. "Then I decided to move into the field."

"What changed your mind about cooking?" she asked, making a turn into a parking lot.

Ry could see the event center lay ahead of them. Instead of answering her question, he turned his attention to the facility.

"Wow. I really like what Harper did with this. I can't wait to see the inside. And meet her husband. Ivy's husband, too."

Emerson got out of the car before he could unfold himself and get her door for her. She told him to leave his things in the car for now. They walked across a bridge and toward the event center together.

"Harper said business is brisk," he commented.

She laughed. "You've arrived in the middle of wedding season, Ry Blackwood. This place is hopping on weekends and even several days during the week. Harper offers a discount on renting the facilities during the week, and she has her fair share of Tuesday and Thursday weddings."

"But not Wednesdays," he noted. "She and Ivy told me a group of you get together each Wednesday night and share a meal. I've been invited to the next one tomorrow night. It seems you're the one who provides desserts, and we serve as guinea pigs testing them out."

She laughed again, rich and throaty, making him want to stop and pull her to him for a kiss. This was unbelievable. He had never been attracted to a woman so quickly. Ry didn't even know if she were seeing anyone although he hadn't spotted a ring on her left hand.

"Yes, I do like to try things out on the group. Braden and Finley do the same. Both are fantastic cooks, and they alternate who makes the meal each week. We've had everything recently from Thai to Italian to Peruvian food."

He opened the door, ushering her inside the building, and gazed about, taking in the place. Whistling low as he spied one wall made entirely of glass, he began wandering through the facility, seeing where weddings would occur and the set-up on the other side where receptions could be held. A couple of tables were decorated for his homecoming. He saw Harper had gone with a patriotic theme of red, white, and blue. A banner hung on the wall, proclaiming *WELCOME HOME, RY,* the block letters in a stars and stripes pattern.

A tall, lean man approached him, holding out a hand in greeting.

"Braden Clark. Husband to Harper and winemaker for Lost Creek Vineyards."

Ry took the hand and pumped it enthusiastically. "Glad to meet you, Braden. Harper and Ivy are like little sisters to me."

Braden smiled. "They've told me how much you're like family to them. Thank you for your service."

Another man joined them, dark-haired and with chocolate brown eyes. "I second that," he said, offering his hand. "Thank you for what you've done for our country, protecting us at home and abroad. Dax Tennyson. Ivy's husband."

"I hear you run a coffeehouse. I'll definitely stop by and check it out." He glanced to Braden. "Hate to say it, but I'm not much of a wine drinker."

Both men laughed, and Dax said, "I was a beer drinker until I moved to the Hill Country. Yes, they've got a lot of great craft beers on tap here, but marrying someone who comes from a wine family and has a terrific nose for the bouquet of wines, I've come to appreciate wine."

"And I grew up in a winemaking family," Braden told Ry. "I practically had wine in my sippy cup."

He liked the easy camaraderie he felt with these two men and decided to ask them a question.

"I've been invited to your group gathering tomorrow night, and I wanted to check and see if Emerson is seeing anyone."

Braden and Dax exchanged a knowing look, and Braden said, "Nope. Emerson hasn't dated anyone for as long as either of us have been in Lost Creek. You interested in her?"

Shrugging, he said, "She gave me a ride to the winery just now. She seems really nice, but I didn't know if I should ask her out or not."

"I'd do it," Dax encouraged. "Emerson is a really kind, thoughtful person. A little quiet until she gets to know you, but then she can be a real chatterbox."

"Good to know," Ry said. "I think I'm going to go find her."

"She was heading toward the kitchen when I passed her," Dax volunteered. "But your parents are already in the kitchen prepping, so you better avoid that area."

"Thanks."

He ventured toward the glass wall and was stopped on the way by a blonde with brilliant aquamarine eyes, recognizing her. "Finley Farrow. It's good to see you."

She gave him a hug. "And here I thought a popular guy like Ry Blackwood wouldn't even know me. I'm sure Harper and Ivy mentioned me when they picked you up at the airport. I hope you don't mind if I take a few photos tonight of your homecoming."

"Please do. Mom'll love that. In fact, I had a photo session before I separated from the army. Had the opportunity to have my picture made in my dress and everyday uniforms. I have the digital copies and need to print out a few of them so Mom can frame them."

"I'd be happy to print and frame those for you, Ry," Finley offered. "I'm moving into photography full-time now. It's something I do all the time."

"I'd appreciate that. We can exchange info later."

A tall, handsome man with wire frame glasses stepped up to Finley, wrapping an arm around her waist as he stuck out a hand to Ry.

"Holden Scott. Finley's other half."

"Ry Blackwood," he said, shaking Holden's hand. "I hear the two of you recently tied the knot. Congratulations."

Holden and Finley exchanged a tender yet heated look, and it caused a rush of emotion to fill Ry.

This is what he wanted. Someone to love. Someone to share life together.

The couple turned back to him, and Holden said, "We're still newlyweds, going on a month of marriage now. I hear you'll be at dinner tomorrow with the gang. We'll talk some more then. I know things will be starting up soon, so we'll free you up."

"Thanks," he said, seeing Harper fussing with the flower arrangement on one of the tables.

He walked toward her and asked, "I hear Mom and Dad are already in the kitchen, working on our dinner?"

"They should be ready to serve in the next ten minutes or so. That means no going to the kitchen for you. I want you out of sight while they're doing their set-up there. It won't take them long since it's such a small group of us.

Nothing like the hundred or more plates they prep during a wedding reception."

Harper glanced up as Emerson rolled a cake by them and said, "Em, once you get the cake fixed how you want, would you take Ry to the bridal suite and keep him under wraps until everyone's here and Shy and Shelly have everything plated?"

"Sure can, Harper."

Harper turned to him. "Go with Emerson and stay out of sight."

"Yes, General," he said, saluting her in a teasing fashion.

As he walked over to Emerson, he heard music start up and saw Dax was at a station with speakers. He recalled Ivy's husband acted as a DJ or had his band play live at receptions and supposed he would provide music for this evening.

Wandering over to Emerson, he took a good look at his welcome cake and smiled.

"My mouth is already salivating," he told her.

"Harper told me you were a chocoholic, so I did my best to come through. I've baked a molten mocha chocolate cake for your party tonight. I hope you'll enjoy it."

"It's beautiful, Emerson. A true work of art. I can see where your creative juices were flowing as you put this dessert together." He looked over his shoulder, seeing Harper point impatiently, and asked Emerson, "Ready to go hide?"

"Yes."

She led him to a group of rooms, and they entered one

which had a large mirror running the length of one wall. Several chairs sat spaced out in front of it, and he assumed it was for brides and their attendants to sit and have their hair and makeup done before the ceremony. Several other comfortable chairs were scattered about the room, along with a slightly raised platform.

"This is where the bride and her bridesmaids get ready," Emerson explained. "Harper always has the bride step up here to make certain that the hem of the gown is intact. She's a stickler for details, our Harper, but her weddings turn out flawlessly every time."

She began wandering the room. "Your parents also do a wonderful job catering many of the receptions. Since it's a Hill Country wedding, Harper is always quick to suggest that the bride and groom go with a Texas theme for their food, and that means barbeque. Your dad smokes the best meat on the planet."

He stepped closer to her and said, "That's because you haven't sampled *my* smoked meats, Emerson," he said quietly. "And I've learned a lot from my time in the army. I told you I cooked during the majority of my first TOD. I was stationed in South Korea. I incorporated a lot of Asian influences into the meals I cooked. I traveled to Vietnam. Laos. Thailand. Cambodia. Japan. I can't wait to bring some of the influences of those cuisines into traditional Hill Country barbeque."

Ry took another step toward her, his heart beating rapidly, as if he were a teenager about to ask a girl on a date for the first time. He caught the scent of sweetness on her, and he wished he could bury his nose against her skin.

"As a fellow preparer of food, I would really appreciate your opinion on some dishes. I'd like to try them out and get your feedback before I bring up any kind of menu changes to my dad."

His hand went to her waist, resting it there, and he heard her breath hitch as her eyes widened in surprise. "I'm even interested in a fusion of my smoked meats placed inside your pastries. I think we could create some special dishes together."

His gaze fell to her mouth as she nervously licked her lips, and he added, "So, what do you say, Emerson? Interested in stepping into my test kitchen and giving me some professional advice?"

Ry wanted to do more than cook for this lovely woman. The attraction between them had the air crackling with electricity. His hand on her waist tightened slightly, and his gaze locked on hers. He started to move in to kiss her.

And stopped.

This wasn't a woman who would appreciate being rushed. He couldn't move too fast with her, sensing she would scurry away like a jack rabbit. He'd been a hunter during his teen years and had learned the patience of waiting on a deer. Emerson reminded him of those deer. Graceful. Soulful eyes. A bit skittish. He needed to take his time. Show her he could be trusted. Calm her fears.

His gaze connected with her unusual gray eyes, seeking answers. Ones which she didn't even know he was questioning her about yet, but Ry was determined to find those answers and pursue the connection he felt with this woman he'd just met.

She said in a prim teacher's voice, "Yes, I would be happy to taste your food and provide some feedback to you, Ry."

Emerson took a step back, breaking the contact between them, and it was a good thing she did so. If she hadn't, Ry just might have kissed her anyway.

The door opened, and Ivy popped her head in. "Come on, Ry. It's time to surprise Shy and Shelly."

He couldn't help himself. As Emerson took a step away, his hand went to the small of her back, guiding her from the room. He sensed the shiver running through her and knew this woman was going to challenge him in ways he'd never experienced before.

Ry couldn't wait to rise to those challenges.

5

---

*R*y Blackwood had almost kissed her...

At least that's what Emerson thought might have happened. She had no experience in reading those kind of social cues, however, because she had never been on a date, much less been kissed. She thought she had to be the only twenty-nine-year-old woman in Lost Creek who fit that particular description. Probably the only one in all of Texas.

Her life had not been an easy one, growing up in foster care. No time was devoted to boys and dating during her high school years. She was always either working or studying, trying to earn top grades in order to win a scholarship in order to have the opportunity to go to college.

Education had been her way out of poverty. She had to maintain a certain GPA in college to keep the scholarships and grants which had been awarded to her. Emerson had also worked long hours at various jobs when not in the classroom. While she was always friendly with other employees, she erected an invisible barrier around her that flashed *FRIENDS ONLY*. Her male co-workers had respected that. Respected her, because she was such a hard worker.

Things hadn't changed when she'd moved to Lost Creek. She was grateful Mary Miller had given her a job in the classroom, and Emerson had thrown herself whole-heartedly into teaching. Many hours outside the class-room also were devoted to being an excellent teacher, which left little time for a social life. She created lesson plans. Graded assessment from papers to projects to tests. Talked frequently with parents, keeping them apprised of their child's growth. All those things took up an inordi-nate amount of time. Once she got her feet under her, she decided to take on the part-time work at Ethel Frederick's bakery. Those hours ate into any free time where she might have gone on a date. Not that anyone had been asking.

Having lived with Finley during the six years they had been teaching at Lost Creek Elementary, she had seen Finley's boyfriends come and go. None of them— before Holden —had made her friend happy. Those failed rela-tionships had Emerson grateful she had isolated herself the way she had. She enjoyed her work and was lucky to have a growing network of close friends she trusted. That was all she needed.

Not a complication like Ry Blackwood.

His hand had come to rest possessively on her waist,

though, and Emerson had not known what to say or do. While her brain told her to move away from him, instinct had been whispering in her ear to step closer instead. There had been a moment when Ry looked at her and she felt a kiss was coming. Then it seemed he changed his mind, which she thought was a very sensible thing. Ry Blackwood oozed sex appeal, and he had probably kissed his way into the lives of dozens of women. She didn't need the former army vet distracting her, not when she was just beginning to figure out things at the bakery and in her own life.

Besides, one kiss— and he would be able to tell how inexperienced she was. That would be downright embarrassing. Someone like Emerson could never truly interest a man such as Ry Blackwood.

Still, a tiny part of her wished that he had kissed her. Just so she could experience what a kiss was like.

Emerson was aware of his palm fitted against the small of her back now, shooting tingles throughout her body. Her mouth had grown dry, and she hoped no one was expecting her to say anything for the next few minutes.

Ivy stopped and turned. "Wait here, Ry. Watch for Harper's signal." She looked at Emerson. "Come on. We're supposed to be seated. Shy and Shelly are about to bring in the plates from the kitchen."

Nodding, Emerson stepped away with Ivy. Suddenly, she felt bereft without Ry's warm palm against her. She fought the urge to glance over her shoulder and was pleased when she didn't give in and look back at him.

She and Ivy went to the two tables which Harper had set beautifully for tonight's dinner in Ry's honor.

Harper approached them. "Sit here, Em," she said crisply as Ivy moved away and went to the other table, where Dax seated her next to him.

Others were taking their seats, as well, and Emerson greeted Bill and Cecily Hart. Harper's parents took a seat to her right. Braden joined them and sat next to Bill, and Emerson counted the empty chairs, realizing she would be sitting at the table with Ry and his parents.

Immediately, she shot to her feet and took a few steps to Harper, whispering, "I should sit at the other table."

Her friend frowned. "I already have the seating arrangements organized, Emerson. I want even numbers at each table. Go back and sit next to Mom."

She knew not to question Harper when she was in coordinator mode. Harper planned every detail, down to the smallest one. Emerson would not rock the boat tonight, no matter how uncomfortable she was.

She saw Shy and Shelly Blackwood appear, both of them rolling a cart filled with covered plates. Shelly went to the table of six, which now held Dax and Ivy, Holden and Finley, as well as Wolf and Ana Ramirez. The director and his producer wife lived nearby at Meadow Creek Ranch with their two children and had started their own production company. They were now filming *Hill Country Homicide*, based on the second novel Holden had written. Holden had written a screenplay from his own novel, and Finley was taking stills and working on an ad campaign for the movie. Emerson liked the couple and thought Ry would, too.

Shy approached Harper, who stood nearby and said, "I see not everyone is seated. Should we go ahead with the service?"

Harper smiled. "Yes, Shy. Distribute all the dinners if you would."

The caterer nodded at his wife, and Shelly Blackwood began setting plates of food in front of those seated at Finley's table. Shy did the same at the table Emerson sat at.

Once Shy had set the last plate on the table, he looked to Harper. "Anything else? If not, Shelly and I will be cleaning up in the kitchen."

"There is one more thing." Harper motioned Shelly over and as the town's diner owner came toward her, Harper glanced over her shoulder.

Ry began walking toward them, and Emerson couldn't help but be attracted to the tall, muscular, former soldier. He was as handsome as sin and had a smile the Devil himself would envy, one he now used to full effect as he marched toward his unsuspecting parents. Both Shy and Shelly had their backs to their son, and Harper pointed, drawing their attention to the banner hanging on the wall.

Emerson watched the couple and heard Shelly's gasp when she understood what was happening. Shelly whirled just as Ry reached his parents, and she threw her arms about her son, burying her face against his chest. Emerson heard her sobs of joy.

"It's okay, Mom," Ry comforted. "I'm here. I'm finally home."

A tearful Shelly Blackwood raised her head, looking into her son's eyes. "Oh, Ry. I never thought this day would come."

Glancing to Shy, Emerson saw tears filled his eyes, as well.

"Come here, son," Shy ordered, and he wrapped Ry in a bear hug, slapping his son on the back several times before clutching him as if he never wanted to let go.

Harper slipped into a seat next to Braden, satisfaction on her face.

Ry beamed at his parents and then said, "Hope you enjoyed the surprise."

Shelly took a napkin from the table and removed the ring from it, mopping her eyes with the fabric. "You certainly know how to make an entrance, son," she said.

"Have a seat," Harper urged. "I know Ry's been looking forward to seeing you and eating some Blackwood BBQ."

Shy seated his wife, and Ry sat next to Emerson. He turned and smiled at her.

"Thanks for being a part of pulling off the surprise," he said, his eyes full of sincerity. Then he glanced to Harper. "Thanks for all you did to make this happen, Harp. Now, if y'all don't mind, I'm ready to dig in to the best barbeque in Texas."

Everyone laughed and for a few minutes, Ry didn't say a word. Emerson watched as he sampled a bit of every-thing on his plate. Brisket. Sausage. Pulled pork. Potato salad and baked beans. Fluffy, yeasty rolls.

As far as the Blackwoods were concerned, both of them would take a bite and then stare lovingly at their only son. In their gazes, Emerson saw great love. It hurt for her to swallow her own food, and she reached for the iced tea in front of her plate, trying to get a few bites of pork down. She was happy for Ry and his parents, being reunited after so long a time apart. She had never known that kind of love or support from her own parents, though. At least she had her friends, who were fast becoming the family she never had.

"I've tasted everything— and it's even better than I remembered," Ry pronounced, causing those gathered to chuckle.

"When did you get in, Ry?" asked Shelly.

"I flew in this afternoon," he told his mother. "Harper and Ivy picked me up in San Antonio and stashed me away so I wouldn't run into you. I wanted to surprise you and Dad, and I think I did."

Shy gestured with his fork, asking, "So, what time will you be at Blackwood BBQ tomorrow morning?"

Again, laughter filled the air.

"At least I'm assuming you want to come to work with me and not your mama," Shy added.

"Smoking meat is in my blood, Dad," Ry said. "No offense to you and the Lone Star Diner, Mom, but I'm a barbeque man at heart."

Shelly grinned at him through tears. "I never thought you would come and work at the diner, Ry."

"Don't say that," he protested. "I put in my fair share of a few summers there. Busing tables. Washing dishes. But

I've always wanted to put roots down in Lost Creek and go to work at Blackwood BBQ."

"You mean that, son?" asked Shy. "You've worked out that wanderlust of yours?"

Ry nodded. "I've seen a lot of the world. More than most people ever have a chance to do." He glanced around at the guests who had come to welcome him home. "Without a doubt, I can say that Lost Creek is the best place in the world to be."

"I second that," Braden said, raising his wine glass.

Lifting his glass of wine, Dax said, "I third it. Is that even a word?"

Everyone laughed.

"I really mean it," Ry told those gathered. "There's something special about Lost Creek that makes it home. I wouldn't want to live any other place." He slipped an arm about his dad's shoulders. "And I can't think of a better boss to work for than you, Dad."

They returned to their dinners, and Emerson ate sparingly. Normally, where Blackwood BBQ was concerned, she would have cleaned her plate.

Things were different, though. Tonight was different. Her insides were churning in an odd way. She felt almost breathless and restless at the same time, being seated so close to Ry. She had a sensitive nose and could smell his very essence. No cologne, just a clean, masculine scent that had her heart racing.

When Emerson saw that people were almost done eating, she slipped from her chair and went to the cake she had baked. She glanced to Finley to make certain her friend had taken a few pictures of it, and Finley nodded, confirming that she had.

The cake was situated on a table which rolled, and so Emerson moved it to where it was close to both tables.

She looked at Harper to see if she should cut it, but Harper shook her head slightly, mouthing, "Wait."

Emerson stepped behind the table and saw Ry glance her way.

"Ah, as much as I was eager to dine on Dad's barbeque, Emerson has outdone herself tonight and baked something ooey-gooey chocolatey for me." Looking to Harper and then Ivy, he said, "Thanks for passing along the fact that I live, eat, and breathe chocolate."

Ry rose and came toward her, offering Emerson a warm smile. "Would you do the honors and dish it up for us, Emerson?"

"I'm happy to do so, Ry," she said calmly, surprised at how even her voice sounded.

As she sliced into the cake and placed a serving on each plate, Ry distributed them to the guests. He placed the last two dessert plates in front of their empty seats, and Emerson returned to the table.

Ry continued to stand, however, and it was obvious that he wanted to address those gathered.

"I missed this place more than I thought possible. I'm eager to be back and become a part of this town again. I want to thank everyone who came tonight to welcome me home, both those familiar faces and the new ones which have become part of the fabric of Lost Creek, people who are important to those I already love. Thanks again for such an incredible welcome home."

He paused. "And nobody better ask for seconds on desserts— because those leftovers are coming home with me."

Laughter broke out, and Ry returned to his seat. Emerson watched out of the corner of his eye as he took a bite of her latest concoction. He let out a soft moan.

Turning to face her, their gazes met. "I may just have to marry you, Emerson. Just for your ability to make my belly happy."

She felt the heat rise in her cheeks as everyone at their table laughed at his teasing remark.

"You don't have a husband to divorce or a boyfriend I have to compete with, do you?" Ry asked playfully.

"No," she said softly. "I'm married to my job, but you're welcomed to come to The Bake House and purchase whatever you want."

She turned back to her cake, lifting her fork and taking a bite of dessert, pleased with how it had turned out.

Suddenly, her free hand in her lap was engulfed with warmth, and she quickly glanced down, seeing Ry's large hand atop hers. Her eyes flew to meet his gaze.

"Since there isn't a husband or boyfriend in the picture, Emerson, maybe you'd like to go out with me Friday night."

6

Ry flashed his winning smile at Emerson, a smile which had always gotten him whatever he wanted.

It obviously had no effect on this woman.

Instead, Emerson's face reflected the stereotypical phase *deer caught in the headlights*. She looked as if she was panicked by his innocent, flirtatious question. She tried to pull away from him, but he held her hand firmly.

In his most soothing voice, as if trying to comfort a frightened animal, he said, "It's all right, Emerson. I know you don't know me at all. But you know people who do know me well. If asking for a date is too much at this point, maybe we can simply go for coffee and get to know one another a little better. I hear that Dax owns a coffeehouse in town. We could sit and chat over a cup of coffee and you could see if you might like to go out with me sometime."

She still appeared incredibly unsure, and so he added, "You don't have to give me an answer either way right now. You'll be around me some tomorrow night at the group dinner and Harper and Braden's house. Let's see how that goes. Then I'll ask again and see if you're interested in having coffee or dinner with me sometime."

Ry removed his hand from hers, thinking she still looked as if she were ready to bolt from her chair. For the life of him, he couldn't understand why the thought of going out with him had put her in such a state of terror. Being asked on a date shouldn't cause a woman to want to flee a room. At another time in his life, Ry would've let it go. Let her go. Not worried about it.

He was older now, though. And something about Emerson drew him to her. Something he didn't yet understand. Whatever it was, he wanted to find out more about her.

And why the thought of spending a few hours in his company seemed to bring her to a state of chaos.

Dax had gone to a music station and called out, "Let's make this a party for Ry's homecoming."

All of a sudden, *Ain't Too Proud to Beg* began playing over the speakers. People pushed back from their chairs, ready to get up and dance to the infectious song. Ry started to ask Emerson if she might at least care to dance, but she told him, "I need to leave now. We should get your bags from my car."

She came to her feet and was halfway to the door by the time he reacted.

Something wasn't right. Braden and Dax had

mentioned that they hadn't known Emerson to date anyone since they'd come to Lost Creek. Ry couldn't help but wonder if something in her past had turned her off men. He stood and turned to his dad.

"Be right back."

Hurrying toward the door and leaving the building, he saw Emerson ahead of him. Following her with long strides, he reached her as she got to her Mini Cooper. She'd already raised the hatch.

"Sorry. I need to go," she said breathlessly. "I've got to get home and get some sleep. I have to be at the bakery at three."

"Three in the morning?" he asked.

She gave him a nervous smile. "All those donuts and breakfast pastries don't bake themselves. The Bake House opens early, and we have to have fresh items for customers to purchase. The community depends upon us. I would never let Ethel's legacy down."

He reached in and slung his backpack over his shoulder before picking up his duffel bag. Emerson closed the hatch.

"Can I return the favor and at least pick you up tomorrow and drive you to the group dinner?" he asked quietly.

She had been avoiding his gaze, but she met it now. "I… I… guess so."

He pulled out his cell. "Let's exchange numbers. You can text me your address."

They did so and he asked, "What time is dinner?"

"Five-thirty," she replied. "We meet early because several of us have jobs that get us up early."

He supposed like the bakery, Dax's coffeehouse would open early.

"Early isn't a problem for me," he told her. "I'm always up before the sun, courtesy of Uncle Sam. Old habits die hard. What time should I be at your house?"

"Five-fifteen should do it. I live a few blocks off the town square. Braden and Harper's house isn't far from me. I'll see you then," she said stiffly, going to her driver's door and unlocking the car.

She got in, and Ry stepped between her and the door, not wanting her to close him out just yet.

"Thanks again for picking me up and bringing me to the party tonight," he said. "Your dessert— and your company —were the highlights of my evening."

Her eyes narrowed at his words. "You don't mean that," she said. "Seeing your parents and your friends. That was what was important."

He wasn't going to let her push aside what he'd said. "I am thrilled to be back home in Lost Creek, but I know the time and effort you put into that dessert. You didn't even know me, but you put heart and soul into making it. I appreciate that, Emerson, and I do want to get to know you better."

He stepped back. "Thanks again. I'll see you tomorrow night."

Ry closed the car door and waited as she started the car and drove away. He raised a hand, waving at her as she left. He couldn't help but wonder what her story was and how to unlock it.

And he decided Finley might be just the person to clue him in.

Returning to the building, he dropped his gear just inside the front door. He joined the party, which was now in full swing, thanks to the upbeat music. He danced with his mom to Luke Combs' *Fast Car* and then took turns dancing with the other women present, including Ana Ramirez. He learned a little about her and Wolf's new production company, and she invited him to come along with Holden and Finley and watch filming one day.

When he came to Finley, he asked, "Can we talk as we dance?"

A knowing look came into her eyes. "You want the scoop on Emerson, don't you? I saw you talking to her throughout dinner."

Ry nodded. "She intrigues me. Not many women ever have. I asked her out, and she was ready to run from the building like it was on fire. Has she been hurt badly by a man in her past?"

Hesitation crossed her face. "I don't want to share too much of Em's story with you, Ry," Finley answered. "It's her story to share. I will say that she had a really rough childhood. She was given up by her mother and placed in foster care when she was about thirteen or fourteen. She was too old for anyone to want to adopt and never really had anyone cheering her on all those years before she arrived at UT. Em worked hard to land scholarships and grants to pay for her education. She knew that a college degree was her way out of poverty."

He couldn't imagine not having a support system all those years. He'd had loving parents, great friends, and encouraging teachers and coaches all his life. The thought of Emerson having no one but herself weighed heavily on his heart.

"I really want to get to know her," he shared. "Right now, she doesn't know me— much less trust me —but I want her to see me around people she does know and trust. I hope that it'll encourage her to say yes to a date."

Finley smiled at him. "Emerson has a tender heart and is the kind of person who would give you the shirt off her back. You're right. She doesn't trust easily, but once she knows someone? She is a loving, giving soul."

She studied him a moment. "You might be the one to finally break through all the walls she's built around herself, Ry. I hope that's the case."

He returned Finley to her husband and then danced some more, glad to be back in the town he loved and free of his army obligations.

When the party finally broke up, he gathered his gear and accompanied his parents to their catering truck. He helped them clean up in the kitchen and then his dad drove them home to the house he'd grown up in.

"I wish I would've known you were coming, Ry," his mom said. "I would've put new sheets on the bed. Dusted your room."

"It's fine, Mom," he said. "It won't take us two minutes to make up the bed together."

She leaned into him. "It's so good to finally have you here, baby."

As they put the sheets on the bed, he said, "Do you know much about Emerson?"

"Oh, she's a lovely girl. So kindhearted. She just inherited The Bake House, so she'll be leaving teaching. She'll run the bakery, as well as baking cakes for Harper's events. We went to a wedding at the winery a couple of weeks ago, and I swear it was the most beautiful wedding cake I've ever seen. Emerson is incredibly talented."

"What she made for my homecoming was delicious," he said. "I'm actually going to dinner at Harper's house tomorrow night, and Emerson is making dessert for that, too."

Mom beamed at him. "Oh, that's wonderful, honey. I know how close you were with Harper and Ivy. They do have a nice little group of friends." She finished fluffing a pillow and then asked, "Are you going to take a few days off and get acclimated to being home again?"

"I'm not sure," he told her. "I guess I need to talk with Dad."

"HE WON'T EXPECT YOU TO BE AT WORK FIRST THING tomorrow morning. I say take some time to relax before you start working. You'll be doing that the rest of your life."

"One thing I need to do is pick up some civilian clothes. I only have a couple of things to wear."

She brightened. "I can let Joanie handle the diner tomorrow. Why don't we go into San Antonio for the day and do some shopping?"

He grinned. "I'd love to spend the day with you, Mom."

Ry wrapped her in a tight bear hug and kissed the top of her head.

"Let me go in and get things running in the morning. You can stop by about eight-thirty. I'll feed you breakfast, and then we can drive into San Antonio and be there in time for the stores to open."

"Sounds like a plan, Mom. Looking forward to it. Let me go say goodnight to Dad."

Ry headed downstairs again, finding his dad in front of the TV, watching the news.

"Sports is almost on if you want to watch that. Have a seat, son."

He sat on the sofa and said, "How are the Rangers doing this year?"

"Pitching's been solid," Dad replied. "The hitting has been sporadic, though. They'll have ten runs one night and one the next. I'm hoping they'll get their act together after the All-Star break next week and aim for more consistency." His dad paused. "What are your plans, son?"

"Tomorrow, Mom and I are going shopping in San Antonio." He chuckled. "I only have a couple of things to wear. Long range? I hope you and I can sit down and talk about my future at Blackwood BBQ."

Dad smiled at him fondly. "I was hoping you meant it when you said you wanted to come to work with me."

"I know you have your way of doing things, Dad, but I

learned a few things in the army when I was cooking. I'd like to try some of them out. They'll be a little bit out of your comfort zone."

Shy Blackwood frowned. "We'll have to see about that, Ry. What I do works. Let's just get you back in the groove of smoking meats and doing things the Blackwood way before you start trying to change everything up."

Ry's heart knew his dad wouldn't go for many of the ideas he wanted to implement. Something told him that somewhere down the line, he was going to have to make a decision. Whether to stay at Blackwood BBQ— or open his own place. He didn't want to compete against his dad, but Ry also didn't want to take orders the rest of his life. He wanted to be his own man, calling the shots his way.

For now, though, he needed to get back into the swing of things. It had been several years since he'd cooked. While he knew it would be like riding a bicycle and he'd easily pick it up again, he would work for his dad.

And bide his time.

7

$\mathcal{E}$merson put the finishing touches on the cake she was decorating for Mayor Bennett's birthday this evening. She was glad she had been able to have something to keep her mind occupied.

Because Ry Blackwood kept dominating her thoughts.

Usually, she fell asleep quickly. Last night, however, she struggled to do so. Thoughts of the handsome, ex-military man continually flooded her mind. If this was what it was like to be taken with someone, she was glad no man up until this point had ever distracted her so. It made her a little more sympathetic to the failed relationships she had watched Finley go through over the years.

Rhiannon asked, "Are you done with the mayor's cake, Emerson?"

"I am. I was just about to put it in a cake box and mark it for Mrs. Bennett."

Rhiannon nodded crisply. "Do that and then come

upstairs. I'd like to run some things by you regarding The Bake House."

She set the cake onto a piece of cardboard and then folded the box around it.

"I'll take care of the rest, Emerson," Frank said cheerfully.

"Thanks," she replied, heading toward the stairs and up to the apartment.

The door was open, and Emerson walked in, finding Rhiannon at the small kitchen table, her laptop open.

Rhiannon asked bluntly, "Am I truly the manager of this bakery?"

"You know you are," Emerson assured her old friend. "I trust you implicitly. You're a talented baker, and you've also got a great head for numbers. That's why I brought you in as manager."

"Then I hope you'll take everything I say in the spirit in which it's offered." Rhiannon paused. "You were in the way this morning, Emerson."

Reflecting on how crowded the kitchen was this morning, she nodded in agreement. "You're right. The kitchen is set up for two bakers. Not three. You and Frank had a good system going, and I realize I was a third wheel in your way. What do you suggest?"

"It's summer. That has to be your busy season as far as baking wedding and groom's cakes go," Rhiannon pointed out. "I know we'd talked about you coming in three mornings a week, but I just don't see that being necessary. Or feasible. Between Frank and me, we can get everything baked that needs to go out on the shelves each morning.

As far as specialty cakes go? I can actually bake those cakes and have you come in and decorate them once the morning rush is done. I'm good at decorating, but you have a true creative flair."

"When do you suggest I show up?"

"Our big baking rush is three to six in the morning," Rhiannon said thoughtfully. "Then there's the morning crowd coming in for their donuts, bagels, and kolaches. Things slow down by nine o'clock. I think that would be a good time for you to show up. Nine, ten. And that's only *if* you have cakes to decorate on special orders. Then you could leave. It would be a better use of our time and the baking space."

"That's a smart plan. I'm glad you decided this. It's the reason I hired you to manage The Bake House for me."

"I can always text you pictures of the request forms for special orders and the dates they'll be picked up. You wouldn't be bound to come in daily. Just when needed."

"Communication is the most important aspect in a business to me," she told Rhiannon. "If you'll simply keep me apprised of the cakes I'm responsible for, I can come in and do them during off-hours. Even late afternoons or evenings once the bakery has closed."

"I'll take as many orders off your plate as I can," her new manager assured her. "You said you trust me, and I want to do right by you. I know how busy you have to be at the winery with weddings. Maybe we can adjust things once summer ends. That is, if the wedding season slows down for you. I'm glad you're comfortable with me baking special order cakes and simply letting you decorate them."

"I'm good with that. I'll only come in to ice and decorate cakes that you text me about. You baking the cakes will save me time. I still want to check in on a regular basis, though."

"That's fine with me," Rhiannon said. "After all, The Bake House is your bakery." She hesitated and then added, "I already know of some changes I'm ready to make, however. Things which will streamline things for us."

"Such as? Give me a few examples."

"I've been going back through inventory and records. I think for efficiency's sake, we can cut down on the variety of some items we bake. Kolaches are one of the most popular items at The Bake House, but Ethel— and now you —are offering a dozen flavors a day. That doesn't make sense to me. My idea is to stick with the four basic ones which are the best sellers. Sausage, apple, peach, and cream cheese. Have those available every day since they're our big sellers and then have an extra one or two flavors each day beyond that. Rotate those. So, for example, only bake plum on Tuesdays and pear on Saturdays. It would really make baking kolaches easier. It might even pull in people a little more often if they didn't know when one of those flavors is available. Or I could post on the website and here in The Bake House. Put up a daily whiteboard special of things only available that day."

"I like that idea a lot," Emerson said enthusiastically. "As you said, you'd be offering the four basics that sell the most. As long as we offer those every time the doors open,

I think we'll be fine alternating other flavors. Anything else?"

Rhiannon launched into her analysis of the different pastries, cakes, cookies, and pies, sharing with Emerson which ones she wanted to make on a regular basis and which ones should only be offered a couple of times a week.

"I've run the numbers. We won't lose any business by cutting down on our offerings. It could save on waste, actually."

"I trust your opinion," Emerson said. "Have on hand the items you know sell the most, and you can supplement as you go along. That's why I have you in charge. For the knowledge you bring, along with your baking skills."

Rhiannon took Emerson' hand and squeezed it. "Thanks for your faith in me. I never want to shut you out. I'm merely trying to make the bakery run as efficiently as possible."

"I get that. If I were only focused on The Bake House, I probably would've implemented some of the very ideas you've mentioned. With my attention torn between here and Weddings with Hart, it would've taken me longer to figure these kinds of things out. You've got the expertise, Rhiannon. Make the changes you want. In the future? I appreciate you running those big changes by me, but don't think I have to hear every little idea. Go with your gut. You're the manager. You make the call."

They decided to set up a bi-weekly meeting, where Rhiannon would share the figures of what The Bake House had pulled in during the two-week period, and they could study what was selling, what wasn't, and what they would add and delete from the menus, especially when it came to seasonal items, such as pumpkin bread in the fall and Santa sugar cookies at Christmastime.

Emerson sat back in her chair and expelled a long breath. "I can't tell you how relieved I am that you've come on board. I don't feel the pressure of my attention split in two directions, not giving either of my ventures the time they need to thrive. Have you settled into the apartment okay?"

"Everything's fine. It's nice to have a furnished kitchen and all the linens provided. And the furniture already here was a huge help."

"I'm glad it's all worked out for you, Rhiannon."

"How are you doing?"

She felt herself flush, thoughts of Ry Blackwood coming to mind. "Good. Really good. As you mentioned, I'm incredibly busy, baking cakes for Harper's clients. It's really been a lot of fun, exercising my creativity in designing and constructing cakes for weddings. I have the most fun with the groom's cakes, though. It's the one time a guy can really own a part of the planning process. Yes, some of them come to the food tastings, but they don't really get too involved in how to decorate tables or what flowers are used in bouquets. The groom's cake is their time to shine. Bring a bit of themselves to the wedding."

"Do you ever bake any wedding cakes for The Bake House now?" her friend asked.

"I used to occasionally, before Harper opened her event center. Ethel encouraged me to bake exclusively for

Weddings with Hart, so I quit my part-time job here. I'm not sure how many wedding cake orders come into the bakery now."

"I couldn't find any in the last three months," her manager told her. "Maybe for a small wedding, people might have come in and bought a plain, unadorned white sheet cake and then Ethel could have piped on some rosettes or labeled congrats to the couple on it." Rhiannon smiled. "I'm so glad you took everything I recommended the way you did, Emerson."

"You're the boss of The Bake House," she assured Rhiannon. "I needed to be told that I was in the way. I get that you and Frank can handle all the baking needs here. Two bakers are more than adequate. I'll look for texts from you and drop by when I need to, but I'm happy to focus the bulk of my time at the winery. Since The Bake House is closed on Mondays, maybe we could get together and have lunch next Monday. Not as employer and employee, but as two friends catching up."

"I'd really like that, Emerson. I'm so happy to have a fresh start here in Lost Creek. Already, I can tell this is going to be the job of my dreams. And I also have a good friend here, too."

They made plans to meet at Lone Star Diner at ten Monday morning since Rhiannon was wild about break-fast foods and diners were her favorite.

"I may not see you before then," Emerson said. "I've got several weddings coming up in the next few days. Text me if you need anything, though."

"I will," Rhiannon promised.

Emerson drove to Lost Creek Winery. Once she was in the event center kitchen, she opened her tablet and consulted it for what needed to be baked today. Weddings were booked on Thursday, Friday, and Saturday, as well as an anniversary party Sunday afternoon.

She began pulling out her supplies and mixing bowls, setting the ovens to preheat as she mixed various batters based upon the notes she'd taken from cake tastings with these brides and grooms.

While cakes baked, she played with some new designs to show future clients.

"Hey, you," Harper said, entering the kitchen. She inhaled deeply. "Oh, I love to come in here and smell your cakes baking. You should figure out how to bottle the sweetness in the air and sell it as a perfume. It would rule the market."

Emerson laughed. "Not everything can be monetized, Harper. You did a great job for last night's surprise party. Shelly and Shy looked so happy to have their son home."

Harper took a seat at the table. "It did go well, didn't it?" She studied Emerson a moment. "You seemed to be having a pretty good time."

"It was nice of you to include me, especially since I don't know Ry."

"Braden didn't know him either, but I still had him come." Harper laughed. "I think he and Ry will become good friends, though." She grew quiet a moment, her face thoughtful. "Ry was my brother Todd's best friend from the time they were in diapers. They left Lost Creek right after high school graduation and joined the army together. It was what Ry wanted to do. See the world. Todd was happy to accompany him. They were as close as brothers."

Harper paused. "I know Ry still blames himself for my brother's death. He shouldn't. He wasn't even part of the training exercise when Todd was killed."

Though Emerson didn't know Ry Blackwood well, she understood him. He would feel a responsibility for the death of his friend, someone he'd talked into tagging along to see the world.

Harper brightened. "Ry seemed pretty interested in you."

She shrugged non-committedly. "We were the only two unattached people in the room last night. Everyone else was a married couple."

"I saw how he was looking at you," Harper pushed. "I think Ry is interested in you, Em. It wouldn't surprise me if he asked you out. And I hope you'll go."

"Why?" she asked.

"You've lived like a nun ever since I've known you. You have an incredible work ethic, but life isn't all about work. You need balance— or you're going to burn out. Braden has taught me that. Ry is a lot of fun to be around. I think you would have a good time with him."

She shook her head. "Don't take this wrong, Harper, but he's too good-looking a guy to be interested in someone like me."

"Are you *kidding* me?" Harper asked, slamming her palms on the table. "You're beautiful, smart, and kind. Really funny, Em. You're exactly Ry's type."

"Nope. I know you're friends with him and that he's like family to you, but I think he's a big flirt. I don't' want to get involved with someone who's a player. Remember that coach Finley dated? He was really nice-looking, but he thought way too much of himself. I don't need that kind of drama in my life, Harper. No matter how hot the guy is."

"Ry may have been a ladies' man in high school. Correction. He definitely was a ladies' man in high school. That smile of his could charm the socks off any girl. I noticed a maturity about him, though, last night, Emerson. He's come home to Lost Creek and is ready to settle down. I think Ry might surprise you. All I'm asking is that if he does ask you out, give him a chance. He's a really good guy."

Emerson kept to herself that Ry Blackwood had already asked her on a date for this weekend —and that she had become paralyzed at the idea. She'd barely been able to string two words together after he offered to take her out this coming Friday night. She decided to stay quiet about it.

Instead, she said, "I will see him tonight at your house. Braden told me he's cooking Mexican food for our dinner because he thought Ry must've missed eating it."

Harper's eyes lit up. "That's my favorite kind of food. And what dessert are you going to be bringing to match that theme?"

"I'm going to be making chocolate tacos. In fact, I better get started on them as soon as my cakes come out of the oven."

The timer went off for the cakes and she smiled. "See? I've got lots to do."

"I can take a hint," Harper said, standing and pushing her chair in. "I'll see you— and Ry —tonight."

After Harper left, Emerson removed the various cake layers from their pans and let them cool. She had researched the idea of chocolate tacos previously and would now merge several of those recipes together to come up with her interpretation of the dessert.

As she worked, she couldn't help but think chocoholic Ry Blackwood was going to approve of tonight's dessert.

8

As they pulled into the driveway, Ry told his mother, "Thanks for spending the day with me, Mom. I had a lot of fun."

She cut the engine and turned to him. "So did I, honey. It's just so good being around you after so many years apart. You left here on the cusp of manhood, and now it's a little hard to believe the years have gone by and you're an adult."

"I meant what I said last night, Mom. I'm very happy to be back in Lost Creek, and I'm ready to settle down."

"I assume by that you mean more than going to work at Blackwood BBQ. Are you thinking about marriage and a family?"

"I am," he confirmed. "You know I never liked being an only child, so I've got to find someone who can love me and who wants more than one kid."

She took his hand, bringing it to her cheek. "You have

so much to offer a woman, Ry. I know the right one is waiting somewhere in Lost Creek for you."

"I hope so," he said. "Let's carry all these packages in."

They spent the next several minutes unloading the bags from her trunk and back seat. He hadn't spared any expense as he'd refurbished his wardrobe. Ry had banked almost every cent he'd earned in the army. The only exception had been money he spent on brief R&Rs to different countries. Now, he had everything from shirts to pants to socks and underwear. Even a navy blazer and one tie for formal occasions. Best of all, he'd picked up a new pair of ostrich cowboy boots and couldn't wait to break them in.

He carried all his purchases upstairs to his childhood bedroom and removed all the clothing in his closet from their hangers, folding and placing everything on the bed, as well as emptying the drawers of the dresser. He went to the kitchen and retrieved a roll of lawn bags and filled several with the clothes and shoes from years ago that no longer fit him.

Carting those bags downstairs, he piled them in the foyer. He found his mom in the kitchen, starting dinner, and told her that he had several sacks of items to donate.

"It's a lot. T-shirts. Jeans. Flannel and dress shirts."

"I'll take them to Lost Creek High School. They have a clothes closet there for students in need. I'm sure they'll find several young men who can wear what you're passing along."

"Remember that I'm not having dinner at home tonight," he reminded her.

"I hope you have fun with your friends, Ry. I know with Todd gone, that's left a huge hole in your heart. Most of your friends did move away after graduation from high school and college. It's nice that Harper and Ivy have recently returned to Lost Creek. I believe you'll enjoy getting to know their husbands."

"I liked what I saw of them last night," he told her. "I also enjoyed meeting Finley's husband and Wolf and Ana Ramirez, Holden's friends."

Mom grinned. "They've stopped in the diner a few times. Such lovely people, and their children are so well behaved."

"They asked me to stop by and watch a day of filming. I think I'm going to do that this week. Take a few days off, as you suggested, and then start at Blackwood BBQ next week."

"Your father will be pleased to hear that, Ry. He's been looking forward to you coming home and joining him in the family business. Your grandfather would also be proud."

"I'm going to jump in the shower and then head out," he said.

Twenty minutes later, Ry was in his mother's borrowed car, heading to pick up Emerson. He told himself not to rush things with her. Not to push her. Well, maybe he might nudge her a little bit. He was curious to learn more of her story, especially hearing from Finley what a rough time Emerson had growing up. No wonder she was so guarded. She had never really had anyone she could depend upon as a child or teen. It made him even more thankful for the childhood he'd experienced in Lost Creek, with loving parents he'd taken for granted.

He found her house easily and exited the car, walking up the sidewalk and ringing her doorbell.

She answered immediately, waving him in. "I need to get a few things for tonight's dessert. I wanted the ice cream to stay in the freezer until you got here."

Ry looked around the small, neat living room, which was open to the kitchen. His eyes followed Emerson as she went straight to the freezer and removed a carton of ice cream.

Walking her way, he exclaimed, "Blue Bell! That's my favorite ice cream." Glancing at the label, he added, "Homemade Vanilla. It doesn't get much better than that—unless you pour a little Hershey's dark chocolate syrup over it."

She smiled. "Funny you should say that."

Emerson opened the fridge, removing a bottle of dark chocolate syrup, as well as one of caramel.

"If dessert is just ice cream topped by these two, I'll be forever happy."

"There's more to it," she said, retrieving a covered 9 x 12 container from the fridge.

"What's inside that?" he asked, curiosity eating him up.

"You'll need to wait and see," she said, mischief glinting in her gray eyes.

Emerson opened a canvas bag and slipped everything inside it before saying, "Ready."

"I'll get that for you." He picked up the bag by its handles and followed her out the door.

"I'm in Mom's car tonight," he explained. "I had an old Ford Mustang in high school. Todd and I spent hours restoring it. When I left for the army, Dad promised to keep it running and in shape for me."

Once in the car, he continued, saying, "I thought I'd be coming home after my first TOD. When I decided to re-up, I told Dad to sell the car. He got a really decent price for it. I'll use that as a down payment on a truck."

"Boys and their toys," she said teasingly. "Does every male in Texas think he needs to drive a truck?"

"Have you ever thought about trading in the Mini Cooper?" he countered.

Emerson chuckled. "I do have plans to do so," she shared. "I bought it used. Very used. I've been good about keeping up with oil changes and tire rotations, but it's on its last legs. Not only did Ethel leave The Bake House to me, she also left me some cash. I plan to use that to buy something new. Well, new to me. I'm sure I'll buy a used car."

"Can you afford something brand new?"

She grew thoughtful. "I suppose I could."

"Then buy new," he recommended. "You seem like a careful, meticulous person. If you buy new and treat it right, you can drive a car for a decade or more. When you buy used, you don't know how much use— and abuse — that car's been through. New is a sound investment." He paused. "Maybe we should go car shopping together," he tossed out, wanting to see her reaction.

"Maybe," she said.

He recognized that tone. It was reminiscent of his

mom's when she would tell Ry maybe when he was a boy. But she'd always meant no.

Changing topics, he asked, "You said we're eating Mexican tonight."

Emerson nodded. "It's Braden's turn to cook for us. He's fallen in love with Tex-Mex cuisine since he arrived. Finley will contribute her famous sangria. I know Ivy is making guacamole."

"Sounds like a feast. It's great that you get together once a week with friends."

"It's something we really look forward to," she shared. "Everyone has busy lives. Harper's will get even busier once the baby comes. I hope she'll still be up to hosting our Wednesday dinners after that happens. She and Braden bought a house which has a large dining room. We gather there each week. Turn here," she said. "And then turn at the first street."

She pointed out the house to him, and Ry parked in front of it. In the rear-view mirror, he saw another car pull in behind them. Dax and Ivy got out of it and joined them as Ry removed the canvas bag from the car.

Dax looked at the bag with interest. "That's dessert, I'm guessing. I'm hoping it's chocolate."

"Yes," Emerson said. "And that's all you're getting out of me, Dax Tennyson."

"Whatever it is, Emerson also brought vanilla Blue Bell to go with it," Ry revealed.

Dax smiled. "If you just give me a spoon and the carton, that's all I'll need tonight."

They made their way to the front door, and Harper let them in.

"Come inside. Finley is busy pouring sangria. There's also iced tea or sparkling water if you want either." She patted her belly. "As eager as I am for this little one to arrive, I think Finley's sangria might be the first thing I ask for after I give birth. I miss it."

Ry followed everyone into the large kitchen, greeting Finley and Holden.

"Are Wolf and Ana coming this evening?" he asked the writer as Finley handed glasses of sangria to the new arrivals.

"No," Holden said. "They took off last night for your welcome home party. Ana doesn't like to be away from Bear and Eva two nights in a row. She did remind me about asking if you want to come to set."

"I think it would be fascinating. Count me in." He glanced to Emerson. "Have you ever visited while they're filming?"

"No, I haven't."

Finley brightened. "You both should come. Tomorrow will be a really fun day."

"I'm usually at the bakery," Emerson said.

"You told me you'd hired your friend, Rhiannon," Finley pointed out. "Can't she cover things? You said you were putting her in charge so you could focus more on cakes for Weddings with Hart."

When Emerson didn't respond, Finley added, "I think you need to take the time off and go see the filming. It would mean a lot to Ana and Wolf."

Ry held his breath, seeing Emerson think it over. Finally, she said, "Okay. I guess I could come for a couple of hours before I head to the winery."

Holden consulted his phone. "There's a lot of little things being shot first thing. The big scene will probably begin shooting about ten. If you could be on set about nine, you could see a lot behind the scenes, and then we could watch the actors in action."

"I'll pick you and Ry up," Finley volunteered. "Holden will already be there. Say eight-thirty?"

"That's fine with me," Ry said easily. "I'm not going to report to Blackwood BBQ until next week." He glanced to Emerson. "Does that work for you?"

She nodded. Looking to Finley, she said, "Pick me up at the bakery."

"I'll be there, too," he said quickly. "That way, you'll only have to make one stop. I've been hankering for a kolache, so I'll get my fill tomorrow morning."

Braden opened the oven door and removed two large pans. He set both on the massive island in the center of the kitchen and pulled the foil from them, revealing enchiladas. The island already held a large bowl of Spanish rice, refried beans, guacamole, and chips.

"Everybody grab a plate," Braden announced. "Left side is beef enchiladas. Right is chicken."

Ry went around the islands, getting one of the beef and two of the chicken enchiladas, his mouth salivating at the sight and smell of them. He went to the dining room, where others were taking a seat. He hoped he'd be able to sit by Emerson and saw a spot open next to her, claiming it.

As he sat, his stomach grumbled loudly.

"Sorry," he apologized. "I just haven't seen good Mexican food in a long time."

Braden took a chair at the head of the table. "I grew up on Fresh Mex, thinking it was the best. When I relocated to the Hill Country and was introduced to Tex-Mex, I saw I'd been missing out. Fresh Mex emphasizes seafood and fresh herbs. Tex-Mex goes heavy on beef, with a little chicken and pork thrown into the mix. I've had fun playing with recipes and adding to my cooking repertoire."

"You should taste Braden's chicken tortilla soup," Ivy told Ry. "It's better than any bowl you'll get at a restaurant. If Braden wasn't our family's chief winemaker, I'd encourage him to open his own restaurant."

Ry grinned. "You're speaking my love language when it comes to tortilla soup. Do you ever share your recipes, Braden?"

"I'm happy to do so. Finley also shares, but hers are a little harder to follow."

Finley laughed. "I have a basic recipe, then I simply toss in a little of this and some of that. Unlike Em, I don't measure anything. And my one hard and fast rule? Double the cheese in any recipe."

Emerson said, "Baking is different from the meals you and Braden prepare for us. The difference between a teaspoon and a tablespoon of baking powder in a dessert can totally change its taste, texture, and baking time."

"That's why you taught math and science," Finley told her former roommate. "I was a little more freewheeling in the classroom."

"Two plus two will always equal four," Emerson said. "Yes, there are different ways to get to that final sum. One plus three. Two plus two. One times four. Five minus one. But that's what math is all about. Precision. Same as baking."

Braden said, "Winemaking is a blend of both of those. Yes, I go by established amounts as I'm blending grapes. Then, there are times I need to go with my gut and taste as I add a little of one wine and some more of another to create the different wines for the current season."

Talk through dinner range from wine to politics to entertainment and sports. Ry felt at home with this group, as if he'd known them for years. He noticed not only the easy camaraderie between everyone, but he also observed how the three married couples interacted with one another. They weren't just in love with each other. They all seemed as if they were best friends with their spouses. If these three couples could find happiness, it gave him hope that he could, as well.

He glanced at Emerson, her cheeks flushed with excitement as she was talking about a book she'd recently read. She and Holden were going back and forth about the protagonist and his ability to solve the crime which was central to the novel's plot. Ry would need to read one of Holden's books. Harper had even mentioned a movie had been made out of one of them, so that would be fun to watch. He decided to ask

Emerson if she had a copy of Holden's book or if she might want to stream the film with him. That would be a low-key date, an activity he hoped she wouldn't object to.

In the army, Ry hadn't had time for leisure reading. Or leisurely anything. While he'd been a mediocre student, he'd always enjoyed getting lost in a book and was ready to pick up that habit again.

"I'm ready for that tempting dessert," Dax told the group.

Harper stood. "Let's get everything cleaned up. Emerson can get dessert ready for us."

He glanced to her. "Can I help you with that?"

"All right," she said softly.

Everyone took their plates into the kitchen. Holden and Dax took over, rinsing dishes and placing them in the dishwasher, while Braden and Harper sealed the leftovers and placed them in the fridge. Finley made sure everyone had fresh drinks. Ry noticed Ivy turned down sangria and asked for sparkling water instead.

Ivy then brought dessert plates to the island, saying, "I can't wait to see what you've brought tonight, Emerson."

While the others were cleaning up, Emerson had taken the items she'd brought from the freezer and fridge.

She handed him the carton of Blue Bell and said, "Microwave this for eleven seconds. Lid off."

Ry laughed. "Eleven seconds exactly? Not ten or twelve."

"I know what I'm doing," she said, "I told you. It's all about being exact."

"I learned how to follow orders in the army. Eleven seconds, coming up."

The others returned to the dining room, leaving them alone in the kitchen. Ry retrieved the ice cream and microwaved it before bringing it back to Emerson, who had opened her containers and placed taco shells made of chocolate on each plate.

"Wow!" he exclaimed. "I've never seen a chocolate taco shell before."

"It's actually a lace cookie which I folded right as they came out of the oven. They were warm enough for me to shape and then dip in chocolate before I rolled the edges in sprinkles."

Spooning ice cream into the first shell, she said, "That's the amount of ice cream needed in each taco shell. Are you up to the task, Soldier?"

"You bet."

Ry took over the ice cream portion, with Emerson following behind, squeezing chocolate syrup and drizzling caramel on top of the ice cream before placing a dollop of whipped cream as a finishing touch.

"These are a work of art," he declared. "You are really creative."

She blushed. "Thank you. Let's take the plates into the dining room."

Emerson picked up two plates, but Ry was able to set two on his forearm and carry one in each hand.

"I'd be afraid I'd drop them if I tried to carry them that way," she said.

"Part of my army training," he said, laughing. "Cook

and carry."

Everyone exclaimed how beautiful the tacos were, and silence followed, all conversation ceasing as people bit into their desserts. A few moans and groans were heard around the table.

"You've outdone yourself, Em," Finley said. "This may be my favorite dessert yet."

"It's so simple," Emerson said. "And you can really stuff them with whatever you want. If I try this again, I might go with pecans or walnuts. Some fruit. Cherries or raspberries might be nice."

"If you brought these every time, I'd never get tired of them," Braden said. "They're the perfect way to cap off a meal."

Once everyone had finished their desserts, the group went into full cleanup mode again. Ry supposed they did so without having to think, the division of labor occurring over weeks of sharing meals together. As he expected, goodnights were then said. Holden had to be on set by seven tomorrow morning. Dax said he jogged mornings before he arrived at Java Junction, which opened at six each day. Ivy said she always got up early with Dax and then headed to her studio to paint for several hours before showing up for her shift at the winery's tasting room.

After they said their goodbyes and got into the car, Ry said, "You were right. It's a true early bird group."

"We enjoy meeting and eating, and everyone is very understanding about the need for things to break up early. Harper is really the only one who doesn't go into work until nine or ten each morning, and she puts in long hours on the weekends. I know Braden gets to the vineyards or his lab early."

"Your dessert was the hit of the night," he complimented. "Blackwood BBQ only had two desserts on the menu when I left for the army. Peach or apple cobbler."

She chuckled. "That's still what they serve. No additions."

"Maybe I can talk Dad into expanding his horizons where dessert is concerned. It might help him warm up to some of the changes I might want to bring."

"What are those?" she asked as he pulled into her driveway.

"I'd rather show you— and let you sample some of them —rather than merely tell you about them." Pausing a moment, he gazed at her until her eyes met his. "Would you have time this weekend for some taste testing? Maybe Friday? And maybe watching the movie of Holden's book? I've never seen it before. Hell, I've never even read either of his books. I'd hadn't heard of him before I met him. Then again, the army doesn't give you time for reading."

Emerson worried her bottom lip, causing desire to surge through him. "I need to set up cakes at a wedding on Friday."

"Do you have to stay around and serve them, too?"

"No. Harper has assistants who help with food service or supervise anyone whom the bride has designated to be a cake cutter."

"So, you'd be free once you did your setup?" he nudged.

"Yes. I could be home by six. If… if you'd like to come over then."

"That would be terrific," he said eagerly. "I can bring a few items for you to try. Would you be willing to give me free rein in your kitchen? I promise I'd clean up."

"Yes," she said, her voice strong, as if she'd come to a decision about him.

"Thank you, Emerson," he said, leaning over and kissing her cheek.

Ry wanted to do a lot more, but he wasn't about to scare her off at this point.

Her face flamed, and he thought it sweet she blushed so easily.

"Let me walk you to the door," he offered, going around and helping her from the car, taking the canvas bag from her hand as he escorted her up the sidewalk, his hand resting against the small of her back.

They reached the porch. She turned, taking the bag from him.

"I appreciate you driving me to dinner tonight."

"I was happy to do so. I hope you feel a little more relaxed in my company now."

"If I didn't, I wouldn't have invited you over to cook," she said bluntly.

"Good. I'm looking forward to Friday," he told her.

While Ry wished he could see her before then, he didn't want to demand too much of her too soon. As it was, he now was spending Friday night in her company. Cooking for her. Talking with her. Maybe even exchange a few kisses.

"I'll see you at six then. Goodnight, Emerson."

He turned to go, but she caught his elbow, pulling him back. Ry looked at her questioningly and was shocked when her hands went to his face, cupping it, pulling him down. Her lips brushed his quickly in a soft kiss, and then she released him.

"Goodnight, Ry."

Before he could speak, she unlocked the door and was already inside, the door closing.

He stood on the porch a moment, a bit dazed, thinking the kiss a bold move on her part.

And deciding he might also make a bold move or two come Saturday night.

9

———————

hy had she kissed Ry Blackwood?
Because she had wanted to...
Emerson still couldn't believe she had acted so spontaneously. She was the most methodical, practical person she knew. Yet the handsome ex-soldier's good looks made all of her common sense fly out the window.

He must have thought it odd, her making a move like that, much less making the kiss so brief. Actually, she had no idea how long a kiss should last, other than what she'd seen in the movies. It wasn't as if that was a topic which came up in everyday conversation. She was dreading being alone with Ry tonight and yet excited at the same time. Such a mixed bag of emotions had her thoughts scattered, and she forced herself to focus on the cake she was moving from the kitchen to the reception area.

Shy Blackwood was already on site, getting the meal

ready for tonight's reception. He walked over now and grinned at her.

"You just get better and better, don't you, Emerson? That wedding cake is a true work of art. Just look at all those tiers and beautiful flowers on it."

"I just hope it'll please this particular bride. She's been a handful."

Shy nodded in agreement. "She changed the menu on me three— no, four —times. Finally, Harper told me to stop accommodating her and tell her things were set. If not, she'd be needing a new caterer. That shut the little lady up pretty fast."

A worker asked Shy a question and he excused himself, allowing Emerson to roll the cake out to the area designated for the wedding and groom's cakes. One of Harper's assistants came over and helped her to remove the cake from the rolling cart and place it carefully on the display table. While the assistant began arranging dessert plates and napkins around it, Emerson returned to the kitchen to claim the groom's cake. She was pleased at the sports theme and hoped the groom knew what he was doing by marrying this particular bride.

Once more, she brought the second cake to the reception hall and the assistant helped her set it on the groom's table.

"This design rocks, Emerson," the assistant praised. "I feel sorry for this groom. He's got a tiger by the tail, and I think she's going to gobble him up."

Harper appeared, her eyes sweeping over the two cake tables, giving Emerson a nod of approval.

"Wonderful job, Em."

"You seem a little uptight," she commented.

Harper gave her a rueful smile. "If I call and ask you to bail me out of jail, it's because I've been arrested for murder. Friday's Bridezilla is wearing me out."

"Stay firm, Harper," Emerson recommended. "I know not every client is pleasant to work with. Hopefully, you'll never have to lay eyes on this one again."

"I don't think this marriage is going to last. If she returns for a second round, I'll tell her she needs to find some other venue to work with. Life's too short to deal with women like her. Changing subjects, how did you like being on the set of a movie?"

"It was interesting. It amazed me how long it takes to get set up to film a scene. Lighting. Sound. I thought stand-ins were people who performed stunts, but I know now that they're used to help light a scene before the actors step in and do their thing. We got to watch a few scenes filmed, and we also went through the makeup trailer and talked to the lady in charge of costumes. I have a lot more respect now for what it takes to get a movie completed."

"How is Wolf as a director?" Harper asked.

"He's got a quiet yet commanding presence. Ana told us that he likes rehearsing a scene several different ways, getting the actors' input, before the cameras roll. He really picks up on the tiniest of details. He pulled aside the lead who's playing a detective and spoke to him briefly after the first take. They filmed the scene again, and it played out totally different from what we'd witnessed previously, even though it was the exact same dialogue. I can't wait to see the final version of the movie."

"Ana told me they'll do the premiere at an upcoming film festival in Austin," Harper shared. "We'll all be invited to attend. They will do the wrap party here at the winery, though. Ana wants you to do a few different desserts for it. Not necessarily cakes."

"She mentioned that to me while we were on set. Ry told her about the chocolate tacos I'd made, and Ana definitely wants those prepared for the cast and crew. We talked it over, and I'm also going to do a blueberry chiffon mini-pie, honeybee cupcakes, and strawberry cheesecake bites. I haven't yet put a date on my calendar, though. Do you have any idea when filming might wrap?"

"Ana gave me a tentative date in August," Harper said. "I'll check my calendar and text that to you. She thinks things are going so well that they might finish production sooner than planned. Maybe by a few days to as much as a week. You'll have plenty of time to prepare for it, though."

Harper told her how many cast and crew members were involved in the production of *Hill Country Homicide* and said to add another twenty people to that total, saying that Ana wanted their friend group to attend, as well as a few others from Lost Creek.

"They'll be using Lone Star Diner in a couple of scenes," Harper explained. "Shelly is over the moon about that. They'll film those after she's closed the diner for the day. I know there's also a scene set at a library, so Ana and Wolf will want Dorothy Prigmore also invited to the party as a thank you."

"Sounds good. I'll be out of here once I get the groom's cake situated."

Harper smiled encouragingly. "I hear you are having company for dinner tonight."

Heat filled Emerson's cheeks. "Who told you that?"

"Braden. He heard it from Dax. Ry stopped in at Java Junction and had coffee with Dax. He brought it up." Harper touched Emerson's arm. "I think this is a good thing, Em. I told you that Ry is a great guy. I hope this is a match that sticks."

"I'm not sure if I have time to see anyone, Harper," she said brusquely. "Between The Bake House and Weddings with Hart, my time is pretty well taken up."

Harper smiled reassuringly. "There's always time for friends. And love."

Emerson stiffened. "You're jumping to conclusions, Harper. I know you're very fond of Ry and think of him as a brother, but I'm not Ry Blackwell's type."

Her friend studied her a moment. "Then why is he coming over tonight? He's interested in you, Emerson. I can tell. Don't be so prickly. Give him a chance."

"He's seeking my help as a professional," she said coolly. "I'm going to be tasting a few dishes he's prepared and giving him feedback on them. That's all."

Harper pursed her lips. "If you say so. Gotta go."

Emerson fiddled some with the groom's cake before leaving the event center. The entire way home, she kept telling herself that Ry Blackwood wasn't interested in her. That he really only wanted her opinion regarding what he cooked. She would keep her lips and hands to herself and expected him to do the same. She had acted foolishly when she'd kissed him.

She wouldn't make that mistake again.

Once she arrived home, she went into the bathroom and studied her image in the mirror. Color dotted her cheeks. She applied a coat of lipstick and tossed the tube in a drawer, refusing to remove the elastic band which held her hair in a high ponytail. She usually wore it this way to keep it out of her way as she worked and wasn't going to go to any trouble for the man who would be stopping by tonight.

She did decide to open a bottle of wine, though. Lost Creek Vineyards had several wonderful whites and reds, but they were fast becoming known for their blends, thanks to Braden. Emerson chose a red blend now and opened it in order to let it breathe.

When the doorbell rang, she sucked in a quick breath, telling her racing heart it was no big deal that Ry had arrived. She would treat him as she would any of her friends who stopped by.

Opening the door, though, her heart slammed against her ribs, leaving her breathless. Ry held a large pan in his hands. It was covered with foil, and she assumed whatever he wished for her to sample was inside it.

"Hi," she said brightly, stepping aside to let him enter the house.

"Hi, yourself," he replied, going straight to the kitchen and setting the pan on the countertop. "I spy wine."

"I opened some for us," she said casually. "Being a

barbeque man, I knew you'd be bringing meats and thought a red blend would go well with them."

"You're right about that. I actually went to Lost Creek Winery today and did a tasting with Ivy. I knew next to nothing about wine. Only that it came in red and white."

She laughed. "Ivy has taught me a lot about wines, so much that I actually have a few I prefer now and even know what foods to pair with them."

He picked up the bottle, nodding approvingly. "This is one I sampled. Probably my favorite."

"Mine, too," she confirmed. "Braden has really contributed some great flavors to the Lost Creek Vineyards label."

A shadow crossed his face, and Emerson recalled how close Ry was with Todd Hart, who had been slated to take over from his dad and become the chief winemaker at the winery.

"I'm sorry," she said softly. "You must really miss Todd, especially now that you're back in Lost Creek."

Tears misted his dark blue eyes. "I hate to say it, but it's like I've lost him all over again by coming home. When Todd died, a part of me died, too. We had left Texas to see different countries and have a few adventures. Then Todd came home in a box. I stayed. Did another TOD. Then two more after that."

Understanding dawned within her. "That's why you left cooking after your first tour. Did you think fighting in the field would make up for Todd's death?"

"I don't know what I was thinking back then," he admitted. "I only knew Todd was gone, and I felt like it was all my fault. Cooking had always brought me joy, so I denied myself that joy. Todd was dead, and I felt guilty as hell about that. I learned a lot, being in combat, though I never made another friend. I had my fellow soldiers' backs. I knew a lot of people as acquaintances, but I never really believed I could let my guard down and open my heart to another friend. Todd was my brother from another mother."

"Do you still feel the same?" she asked quietly. "Or have you reached a point where you can move on, remembering the many good times?"

He grew thoughtful. "Coming back to Lost Creek, everything here reminds me of Todd again. I do have a little more maturity about me, however. I appreciate the bond I had with him. I've apologized to Ivy and Harper—and the Harts. They've all told me there's nothing to forgive. I wasn't even around during the training exercise that went wrong. Still, I've carried that burden of Todd's death on my soul for a long time."

She stepped toward him and squeezed his arm, feeling the hard muscle beneath her fingertips. "Believe the Harts, Ry. They're good people. They would never hold you responsible for what happened. And you shouldn't either."

Emerson let her hand drop but stayed close to him, feeling the heat vibrating off of him, inhaling that wonderful, masculine scent.

"I'm ready to move on," he said determinedly. "I've made peace with the past. I'm ready to live in the present — and I'm open to whatever the future brings. I'm already feeling a connection with others. No one will ever replace

Todd, but I realize now that I can make new friends and build memories with them."

"That's very mature of you," she praised, knowing he'd reached a turning point in his life. The men in their friend group were wonderful. Kind and generous. They would welcome Ry and help him get over the past.

For a long moment, they gazed at one another, Emerson's heart beating rapidly.

Then Ry turned away, focusing on the bottle of wine. "Let me pour us some wine, and you can try what I've brought."

He poured the wine into the two glasses sitting next to the bottle and offered her one.

"To new friendships— and good times to come," he toasted, tapping his wineglass against hers.

She took a long pull of the blend, feeling it warm her as she swallowed.

"Let me get some plates for us."

As she walked to the cupboard and removed them, she added, "Why don't we eat at the breakfast bar? It'll be convenient for you to serve us here."

"Fine with me."

Ry began removing the foil from the large pan, and Emerson saw within it were separate packets of foil-wrapped items, along with a few Styrofoam containers.

He pulled those out first, saying. "These are some different sauces I'd like you to try before we even pour them over the meats."

While he removed the lids, she got napkins and silverware for them. She also poured each of them a tall glass of water, placing those beside their plates.

"We can cleanse our palates with the water," she told him.

"Good idea."

He had her taste each sauce, describing the base and what herbs he added to it, noting the heat level and what kinds of meat he'd use with the sauce. Emerson had a great palate and even asked him about one of the sauces.

"Did this one also have thyme?"

He grinned. "It does. I'd forgotten I'd added that. You really do have good taste buds."

"I mostly deal with sweets, but I can pick out different herbs. I use some of them in breads I make."

"Let's see what you think of my meats. I was up at six this morning, letting them cook slowly. That's the thing about barbequing. You have to practice patience. Nothing can be rushed." He paused. "Kind of like relationships. You have to feel your way. Take your time. Sample different items until you hit upon what you like."

She looked away, sensing the blush filling her cheeks, and sipped some of her wine as he unfolded the first item.

"This is smoked brisket. I'm sure you realize that beef brisket is at the heart of any barbeque joint."

He plated some for her. "Try it first without sauce."

Emerson did so, the brisket tender as she chewed. "It's fabulous."

"I used chili antique and Thai herbs on it." He lifted a container. "Try this sauce with it."

She did and said, "I like it with and without. It can stand alone, but the sauce really enhances the flavor."

As they ate, she asked, "Would you tell me about how you smoke meat? I've eaten your dad's barbeque a bunch of times, but I really don't know much about how it's prepared."

He grinned, looking boyish and very appealing. "Smoking meat low and slow really changes its taste and texture. The heat isn't just low. It's indirect. The smoke changes the composition of a cut of meat, infusing it with vapors and soot. The type of wood you use also flavors meat in unique ways."

Ry paused. "You understand science, so you'll get how a gradual heat crispens and dehydrates the outside of a cut of meat, making the outside browned or even blackened, like with brisket. Slow cooking a brisket twelve hours or more gives it that distinctive, smoky favor. It's melt-in-your-mouth tender."

"You mentioned the wood also flavoring your meat. What kind do you prefer? Or do you change it up for different cuts or varieties of meat?"

"I'm partial to apple and maple when it comes to pork. They both give pork a sweet, mild flavor. But the heart and soul of Texas barbeque is beef. For that, I like hickory. That provides a strong smokiness to your beef. Almost bacon-like. Oak and mesquite are also good choices. Oak is middle-of-the-road, as far as smoky flavor goes. Mesquite can be really strong. We only use it in our outdoor smokers."

Emerson saw how his eyes lit up now, comfortable talking about a subject he knew a lot about.

"Then there's the whole argument about whether to use chips, logs, or pellets. Personally, I'm into wood chunks since I've got tons of experience smoking meats and prefer them for smoking brisket or pork butt. As for whether or not you wet the wood? I'm a firm believer in…"

His voice trailed off, and she frowned. "You wet the wood?"

Ry shook his head. "You asked a simple question, and I'm going off, spouting about all kinds of things you couldn't possibly be interested in. I'm sorry."

"Don't be," she told him. "I can tell you have a passion for smoking meat. Returning to your roots in Lost Creek, you'll get the opportunity to do that again. Really, I'm interested in what you have to say."

"Why don't you finish tasting what I brought instead?" he countered. "I've got a pork loin and would be interested in your feedback."

Removing another packet, Ry opened it, placing some on her plate.

"This is grilled pork loin. I used oak. It's accompanied with cucumber pickles and chicharrónes— fried pork belly. My spin on it includes a walnut bagna cauda. That's made up of garlic, anchovies, and olive oil. Not really Asian. Just something I've played around with."

Emerson tasted it, letting it sit on her tongue a moment. "I like the garlic. I'd cut back slightly on the anchovies, though. Those are an acquired taste as it is, and you don't want them to overwhelm the dish."

"Got it."

She also sampled what Ry called a smoked butcher's cut covered with shishito salsa verde and sprinkled with chopped cilantro and pickled onions.

"This is even better than the brisket, and I was a fan of that," she said. "I could eat this all day."

"One more thing to try. Some braised ribs. I actually wrapped these in foil with hoisin sauce."

"What's hoisin got in it?" she asked.

"It's a glaze that's a mixture of sweet and salty. It contains soybeans, garlic, fennel, and red chili peppers. I also added some five-spice powder, as well as vinegar and sugar, then finished it off with a healthy dose of soy sauce. Braising infuses the liquid into the ribs and softens the connective rib tissue. Try dipping them in this sauce after you've sampled the rib."

He opened a container and placed it in front of her. "I made this from the reserved braising liquid. Added some red pepper jelly and a dash of vinegar."

First, she bit into the rib and tasted the meat alone. Then, she dipped it into the sauce.

"Wow! I'm not kidding, Ry, this is terrific. Everything has been excellent. You're really on to something."

He looked worried. "Do you think Texans would eat this?"

"Honestly, I think they'd be reluctant to order it if they saw it on the menu. Blackwood BBQ has been around for decades. People like the tried and true, their go-to orders.

But," she added, "if they sampled these dishes, you would have some real converts."

"I doubt Dad will consider putting any of these on the menu," Ry said. "He's more set in his ways than his customers are."

"Then you need to convince him otherwise," she advised. "Have him taste what you made me. He's a businessman. He's not going to turn down a good idea. Adding some of these menu items to what he already serves would be good business. It would also add a new dimension to the catering menu. Harper would go crazy for all of these. In fact, why don't you take over next Wednesday's dinner and try out your recipes on the group? They would give you honest feedback."

"You really think I should?" he asked.

"Definitely. Don't just go with my opinion. I'm telling you, though, that everyone is going to go wild over your spin on traditional Texas barbeque."

He reached up, his fingers lightly grazing her chin as his thumb rubbed against the corner of her mouth.

"You had a little sauce," he explained, wiping his thumb on a napkin.

For a moment, Emerson couldn't breathe as his gaze penetrated her, seeming to see into her very soul.

Then Ry leaned over and brushed his lips against hers.

Magic...

10

*R*y had wanted to kiss Emerson ever since he stepped across her threshold. The brief kiss they had exchanged had only whet his appetite for more. She had surprised him with that kiss, and it had ended almost as soon as it had begun. He hadn't known if she had wanted to kiss him and then changed her mind or if she had been embarrassed about taking the lead.

He wasn't shy about that— and was ready to have a proper kiss with her.

Leaning toward her, he fought the urge to touch her and merely brushed his lips against hers slowly, wanting to see how she responded. Her lips were full and pillowy soft, the most tempting lips he had ever touched. She didn't move, merely letting him make light contact. Since she didn't pull away, Ry decided to crank it up a notch.

His hand went to her nape, cupping it, holding her in place as he gently pressed his mouth to hers. He thought it odd that she hadn't moved. Hadn't responded. It was as if Emerson was frozen in time.

Or too scared to move.

Ry still thought something had happened with her—or to her —that made her wary around men. That kept him from advancing too fast now. Instead, he alternated kissing her lips softly with moving to her cheek. Her ear. Her throat, where her pulse throbbed wildly. Just easy, sweet kisses. Nothing demanding.

Damn, if she didn't move or react or make some kind of noise soon, he was going to stop and ask why.

He gave it another minute, pressing his lips a little harder against hers. Still, nothing.

Breaking the kiss, he looked into those sad, gray eyes, seeing them clouded. With doubt? Frustration?

Ry couldn't say.

"Why did you stop?" Emerson asked, her mouth trembling slightly, her brow creased with worry. "Oh, never mind," she said, pushing off her stool to escape.

Something in her tone gave him pause. He stood, reaching out and clasping her elbow, spinning her to face him. Surprise filled him as he saw tears welling in her eyes. She blinked and then looked away.

"Emerson?" he asked, taking her chin in hand and turning her back to face him.

This time when she looked at him, he saw disappointment, which was like a knife to his heart.

"I'm sorry about the kiss," he apologized. "It was impulsive of me. I should've asked you first."

"I'm not the kind of girl you kiss," she blurted out,

biting her lip once the words sounded. She pulled away and went to where their plates were sitting. Picking them up, she said, "You can leave now. I'll clean this up. I'll wash your pan and return it to you."

She brought the plates to the sink and set them down, turning on the water to rinse them.

He was usually good— really, really good —about reading women.

In this moment, he had no idea what had gone wrong. But he was determined to find out and make things right with her.

Going to stand behind her, Ry leaned around and turned off the faucet, his body brushing against hers. He felt the electricity spark between them and turned Emerson to face him.

"Have I done something wrong?" he asked. "And what did you mean, you're not the kind of girl I would kiss. How would you know who I like to kiss?"

His hands went to her shoulders, keeping her firmly in place. He wanted answers.

She bit her lip again. "You're… well, you're Ry Blackwood. I'm guessing you were the most popular guy in your class. The guy every girl wanted to go out with. The one even the nobodies had a crush on." She wet her lips. "You're handsome. Smart. Outgoing. And you're built like a hero in a romance novel."

"Huh?" he said. "I'm not following this conversation at all, Emerson. Spit it out."

Frustration filled her eyes. "You're so far out of my league, Ry. I'm a cipher. I could never hold the attention of a man like you. I... I... don't even know how to kiss."

Without warning, she burst into tears. She tried to pull away, but he wasn't willing to let her run off after what she'd just told him. When she realized that, she collapsed against him, her entire body shaking as she cried her heart out. Instinctively, he wrapped his arms about her, stroking her hair.

"It's okay," he murmured. "You're safe."

His words had the opposite of his desired effect, making her cry even harder. Baffled by her outburst, he swept her off her feet and carried her to the sofa. He sat, cradling her in his lap, her face buried against his chest. He decided to remain quiet and let her simply cry it out. Hopefully, he would get to the bottom of things after that.

She wept for another few minutes and then began to quieten. He'd been rubbing her back, trying to comfort her. Kissing the top of her head. She didn't wear perfume, but she had a sweet smell about her, as if the desserts she baked enveloped her, causing her to give off a delightful scent.

Finally, she lifted her head, staring at his chest and not looking him in the eye.

"Thank you for being nice to me when you didn't have to. You can go now."

"What if I want to stay?"

His question caused her to suck in a quick breath. Her gaze met his, and he saw yearning in hers.

"Have you ever been kissed, Emerson?" he asked quietly.

Fresh tears welled in her eyes. "No," she whispered.

Her words shocked him. No wonder she hadn't responded to him. She didn't know how. Good Lord, she had to be in her late twenties— and yet no man had ever kissed her?

Ry would ask her about that later. Right now, he wanted to soothe her. Assure her.

"Would you like me to teach you how to kiss?"

"Yes."

It was a start.

"Okay. First, you shouldn't hold back. You didn't really move when I kissed you before. It's okay if you do. You'll feel things, all kinds of things when you kiss. You can react. Make a noise if you'd like."

"A noise?" she questioned, her brow furrowing.

"A sigh. A moan. Whatever feels right, go with it."

"Okay."

"It's also okay if you touch the other person. Stroke their face. Touch their hair. Kiss them where you want to kiss them."

When she gave him a blank look, he said, "On the mouth. The chin. The brow. The throat."

"Oh. Okay."

"Would you like to try a kiss with me now?"

Emerson nodded.

"Close your eyes. Let the sensations you're feeling guide you. Kissing heightens your senses. Your awareness of your body."

She looked uncertain, but she closed her eyes. Ry looked at her, his heart aching. This woman was special.

She had a lot to give— and had no understanding of how to do so. He reminded himself how alone she must have been for so many years and figured she'd cut herself off from all her feelings. Or at least repressed them.

His mouth moved to hers. Once more, he brushed his lips against hers. This time, he sensed a difference in her. He kissed her. Not too hard or soft. But firmly.

Her hands moved to grip his shoulders.

"Good," Ry murmured against her mouth. "Now, you kiss me."

She stilled a moment but followed through. She moved her mouth on his, gradually increasing the pressure. His blood spiked, running hot through his limbs. One arm was snug around her waist. He allowed his free hand to cup her cheek, his thumb stroking it.

He began kissing her again, and this time, Emerson kissed him back. She might never have kissed a man before, but she was a fast learner. Desire flickered within him, and Ry decided to up the stakes.

Slowly, he ran his tongue along the seam of her mouth, back and forth, urging her to open to him. She did so, and he slipped his tongue inside her mouth, stroking hers. Emerson didn't move for a moment, and he worried he had pushed her too far.

Then she snuggled closer to him. One hand pushed into his hair. Her tongue rubbed against his. His blood caught on fire now, but he knew to rein in the desire. This woman needed baby steps. A lot of them.

And for the first time in his life, Ry didn't want to rush things.

They kissed for a long time, with him exploring her mouth and teaching her to do the same. She tasted as sweet as she smelled, absolutely divine. He didn't think he'd ever spent this much time kissing a woman, but he could have kissed Emerson all night.

Breaking the kiss, he trailed his lips along her jawline and then down to her throat. He nipped playfully at her racing pulse and then licked it, soothing the skin. She had startled when he did so, but she settled against him again as he licked and nipped at her, little sounds of satisfaction coming from her.

"Can I try that?" she asked.

"You can do anything you like," he told her. "Be as bold as you want."

Their gazes met— and he saw those gray eyes had darkened, turning stormy with desire.

"Go for it," he whispered encouragingly.

And she did.

Though she was a novice, every kiss sent his senses reeling. Her tongue glided along the skin of his throat, and he sighed in contentment. She moved back to his mouth and softly bit into his lower lip, something he had yet to teach her.

"Good," he murmured, glad she was following her instincts.

They began kissing again, longer, deeper, more passionately. By now, the student was ready to become the teacher, and Ry's tongue warred with hers happily, his groans becoming louder, even as her moans went from soft to needy.

He was the one to break the kiss. "You pick up things quickly."

She laughed softly. "You make me feel… confident. Alive."

Ry kissed her again, hard, and then broke it. "You taste incredibly sweet, Emerson."

"You taste like… danger," she replied.

He gave her a soft kiss. "Don't ever be afraid of me. I'll always listen to you. To what you say with your voice. With your body. We'll only do what you want us to do."

She frowned. "I'm just learning how to kiss, Ry. I can't think of going beyond that right now. This is all so new to me."

"I'm not asking to make love to you, Emerson. Maybe that day will come. Maybe it won't. But I want you to know that you're in charge. We only do what you're comfortable doing."

Her face softened. "Thank you. I like kissing. I like kissing *you*, Ry."

She rested her head on his shoulder a moment, and he inhaled the sweet scent of her.

Then she raised her head. "I guess you want to know why I've never kissed anyone."

"I'll admit I'm curious," he told her. "But I only want you to share what you want of your story."

"I think I'll get our wine," she said, slipping from his lap and heading to the kitchen.

He watched her fill their glasses again, and she brought them back, handing him his. She sat next to him. While he wished Emerson would've climbed back into his lap, he was happy to take her hand and thread his fingers through hers.

She looked down at their joined hands. "This feels really nice. Almost as nice as kissing."

"You've never held hands with anyone?"

"Nope." She took a large swallow of her wine and set it on the coffee table in front of them. "I don't want your pity. I'm just going to tell you how things always were."

He set down his own glass and took her other hand, smiling encouragingly.

"My dad had a hot temper. I learned early to stay out of his way, especially when he was drinking."

"He hit you?" The thought angered him.

"A few times. Like I said, I got good at avoiding him. Making myself small. Sometimes, I'd even hide under my bed. Or in the closet. With him, it was out of sight, out of mind. Mom never learned that lesson. She would confront him. Yell at him about his drinking. He slapped her around a lot." She winced. "I would put my hands over my ears when they were fighting, but I could still hear them."

Emerson paused, staring into space a moment. Ry knew to let the story unfold at her pace and kept silent.

"He went to prison for killing a man. Frankly, I can't tell you who it was or what it was about. I assume he was drunk and belligerent when it happened."

"How old were you?"

"I was in third grade."

His heart ached, thinking of a frail, skinny Emerson, knowing how her classmates would have teased and even bullied her unmercifully over something like this. His fingers tightened on hers.

"Mom went off the deep end after he went to prison. I thought things would be better with him gone. Or at least different. Well, they *were* different. She started drinking. Got into drugs. Lost job after job. We moved a lot because she couldn't make the rent. The lights would be turned off when the bill wasn't paid. Not much food was in the pantry. She was gone all hours, leaving me to fend for myself."

He leaned over and kissed her softly. "I'm sorry."

"It was hard. It got even harder. I tried to keep myself clean and presentable, but the teachers at school figured out things were bad. They reported her to the Child Protective Services. They came and took me away. I never lived with her after that."

A tear ran down Emerson's face, and he leaned over, kissing it away.

"Even though things were awful, I still wanted her to get her act together. Get clean and sober and bring me home." She paused. "It never happened. I went from one foster home to another. Rarely saw her. And then when I was fourteen, she signed away her parental rights. She OD'd a few years later."

"How did that make you feel?" he asked.

"Her giving me up hurt worse than hearing about her death. By then, I'd written her off. I was too old for anyone to even think about adopting me. No one wants a teenager. I tried so hard, Ry, to be good. Not to cause any problems. I worked harder than anyone at school. Had a teacher who mentored me. Miss Kent saw potential in me and told me a college degree would be my way out of poverty and despair."

She smiled wryly. "I became a teacher because of Miss Kent. I wanted to help other kids, just as she'd helped me." Emerson cleared her throat. "Anyway, I studied and graduated number one in my class. I also worked thirty hours a week."

"So, too busy to date."

"Exactly. No prom for me. No clubs or athletics. Just work and study. College was the same. I had to maintain a certain GPA to keep my grants and scholarships. I also worked in a bakery during the week and as a server and then bartender in a sports bar on the weekends. I had no social life. I built an impenetrable wall around me, Ry. I was friendly to everyone I worked with, but I always gave off the vibe that let people know I had no interest in pursuing any kind of friendship— or relationship — outside of work or class."

"What about when you came to Lost Creek? You're a beautiful woman, Emerson." When she began to protest, he said, "You are. Without question. I can't believe you didn't have a line out your door."

She shrugged. "I suppose I was comfortable with my small world. Usually, people meet others at work, but Lost Creek Elementary didn't even have a single male teacher on staff. And then I started at The Bake House, working weekends during the school year and five or six days a week during summers. I've always filled my time, Ry. I don't know. Maybe I'm afraid to be alone with myself or around others."

"You seemed very comfortable last night at Harper's house."

Her face softened. "I really like everyone in the group. Finley's the one who pulled me along. We roomed together our first year at UT, then she joined a sorority and moved to the house. We were both elementary ed majors, though, and stayed friends. Then when we came to Lost Creek to teach, we rented this house. I saw guys come and go over the years, and Finley never really seemed happy with any of them. Thankfully, Holden came along and changed all that."

Emerson sighed. "I guess I never really thought I've missed out on anything by not dating. Not sleeping with anyone. I loved teaching math and science. I think when the school year starts up again, I'm going to miss doing that. I am happy Ethel left the Bake House to me, though, and I'm thrilled to be working with Harper. Baking and stretching my creativity to the max when I decorate wedding and groom's cakes makes me very happy."

He gazed into her eyes. "Do you think you could add another layer into the mix? Like seeing me?"

She waited a long moment and then shook her head. "I don't think so, Ry. You're a man of the world. You've got a bright future ahead of you. I'm always going to be that awkward, unloved girl. I'm happy in my work and blessed to have some really wonderful friends, but you need a better match than me. Someone lively and outgoing and more—"

"I want you, Emerson," Ry declared boldly. "I can't say if this will work out between us or not, but I'm drawn to you in a way I never have been to anyone else. Are you brave enough to at least give us a chance?"

He waited, not moving, not breathing, hoping she wouldn't shut him out.

Her sad eyes revealed her answer before she spoke. "No. It would never work between us, Ry. I would disappoint you. And you're so nice, you'd feel sorry for me and wouldn't tell me when I wasn't enough for you." She paused. "Until you finally decided to move on. Which you would."

Emerson stood, putting distance between them. "I wish things could work between us. I'm just saving you from wasting your time— and me from having my heart broken when you leave. Let's just try and be friends."

It was not the answer he had expected.

Ry Blackwood always got his way.

And now he was being shut down by a virgin who was too afraid to open her heart.

Emerson may think she was making the right move, ending things before they could ever start up between them.

But he was going to prove her wrong.

Ry was proud he'd made it through the weekend without texting Emerson. He'd decided to give her some space.

And hope she regretted the decision she'd made about keeping him in the friend zone.

He'd kept busy the last several days. Braden had asked if he might like to come and visit the winery and see the production process, and Ry had jumped at the opportunity. They'd walked through the vineyards, with Braden explaining the difference between white and red grapes and the harvest of both coming a little later in the summer during separate weeks. Braden also gave Ry a tour of the facilities where the wines were made.

It was fascinating, and he'd asked a boatload of questions. Just as different woods gave smoked meat various flavors, the wood barrels wines were stored in also impacted its flavor. He and Braden talked about how they both had tried and true formulas for their meats and wines, and yet they also were of a younger generation who liked to experiment.

Braden allowed Ry to sample several different wines, telling him about the subtle differences. Thanks to the wine tasting lesson he'd shared with Ivy, Ry was able to pick up on notes Braden mentioned. His new friend was also excited when Ry shared that he'd like to feed the crew this coming Wednesday night. Since it was Finley's turn, Ry had texted her about holding off a week and allowing him to fill in the gap.

She'd been more than willing and had asked him to stop by the house she and Holden had recently purchased. They'd sat in her spacious office, and he'd shared the digital photo session he'd done just before his separation occurred from the military. Finley had one bedroom in the house devoted to printing and enlarging photos, and she downloaded the two best photographs and had printed out several. When he'd expressed an interest in her help in framing the largest ones of him in his BDU and army service uniforms, she told him she would take care of the matting and framing of both as a welcome home gift, which he thought incredibly kind.

He'd also accompanied Finley and Holden to Java Junction Saturday night, where they sat with Ivy as Dax performed. Ry had learned the coffeehouse owner invited local singers to perform on Saturday nights, and this Saturday was a rare occasion for him to perform. Usually, Dax was either serving as the DJ or playing with his band at a wedding held at Lost Creek Winery. The Saturday night wedding this weekend, however, was definitely a family affair, with the groom's cousin serving as the DJ and the bride's stepfather photographing the ceremony and reception, freeing up Finley, as well.

Ry had enjoyed the night out with friends and was surprised just how well Dax sang and played his guitar. When he learned that every song played had been written by Dax, he was effusive in his praise.

Again, being around the two couples, he had seen the strong connection between them. The small touches. The little glances. Looking at Ivy and Dax, as well as Finley and Holden, it was obvious both pairs were very much in love.

He wasn't in love with Emerson— but he saw potential in a relationship with her. Whether it might lead to love or not, he couldn't say.

But Ry wanted a chance to explore that possibility with her.

Emerson would have to go on the back burner for a while because he was ready to have a heart-to-heart with his dad. Shy Blackwood was one of the nicest men on the planet, but he was also one of the most stubborn. He wouldn't take kindly to Ry coming in and wanting to change things. That wasn't his plan, however. He wanted to see how Blackwood BBQ operated now. Things had to have changed since his teen years, when he would work the dinner service, clean the dining room and kitchen, and then hang around from ten until midnight, helping load the smokers with various meats for the following day's lunch offerings. Then again, maybe they hadn't. His dad was of the *'if it ain't broke, don't fix it'* school of thought. What Ry needed to see was if there were a place for him. His dad seemed to think so, but he wasn't about to step on any current employee's toes or force anyone out.

He showered and shaved and walked several blocks to the town square, glad it was not yet eight o'clock. The past few days the temperature had been climbing, and he was certain triple digits were just around the corner.

Entering the diner, he saw his mom working the cash register and noted the place was busy on this Monday morning.

"Hey, Sweetie," Mom greeted. "Are you stopping by to say hi, or do you want to be fed?"

"Both," he said, smiling at her.

"Why don't you go back and see everyone?" she suggested. "They've been asking about you ever since you got home."

He went to the back, greeting the longtime breakfast cook and his assistant, as well as two servers who'd worked at the diner for a couple of decades. They were all happy to see him, thanking him for his service, and asking what he wanted to eat.

"Surprise me," he said. "Whatever I get, I know it'll be good."

Ry found an empty booth and seated himself. The floodgates opened, and a continual stream of people stopped by, greeting him, telling him how happy they were to see him back in Lost Creek.

His breakfast arrived, brought to him by his mom. She slid in across from him.

"Sunrise Special," she said. "Eggs. Pancakes. Bacon. Sausage. Hash browns. And a biscuit and gravy."

One of the servers had already brought him coffee and refilled it now as he dug into his food.

"Are you going to talk to your dad today?" Mom pressed.

"Yes. I've enjoyed a few days off, but I get itchy if I'm not doing something. After I eat, I'll go over and see how he has things set up these days. I want to hear about his employees and who does what. I'm not going to come in and take anyone's job."

"I know that, Ry. Your dad will make room for you, though. You know that."

"I want to be useful, Mom. I also have some new things I'd like to see Dad place on the menu."

She frowned. "You might want to hold off on that. You know he's not open to changing things."

"I get that. I'll bide my time, but I do think the menu could use a little updating. The website, too. I looked at it, and it's pretty bare bones. In fact, I saw Ivy this weekend. She actually does website designing, in addition to painting. I think it would be worth it to have a conversation with her and see how she could freshen things up."

His mom looked worried. "I don't know about that, Honey. It took a lot of arm pulling just to get him to *have* a website. Please. Take your time. Don't push him right away."

It sounded as if he'd have to use kid gloves with both Emerson and his dad.

"Okay. But I'm not going to stay quiet forever."

"Nor should you," she agreed. "You're a grown man. You have ideas you want to implement. I get that. You have to realize, though, that Shy has been doing things his way for many years. He turned sixty this spring. He's been running Blackwood BBQ since he was twenty and your grandfather passed. And he worked there a decade before that. That's a lot of years doing it a certain way. His way."

"I understand all that, Mom. I'm not going to go in like a tornado and decimate the place. I believe just a few things could be altered, though. Improved."

She glanced up. "I need to get back to work. See you at home."

After he'd eaten, Ry accepted a to-go cup of coffee and set out, traversing the square and then leaving it, turning on to Main Street. It was only a few short blocks to the family restaurant, and he went around back, following his nose to the smokers. He saw almost double the number of smokers from what used to sit here but realized only half of them were in use right now.

Spying Joe Bob, he headed toward the tall, lanky, bearded employee who'd been with Blackwood BBQ for as long as Ry could remember.

"You son-of-a-gun," Joe Bob greeted, enveloping him in a bear hug. "You're all grown up, Ry."

"You haven't changed a bit, Joe Bob," he replied. "Well, there's a little salt and pepper in your beard and hair, but other than that, you look the same. I see you're nursing the meat."

"Yup. I put on a bunch of things between five and

seven every morning for dinner. Keep my eye on them and work the lunch shift."

"Billy still doing the other?"

Joe Bob nodded. "He does the dinner shift and then hangs around and loads the smokers between ten and midnight."

Since smoked meats usually cooked in indirect heat for a dozen hours or so, they were placed into the smokers twice a day in order to have a variety for each meal service. Billy— like Joe Bob —had worked for Shy Blackwood for decades.

"You gonna be spelling me some?" the older man asked.

"I'm going to do whatever Dad needs me to do," he replied. "Don't worry. Your hours won't be cut by me coming to work."

"Hope not," Joe Bob said. "I got a kid in college and one starting in another year. I need all the hours I can get."

"Good seeing you," he said, heading toward the back door, the smell of smoke already clinging to him.

Inside, he found two men in the kitchen and introduced himself.

"I'm Ry Blackwood."

The older of the pair lit up. "Mr. Ry. I'm Carlos. This is my son Jose."

He glanced around. "I bet you two are in charge of sides."

"And desserts," Carlos said. "Jose also runs the cash register during most services."

Blackwood BBQ was set up cafeteria-style, with

customers pushing their tray down a long line, asking for the cut of meats they wished, and then selecting sides. They paid their bill at the end of line, avoiding the need for servers to take orders and distribute meals.

Jose was mixing a large bowl of coleslaw, while Carlos chopped bacon. He finished that now, scraping the bacon bits into a simmering pot of beans on the stove.

"Is my dad around?"

"In his office," Jose said, adding more vinegar to the bowl as he stirred the shredded cabbage and other ingredients for coleslaw.

"Thanks. Good meeting you both."

"You, too, Mr. Ry," Carlos said.

He approached the closed door and took a deep breath before knocking.

"Come in," Shy Blackwood boomed.

Opening the door, he popped his head inside. "You busy, Dad?"

"Not for my son. Get in here. Glad you came. Ready to go to work?"

Ry took a seat in the chair in front of the desk. "I'd like to. But it seems as if you already have a full crew running things. I won't usurp anyone's position, Dad. I'm not going to take paying work away from people who work here. It looks as if Joe Bob and Billy have a great system smoking the meats. Carlos and Jose manage the sides. I'm sure you have a couple of teenagers coming in to bus tables and wash dishes."

He paused. "I know we talked about me coming to

work for you, Dad— but I don't think there's any work to be had. I refuse to put people out of a job."

Shy frowned. "You wouldn't. I just need to juggle things a bit."

"No," Ry said firmly. "No juggling. Nobody's hours get cut."

"What about part-time?" his dad asked.

"Doing what?" he asked.

Shy raked a hand through his hair. "Weekends have gotten a little rough because of all the catering at the winery. Not that I'm complaining. I really appreciate Harper recommending me to so many of her brides. It's brought in a heckuva lot of income."

It dawned on him that the additional smokers he had seen were used for catering weddings and other events at Lost Creek Winery.

"Who supervises the catering?"

"I do. And I do all the smoking for it. With the diner closing at three every day, your mom comes over here and helps me load all the meats and sides into a van I bought. She and I— and sometimes Carlos —spread everything out in the kitchen at the winery. Cut the meats. Keep things warmed until the ceremony is over and pictures are being taken. Harper's got a couple of assistants who take the plated meals and distribute them to guests. Your mom, Carlos, and I then clean up."

Dad sighed. "It's really starting to get to me, Ry. Catering weddings and other events is damned hard work. I never seem to have a chance on a weekend to put up my feet and take it easy. No watching football or playing golf. Just work, work, work."

"You'd like me to take over all the catering then?"

Relief swept across his dad's face. "Absolutely. It would mean you'd be responsible for smoking all the meats for the event. Carlos and Jose can handle preparing the sides, though. Would you be interested in that, son? I know it's not what either of us envisioned, but it would really make a difference."

Ry thought not only would he enjoy preparing those dinners, but he would also pitch a new, varied menu to Harper. It would give him a chance to see how others responded to his new ideas regarding barbeque, and he would be useful to his dad. If things went well, he might even think about investing in a food truck and driving to different places around town during the week. He could serve lunch weekdays. Offer something beyond the scope of Blackwood BBQ.

"I'm in," he said, thrusting out his hand and shaking his father's. "I'll need to see the catering calendar. Become familiar with what the different plates consist of. Since I'd free you and Mom up on weekends, I might even need to hire someone on a limited basis to help with plating and serving."

And Ry had in mind exactly who he'd offer that opportunity to.

12

hy had she pushed Ry Blackwood away?

Frustration filled Emerson as an image of the tall, broad-shouldered, sexy ex-serviceman filled her mind. Thoughts of the kisses they'd shared made her yearn for things she still didn't quite understand— but now knew she wanted.

No. She'd done the right thing, shutting him down, telling him it would be a waste of his time and hers. A man like Ry would never want to permanently be with someone bland and unexciting like her. He needed someone adventurous. Gorgeous. A woman who could offer him much more than dull Emerson Frost ever could. In cooking terms, he needed cayenne pepper— spicy, peppery, and pungent. She was vanilla. Plain, boring vanilla.

Besides, Emerson liked her life the way it was. She'd found her comfort zone and didn't want to stray far from it. Ry Blackwood would have pushed her way out of it. No, knock her the length of a football field. In the end of their time together, he would have grown weary of her. Or worse, been apathetic toward her. She couldn't have taken that look in his eyes. One of boredom or irritation. It was better to not start anything with him.

Yet what she wouldn't give for just one more kiss from him.

She would be seeing him tonight at Harper's. The group text had informed her that Ry was doing the cooking tonight, experimenting on them. Having tasted some of what he'd created, she knew the others were in store for a memorable meal.

He had texted her yesterday. A single line that told her he was preparing barbeque with an Asian twist, and she could plan the dessert accordingly. She'd merely replied with a thumbs up emoji, not wanting to start any kind of conversation with him.

It would be hard to see him again. She knew she couldn't shove him into a corner as she had all the other men she'd met at school or work and go about her business. A part of her would always yearn after Ry Blackwood.

And what might have been. Even if only for a short while.

Harper had asked her how things went with Ry, and Emerson had said she'd tasted his food, and he was an excellent cook. When her friend asked about the rest of the night, she'd shrugged and said there was nothing to report. She'd sampled his dishes and provided her opinion on them. She read the disappointment in Harper's eyes, but her friend hadn't forced further conversation.

How was she supposed to go to Wednesday nights from now on and be around Ry? See him. Smell him. And not want him.

Letting out an exasperated sigh, she glanced at the timer and saw it was about to sound. She switched it and the deep fryer off, lifting the basket and removing the pastries, resting them on paper towels. Emerson had made yakgwa, a Korean honey pastry, wanting her dessert to go well with the meal Ry was preparing for the group. She let the pastries cool while she mixed fresh ginger with honey syrup, pouring the combination into a squeeze bottle to be poured over the yakgwa.

Emerson went to change clothes. She slipped into a sleeveless linen blouse and white capris and then did something she never did.

Painted her toenails.

The bright red made her feel sexy, especially when she slipped her feet into a pair of sandals she'd worn only two other times. It gave her the confidence boost she needed. She brushed her teeth and applied a fresh coat of lipstick before removing her hair tie and brushing her hair. It fell just below her shoulders, thick and dark, and she decided to leave it down tonight.

No, she should put it back up. It would seem as if she were trying too hard to get Ry to notice her. Before she could place it in her usual ponytail, though, the doorbell sounded. Frowning, she set down her brush and went to the door.

Ry stood on her porch.

Emerson's breath caught. She had forgotten how attractive he was in person. He wore a dark navy T-Shirt that showed off his biceps and muscular chest. A pair of jeans that molded to his legs. On his feet were a pair of cowboy boots in rich bourbon.

"What are you doing here?" she demanded, her tone sharper than she wished for it to sound.

He didn't flinch, though. He merely gave her a sexy, lazy smile, one that had butterflies exploding in her belly and thoughts of his mouth on hers.

"I thought I'd drop by and give you a ride," he drawled.

"That's not necessary. I can drive myself," she said primly. "Thank you anyway."

"Come on, Emerson. You said we could be friends. Friends trade rides to places."

"If they arranged to in advance."

"Sorry I didn't text first and simply stopped by. Please. Go with me. We're going to the same place. Save the environment and some gas. Ride with me. Don't be stuck-up."

Anger flared within her. "I have never been accused of being stuck-up." She relented. "All right. But this time only."

He grinned, causing her pulse to leap. "Unless I text you and we make plans in advance to go together."

"Maybe," she said, her anger dissipating as she took in his boyish grin.

"Can I help you carry your dessert?"

"It was cooling. I need to put it into a container." She stepped aside. "You might as well come in."

"Thank you," he said graciously as he inhaled deeply. "Hmm. Gotta follow my nose."

He moved across the room and into the kitchen. "You made yakgwas!" he said excitedly.

Emerson followed. "I'm glad you recognized what they were. I wasn't sure how they were supposed to look. I haven't even tried one yet."

His eyes glinted with amusement. "Then you need an official taste tester to see if they pass muster. "May I?"

"Could I stop you?"

"Nope," he said, scooping up one and popping it into his mouth.

He closed his eyes and chewed, his satisfaction obvious.

"Can I serve them tonight?" she asked nervously.

"Absolutely. Your dough is spot on. The pastry is light and just the right color."

She indicated the squeeze bottle. "I also made a gingered honey syrup to go over them."

Ry lifted the bottle and squeezed some onto the pad of his finger. He slipped it inside his mouth. "Oh, yes. Have you tried it?"

Again, he squeezed a dab onto his finger. This time, he held it up to her lips. Their gazes locked, and she opened for him. He slid his finger into her mouth and her lips claimed it. Slowly, he pulled it out, her tongue brushing against it, causing her heart to race.

"It's… good," she managed to get out, watching him lick the finger that had just been in her mouth.

"Yes. Very good."

Emerson wanted to fling herself at him. It took every ounce of self-control she possessed not to do so.

Turning, she pulled out a plastic container. "Let me load them into this, and we can go."

"I'll help."

Ry did so, placing yakgwas into the container, their fingers brushing against one another's several times. With each contact, her head grew lighter.

"Don't faint," she murmured under her breath.

"What?" he asked.

"Nothing."

She washed her hands when the last pastry had been placed into the container and then placed the lid atop it, sealing it.

"Don't forget the honey," he reminded, and Emerson picked up the bottle.

She locked up, and they started down the sidewalk, to a black truck she'd never seen before.

"New?" she asked.

"Brand new," he replied. "Got a great deal from a dealership in Boerne. Guy I went to high school with owns it. He was two years ahead of me. Played running back. The truck was used as a demo for people to drive to see if they liked the make and model. It's got a couple of thousand miles on it, but it's the current year. Next year's models will be in soon, which really decreases the value of this one."

"It's nice," she said. "I know you were eager to get something of your own."

"I put a healthy down payment on it. Will have it paid off in only a couple of years."

Ry started the truck and put it into gear. "Ready for more of my barbeque?"

"Definitely," she answered honestly. "I've never eaten such tender barbeque before. Have you met with your dad? Will you be starting work soon?"

"Yes. I'm going to handle all the catering for Harper's events," he told her, clearly excited by this prospect. "Dad and Mom have been run pretty ragged by all the extra business those weddings have brought in. He's pleased to get it, but it's spread him pretty thin."

"Will you also take over meeting with the clients?"

He thought a moment. "We didn't actually talk about that, but it would make sense."

"I meet with them once they have a set date at the venue. I have a tab on The Bake House's website. Ivy set it up for me. I walk them through it, showing them different choices of cakes and discussing the variety of flavors and types of icing. I have them decide on several to try, and we schedule a cake tasting. I'm not sure what Shy does."

"I could present whatever menu he gives me— but I also plan to add to it. My spin on different dishes."

"Oh, Ry, that would be terrific. Brides are always look for something new and creative to set their weddings apart. While I know a lot of them will prefer to go for traditional Texas barbeque, I think you'll have your fair share wanting to try something new and different. Congratulations!"

He shrugged. "Dad doesn't know that I want to offer

more than what's on the Blackwood menu. I'm testing some things out on the group tonight to see if any of what I prepared might be good for wedding receptions."

"Anything you prepared for me the other night would work," she told him. "And I can't wait to see what you've brought tonight."

"Some of the same, along with a few other selections."

"Like?" she pressed.

"You'll have to wait and see, Miss… " He paused. "I don't even know your last name, Emerson."

"It's Frost."

He glanced at her— and burst out laughing. She was used to it and let him enjoy the moment.

"Frost. And you frost cakes. Oh, that's too much." He flicked his eyes from the road to her. "But I like it."

They arrived at the Clarks' house, and she brought in her dessert. Ry made one trip and then claimed Holden, who helped him make another three.

"What all did you bring?" Braden asked. "Is this going to be a six-course meal?"

"No," Ry replied. "I brought a little of a lot of things. You people tonight are true guinea pigs."

Ry had them gather around the island as he opened lids to two different slow cookers, three instant pots, and one pressure cooker. He also removed foil from several 9x13 containers.

"I want to tell you what everything is and have you sample small portions of it," he explained. "Then you can fill your plates with what you liked, including some sides. Hopefully, as we eat, you can give me your feedback on what you like and why and what isn't working for you."

He walked them through what he'd brought. They included the items Emerson had tasted Friday night, but Ry had also included new things, such as some interesting side dishes.

"Everything smells heavenly," Finley declared. "I'm going to want recipes, Ry."

"Not a problem. You've all eaten barbeque before. Lots of it. What I've brought tonight is an Asian take on barbeque. Most of it is Korean, since I was stationed in South Korea for three years, but I've also added a little Japanese and Thai into the mix. The biggest difference between Texan and Asian barbeque is in preparation. Here, we throw big slabs of beef, pork, and chicken into smokers and using indirect heat, letting it cook for ten to twelve hours.

"Korean cuisine, as far as barbeque is concerned, utilizes razor-thin cuts of meat or bite-sized pieces. It means cooking time is minimized, but you still get the tender, flavorful tastes. They often eat meat placed on red leaf lettuce, wrapping the lettuce around the meat and turning it into a burrito. Let's try some of the galbi first. These are super-tender beef short ribs."

He spooned up small bites and passed plates around, with Ivy exclaiming, "Oh, I wasn't expecting it to be sweet and savory."

"That's big in Korean barbeque, combining those two flavors." He glanced to Emerson. "I'm even thinking about teaming up with Emerson and getting her to make some plain pastries for me that I could place barbequed meats inside."

"That would rock," Dax said.

She tried not to show her surprise. Actually, it was a great idea.

They sampled bites of spiced chicken thighs, marinated steak and pork, and beef and pork kebabs.

"I don't think I've eaten barbeque this tender," Harper said. "These kebabs are fabulous."

"Do you think something like this might go over with your clients?" asked Ry.

"Yes!" Harper exclaimed. "Blackwood BBQ is always great, but if you could offer even three or four of these dishes, I know they would be a huge hit at weddings."

"I'm going to be taking over the catering end of Blackwood BBQ," Ry announced. "As far as I can tell, looking at the calendar, the events at the winery are the only things Dad is catering right now. Does he have couples do a tasting with him, as Emerson does with cakes?"

Harper shook her head. "No. I merely give them a menu, and they decide which items to offer. Most go with a two-meat plate and two sides. Brisket and pork or brisket and sausage seem to be the biggest crowd pleasers."

"We still need to try some of those things," Holden pointed out.

Ry glanced to where Holden looked. "Oh, the banchan. Sides," he added. "They can really round out a meal."

They sampled sigumchi namul, a seasoned spinach, and bibimbap, which was mixed rice with vegetables.

Emerson's favorite was the japchae, a stir-fried glass noodle dish.

"This cucumber salad has a real kick to it," Braden said. "I like that a lot."

"That's the red chili pepper flakes that bring the heat," Ry explained.

By the time the group had sampled everything that Ry had brought, they were chatting enthusiastically, filling their plates with the new dishes.

Emerson stepped close to him. "This group has tried a lot of different foods, thanks to Braden and Finley, but you've added a new dimension to things. I think you're going to make a big splash when you take over the catering of the winery's events."

Ry locked gazes with her. "I'm going to need some help. With Mom and Dad sitting out for their much-deserved rest, it's going to be too much for me to handle." He cleared his throat. "Would you be interested in helping me plate and serve dinners at wedding receptions, Emerson?"

13

———

Ry drove to Lost Creek Winery, eager for the meeting which lay ahead. The past two weeks had been good ones for him. He was settling into Lost Creek, jogging several mornings a week with Dax. He had also gone with Dax, Holden, and Braden to watch a Rangers baseball game at Hill Country Hangout, the town's local sports bar. Two more Wednesday friends' dinners had come and gone, where Finley had cooked a pot roast with all the trimmings one week and Braden had made chicken fried steak, mashed potatoes, and green bean casserole the next.

He had also worked three different weddings with Emerson's help. Already, they had a shorthand they used between them, words often unnecessary. Ry had taken over the catering end of Blackwood BBQ's business, totally in charge of smoking all meats needed for the three wedding receptions. Carlos and Jose had done a terrific job preparing the sides. While Carlos had volunteered to come work at the winery during the receptions, Ry had given the hardworking employee a pass, saying he would handle things with Emerson's help.

He looked forward to today's meeting with Harper, Ivy, and Finley. Ry had already met separately with Harper, and they had decided which entrées to add to the catering menu available to brides who used Blackwood BBQ. While Harper had liked everything he'd prepared for the group to taste, they looked at time prep and cost effectiveness, settling on an additional three main courses with an Asian flair. These would also include the sides he had made, which went well with the newer cuisine offerings.

Pulling up at the event center, Ry crossed the bridge over the creek which ran through the vineyard and entered the building. He spied Emerson and Ivy already seated at a table and joined them. Finley appeared with a tray of cups and a coffee urn. She poured coffee for everyone and took a seat as Harper arrived.

"I know we're here to talk today in part about the Blackwood BBQ website," Ry began. "Mom told me that she had to practically pull teeth to get Dad to agree to have one, and he never looks at it. She's given us carte blanche to revise it however we choose."

Ivy already had it called up on her tablet and turned the screen so everyone could see the website.

"This is pathetic," Ivy said, causing the others to chuckle. "The only picture is the header, which is a picture of the restaurant itself on Main Street. And a dated one at that. We need to jazz this up in so many ways, Ry."

"I agree. I think we should have tabs for the menu. Catering. Pictures of all items which are available at the restaurant. I'd also like to see pictures of all our employees, as well."

"You read my mind," Ivy said, smiling. "I also think on the catering page that we need to generate a box where people can submit inquiries. I can set up a business email account for you so those could go directly to you."

"It all sounds good to me."

He mentioned which of the new dishes would be offered for wedding receptions and other parties held at the winery's event center. Each of the women agreed those would be the best choices, with Emerson saying she thought they would grow in popularity as word of mouth spread.

"You might even want to have a tab with testimonials on it," Emerson continued. "Or that could even be on the Weddings with Hart website. I think you should include catering tabs on your website, Harper, or at least links that would take people to Blackwood BBQ, The Bake House, and Finley's photography studio."

"Good idea," Harper seconded, looking to her sister. "Ivy, could you handle those updates?"

Ivy made a note. "Got it." She looked at Finley. "What about photographing Ry's dishes? Especially the new ones he's created. People need to see what the food looks like before they commit. Of course, I know Ry will start offering tastings of various barbeques, just as Emerson does for cake choices."

Finley opened her calendar. "I'm really starting to book up with senior portraits. I know it's only mid-July, but school starts in a little over a month. Seniors are wanting to get those photos made before starting classes."

She turned to Ry, pushing her calendar toward him. "I've got a few open pockets the next couple of days. Check and see if any of these might work for you."

He glanced at tomorrow and saw she had open from eleven to twelve and three-thirty to four-thirty. Picking up his pen, he wrote his name in both slots.

"This first one, meet me at Blackwood BBQ. We can get pictures of all the traditional barbeque dishes we serve for the home page and the menu page. Come to my parents' house for the later slot. They won't be home all day, so I can spread out in the kitchen and have at least some of the dishes ready to be photographed."

"That sounds good," Finley said. "Can I also pencil you in for three days from now? I have another time open from nine-thirty to eleven. Maybe we could finish up and capture everything that hasn't been shot up to that point and see if you need additional time or photographs after that."

Ry made a note of all three times in his phone. "I think we're good to go."

Harper said, "I need to bring up one more issue with you, Ry. I've lost two clients over it, and I had to pinch hit to save the third from walking by calling in Rob Owens at

Hill Country Hangout to bring his food truck over to bail me out."

"What are you talking about?" Ry asked.

"It's become the norm for appetizers to be served after a wedding while the wedding party has photos made. Your dad wasn't willing to get out of his comfort zone. He refused to offer any apps. Up until now, brides have simply gone with it, but as I said, two balked and decided to book a different venue over that one issue. Would you be willing to cater apps as well as entrées for the receptions?"

"Absolutely," he responded. "Neither of us should lose business over such a small issue."

As a group, they batted around different ideas for the apps. Emerson even mentioned doing a small puff pastry cup filled with brisket, an idea they all fell in love with.

"Let me refine the ideas we've talked about, Harper," he said. "I'll get in the kitchen and whip up the apps for Finley to photograph, along with everything else. Ivy can then list these on the website."

"The sooner, the better, Ry." Harper told him. "Thank you for being so flexible. You've already done a fantastic job for the three weddings you've catered. Guests were really bragging about how tender the brisket and pulled pork were."

He glanced to Emerson. "I have to give my comrade in arms here a shoutout. Emerson knows how to work quickly and efficiently. Thanks to her —and your assistants delivering the meals —we really have a nice operation set up."

Harper rose. "I think my part is over. I've got to go and meet some new clients now. We'll be finalizing a few things, and then I'll send them here to talk cakes and catering."

Finley also came to her feet. "I've got everything I need, too. I'll see you tomorrow morning, Ry."

The two women left the building, and Ivy said, "Let me show you a few templates I'm thinking about using, Ry."

They spent ten minutes looking at various layouts for the updated website, including fonts. Ivy was able to download the font Blackwood BBQ had used for many years.

"This is your signature brand," Ivy said, "so I don't want to alter it. I do want to bring some color and life to the website, however. I really like the idea of you including the employees. It will mean a lot to them to receive recognition. Once I get the pictures of food from Finley and write the copy, I can show you the pages I've built. As far as employee pictures go, I think it would be more interesting to show them in action, doing what they do, versus a more formal portrait."

"I agree," Emerson said. "Ethel had Ivy do something similar for the employee pictures on The Bake House's website. She's since added Rhiannon to the mix. You might want to look at that, Ry, to see what she's talking about."

"I'll do that."

Ivy closed her tablet. "I have plenty to help me get started since we talked about the layout and colors. Not that I want to do business at our friends' dinner tomorrow night, but if you could show up about fifteen minutes early, Ry, I can show you what I've put together and you can make some decisions about the website."

"Not a problem," he said, and they both told Ivy goodbye.

After she left, he and Emerson talked more seriously about the types of appetizers to be offered.

"I think you should have five to seven choices on your catering menu," she told him. "Most brides go with a package of three or four apps, from what Harper's mentioned. "You want those brides to have a little variety so they can make a choice favorable to all their guests. Although you're a barbeque man, it wouldn't hurt to make one of those selections vegetarian. Even here in the Texas Hill Country, we get a few vegetarians every now and then."

"Good idea," he said, scribbling another note to himself. He decided it was finally time to push forward with Emerson because they had been getting along so well. Patience only went so far, and his was almost exhausted. He needed to know whether he had a chance with her or not.

Ry set down the pen and said, "Thank you for loaning me your copy of *Capitol Crimes*. I need to return it to you. I raced through it. It's hard to believe that I know the guy who authored it."

Emerson smiled. "Holden is immensely talented. I think you'll like *Hill Country Homicide* just as much if you'd like to borrow it next."

"From the limited scenes I saw being filmed when we were on set, I know I'll like it."

"Are you interested in seeing the movie Wolf directed of *Capitol Crimes*? Maybe we could watch it together on Friday night after we work the reception."

"Of course," he said enthusiastically. "I really liked Wolf, and I'd be interested to see how he brought Holden's book to life on the screen."

Ry didn't know if this was a get together as friends— or more —but he wasn't about to turn down time with her.

"That would be great. I can make certain that we have some extra brisket to bring back from the reception with us. We could make sandwiches for dinner."

"Sounds good to me," she said, her head turning as a couple approached them.

They both stood and introduced themselves.

"We're Chris and Laurel," the man said, shaking both their hands. "Harper sent us to talk about our cakes and catering options."

Laurel said, "I want to talk about the cakes first."

Ry sat silently and observed how Emerson walked the pair through what was available. He could tell when Laurel was indecisive, how Emerson nudged her in a direction. She didn't tell the bride what to choose, but she helped narrow choices for the couple.

Within half an hour, the pair had decided on exactly what they wanted, design-wise, for both their wedding and groom's cakes. Emerson had shown them several examples on her website, offering them her card, which also bore the website's address, so they'd have it for easy reference. She'd also sketched a few ideas on a notepad, personalizing both the bride and groom's choices.

"Now that you've decided on design, let's talk flavors," she told the couple.

For the next few minutes, they discussed flavors for both cakes, and Emerson showed them examples of the various types of icings they might use. Once the couple had narrowed their choices, Emerson arranged a date for them to return for a cake tasting.

"I'll have small cakes of the flavors you like best, as well as different kinds of icings on them. We'll taste them together and when you feel strongly, we can make a final decision then. If you want to take the cakes home and share slices of them with anyone— your moms, best friends, siblings —then you can simply call me and let me know what you've decided."

"Thank you, Emerson. I think we're going to have the best wedding cake of all my friends," Laurel gushed. "Your attention to detail and the way you're personalizing both cakes is simply incredible."

"I know you'll be happy with whatever you select," Emerson told the bride.

Chris then turned to Ry. "I'll be honest and tell you up front that Laurel and I aren't sure we want to use you for our reception."

He nodded. "I totally understand. If barbeque isn't your thing, you'll want to serve something that will make your day special."

"It's not that we don't like barbeque," Chris said.

"Laurel and I were going for a more casual feel for our reception. We're not fond of the idea of having our guests seated at tables and staying in the same place while a plated dinner is delivered to them."

"We want more of a fun, loosey-goosey, party atmosphere," Laurel emphasized. "I think the most fun weddings I've attended are the ones which have food stations."

She glanced to her fiancé. "Remember that terrific potato bar at the Clemson wedding?" She turned back to Ry. "They put mashed and sweet potatoes in martini glasses, and then you could add whatever you wanted. Garlic. Bacon. Butter. Chives. Sour cream. To the mashed potatoes. Walnuts or pecans and brown sugar and whipped cream to the sweet potatoes. I liked the fact that everyone was up and moving around. People would grab something from one station and sit at a table. They'd finish with it and head to another station and then sit at a different table."

"We've never done anything like that before," Ry told the couple, "but I'm open to making this day your day."

He began pitching ideas for the various food stations, including the brisket in a puff pastry Emerson had mentioned, as well as a shrimp or chicken jalapeño popper wrapped in bacon. Emerson joined in, making some great contributions, ideas that he couldn't wait to get in the kitchen and try with her. Ry saw the engaged pair's excitement grow as they spoke.

"Oh, I like all these ideas," Laurel told him. "Especially

the brisket pastry, the pulled pork sliders, and the mac and cheese. You could really do all that?"

"I can. I'll have to write up a proposal for you since we've never done this before. How many guests are we talking again?"

Chris told him one hundred and fifty, and Ry wrote the number down, saying, "Let me get your cell number. I can text you an estimate later today. If it sounds good, I can write up a more formal contract for us to sign."

Chris beamed. "I really like this idea. We came to Lost Creek Winery because we wanted something a little different for our wedding. We're also both eighth generation Texans and proud of our heritage. This will really make our wedding perfect."

They bid the couple farewell, and Emerson turned to him once they were out the door.

"You really think fast on your feet, Ry. You tossed out some wonderful ideas for those food stations. In fact, I think it's something you should have Ivy incorporate onto the website."

"You weren't bad yourself," he complimented. "You offered just as many ideas as I did. I'd like to get in the kitchen with you and try some of those things out."

Her smile at the suggestion made him feel he was on the right track. "I'd really like to play around and experiment a bit with you. Really, Ry, I'm just glad you were able to keep their business and make them happy."

"I need to stop by Harper's office on the way out and tell her about this new development. I'll run by her the idea of offering stations in the future, as well, versus sit-down dinners."

His gaze met hers. "We make a really great team, Emerson Frost."

She gave him a warm smile. "I think so, too."

14

*E*merson had made the biggest decision of her life. *She was going to lose her virginity to Ry Blackwood.*

He was much different than what she had thought he would be. In her limited experience, a man with such incredible good looks was usually an arrogant jerk who had little substance and wanted his way about everything. Ry didn't have an arrogant bone in his body. He was easy to get along with. Genuine. Caring. She had enjoyed being around him, not only at their Wednesday night dinners, but also working with him, catering wedding receptions.

Ry was that rare person— handsome, intelligent, and kind to everyone around him. During last week's large wedding, two workers from Blackwood BBQ had accompanied him, helping get out all the plates to guests. Ry addressed Carlos and Jose with respect and kindness. Miss Kent had taught Emerson to treat everyone equally, whether they were the President of the United States or a janitor. She had always followed her mentor's advice, and she saw Ry did the same. People were naturally attracted to him because of his charm and friendliness.

She still didn't think the two of them had long-term potential, but she was tired of missing out on things in life. Emerson had spent almost thirty years keeping her feelings inside her, working diligently, never rocking the boat. It was time to live a little.

And that included learning about sex.

She saw how happy her friends were in their marriages and couldn't wait to be an auntie to Harper's baby. Harper and Braden had announced at their recent Wednesday dinner that they were having a boy and would name him Beau, in honor of Braden's late younger brother.

Who knew? She might one day adopt a child and become a mother herself. Emerson believed she had a lot of love to give to a child who was in the foster system, just as she had been.

But first things first. She wanted to experience the thrill of being in Ry Blackwood's arms. Of coming together and enjoying the physical act of love. She knew he was still intrigued by her, which she found absolutely ridiculous. She had to be the most boring person on the planet, and he would soon come to learn that once he got to know her better. Still, she thought he would be a very considerate lover, the right man to introduce her to a world she had never experienced. This was her chance to find out more about herself— with Ry's help.

She reached the event center earlier than usual because tonight would be the largest wedding ever put on by Weddings with Hart. The wedding cake she had baked was seven tiers high, and the groom's cake was the biggest non-wedding cake she had ever undertaken. The bride had been very specific in what she wanted, but the groom told Emerson just to run with whatever she wanted to bake. She had asked him a few questions about his particular interests, and the cake she had created incorporated his love of the outdoors, fishing, in particular.

Parking in the rear of the event center, she got out just as Ry pulled up in the catering van. He got out and greeted her.

"This is going to be a big night," he said.

He was referring to the reception, but his words made Emerson shiver, thinking of what she hoped might occur between them once they were alone at her house.

"It was a little challenging, preparing this much barbeque," he continued. "Carlos and Jose are following me in my dad's truck, bringing all the sides."

"Let me help you start taking things in," she said.

They began unloading the van, with Harper's two assistants coming out to meet them, helping, as well. Jose and Carlos arrived and began toting in huge bins of sides. Harper had different sets of china in the kitchen, which made it easier for Ry or any other caterer to simply transfer food inside the building and have plates delivered straight to guests.

As the others worked, she rolled out the wedding cake,

possibly the best one she had ever created. Harper met her and assisted in moving it to the display table.

"Everything going smoothly?" she asked her friend, who seemed a little distracted.

"I think so. This is a big day for us. It's the largest wedding we've ever done."

Finley joined them. "I've gotten all the pre-ceremony shots I need except for shots of these two cakes. Also, Ron asked where you were, Harper, and I told him I thought you were here."

"Hmm. I wonder what he wants," Harper mused. "He's been so agreeable. Unlike his bride. Let me help you get the groom's cake out while Finley takes pictures of the wedding cake."

Once they had the groom's massive cake on display, Emerson saw the groom himself heading toward them.

"Is everything all right?" asked Harper, obviously concerned since most grooms didn't seek her out before the ceremony.

Ron smiled broadly. "You have been a dream to work with, Harper." He glanced to the cakes. "And I can't believe what you came up with, Emerson. If I have any friends getting married in the near future, I'll definitely send them your way." The groom paused. "I do have one favor to ask, however."

Harper gave him her professional smile. "Name it, Ron, and I'll make certain it happens."

"I'd like once the wedding party is seated to begin toasts immediately. Could you have your staff have all the champagne glasses out and filled? I know the maid of honor wants to say something. My best man wants to give a speech. Then I want to address the crowd, too. I need by the time I speak to also have as many of the plates out in front of guests as possible."

Emerson thought the groom's request a bit odd, but she saw Harper smile.

"We can accommodate you, Ron. Thanks for letting us know the schedule you want to keep to."

He gave them an enigmatic smile. "No. Thank *you.*"

The groom disappeared, and Harper asked, "Did you pick up a weird vibe from him?"

She nodded. "Sounds like he might have some surprise planned."

"Would you let everyone in the kitchen know what Ron wants, Em? I need to get back to the bride and check on a few other things."

"Will do, Harper."

Finley, who'd finished photographing the groom's cake said, "I'll give you a high sign when I've got about two minutes of photos left to take if that'll help."

Emerson went to the kitchen and explained what the groom's instructions were.

"We can start placing filled champagne glasses on the tables right as the photos are concluding. Harper will make certain that everyone starts moving to their seats then. If all of us serve— and she looked to Harper's two assistants, Ry, and the two Blackwood BBQ employees — we should be able to get a good portion of the dinners out in a timely fashion."

The ceremony began. Emerson went to the door of the

kitchen and looked out. The setting was beautiful, with the solid glass wall looking out over the vineyard as a backdrop for the ceremony.

She continued to monitor things and signaled Ry when to begin opening the champagne bottles. Flutes were quickly filled, and trays of champagne went out as the pictures commenced and guests moved to the other side of the event center where all the tables were placed, and Dax and his Lone Star Rebel band were setting up to play.

After several minutes, Finley made eye contact with Emerson and held up two fingers, letting her know the wedding party photos were almost completed. Harper had also seen the signal and begin gently steering guests to take their seats.

As the wedding party was announced and moved toward their own designated seats, the servers began bringing out the dinner plates. About a quarter of them were in place by the time the maid of honor finished her brief speech. More than half were in place by the time the best man said his piece, praising the newlyweds and remarking how perfect they were for one another.

They worked quickly, continuing to bring out the rest of the dinners as the groom took the microphone from his best man and stood.

"I want to thank everyone who came to see Ashley and me joined in marriage today. Ashley and I have been together four years now, engaged for the past year, and I really looked forward to our lives together as husband and wife."

He paused and added, "That's not going to happen."

A murmur swept through those seated, and Emerson halted a moment, wondering what was about to come. Her gaze met Ry's. He shrugged and placed another dinner in front of a guest.

As they continued serving, the groom said, "I've known Teddy since we played flag football together. He's been my best buddy since third grade, and we've shared everything. Vacations. Team championships. Jobs. And it seems, Ashley, as well."

Her eyes flew to the bride, who audibly gasped.

The groom smiled at his new wife, and his smile reminded Emerson of the Cheshire Cat's in *Alice's Adventures in Wonderland*.

"I know you've been banging my best friend for at least the last year, Ashley. You thought you were so clever in covering your tracks, but you're both idiots."

Ron looked to the bride's father, whose face was drained of color, and said, "I learned about this several weeks ago, Mr. Johnson. I know the honorable thing to do would've been to call off the wedding, but I didn't think Ashley would learn any lesson if I did. She's always gotten absolutely everything she's ever wanted. She never thinks of the consequences of her actions. I know she's hurt quite a few people over the years, but I loved her so much that I tried to overlook a lot. Today, I wanted to teach her a lesson she would never forget."

The groom waved his hand expansively. "So, to our family and friends, drink up. Eat up. I've tasted everything from the wines to the food to the cakes, and you're going to have an unbelievable night. The band is waiting in the wings, and I hope most of you stay and dance the night away, until the wee hours of the morning."

He held up his champagne flute. "As for me, I'll be leaving now and filing for an annulment on Monday." Turning to his bride, he added, "I would say best of luck to you, but I could give a rat's ass what you do for the rest of your sorry life."

Downing the champagne, the new—and soon to be ex—husband walked the length of the room and out the doors. The bride shrieked at the top of her lungs and ran out the opposite doors, sobbing hysterically. Her mother and maid of honor followed her. The best man looked stunned, as did most of the guests.

The bride's father motioned Harper over and said something to her. Harper nodded and went to the table where the groom had placed the mike.

She picked it up and said, "Despite how uncomfortable the circumstances are, Mr. Johnson encourages everyone to stay. He would like you to enjoy yourself and not let anything go to waste. Thank you."

Harper then glanced to Dax, who quickly slipped his guitar strap over his head and asked, "Are you ready to rock tonight?"

The band began playing, and the guests looked perplexed for a moment. Then, some of them started eating. One bridesmaid grabbed a groomsman and moved to the dance floor, and several of the younger guests quickly followed. Emerson watched as the best man slunk from the room.

Back in the kitchen, she took a seat at the table. Ry joined her.

"Well, we couldn't have predicted that would happen," he said.

The others also returned, and he told Carlos and Jose they could go home.

Harper entered the kitchen and said, "I can't ever remember anything like that ever happening at any wedding during all the years I worked in Austin. I'm sure it'll be hitting social media soon if it hasn't already."

Emerson said, "I did see a few people taping the speeches with their cells. I hope it won't reflect poorly on Weddings with Hart."

Her friend shook her head. "I doubt it will. In fact, we'll probably get a lot of free publicity from this. What I do know is what happened tonight is going to take the Internet by storm."

Looking to Emerson and Ry, Harper said, "We'll take it from here. Thanks, as always, for doing a lovely job."

Harper left, her assistants trailing after her, and Ry said, "Are you still up for dinner and a movie?"

Emerson was up for much more than that.

15

Ry told Emerson he was going to drop the catering van at Blackwood BBQ, bring in the empty bins, and then drive his truck to her place. He gave her a basket which had food for their dinner, and she drove to her place.

Nerves filled her as she brought the basket inside. She set it on the counter and opened a bottle of the red blend he'd enjoyed in order to let it breathe. Then she changed out of the white shirt and black pants she typical wore when working at the event center, tossing them and the apron tied around her waist into her laundry basket, and replacing them with a midnight blue shirt and white capris. Removing the hair tie, she shook out her hair and brushed it until the raven waves shone. She dabbed on the tiniest bit of perfume, rubbing her wrists together, hoping she wasn't overdoing it.

The doorbell rang, and her heart thumped against her ribs as she went to answer it.

Ry stood there, his white apron gone, wearing the same black T-shirt and black pants he'd worn while catering.

"You changed. I wish I would've thought to bring another set of clothes," he said, entering the house.

"I had a stain on my shirt," she fibbed as she closed the door, slightly embarrassed now that she had put on a different outfit.

"Do you mind if I pull off my boots and get comfortable? I've been on my feet all day. Like since three this morning, smoking the meats for the reception."

She worried that he might be too tired to go through with what she was going to propose and would have to gauge how things were going before she spoke up.

"Sure. I opened some wine. Let me get you a glass."

He sat on her sofa and removed his boots as she poured glasses for them, using both hands because hers were shaking.

Ry came into the kitchen, and Emerson handed him a glass. He took a long sip.

"Pretty damn good," he growled in that low, sexy voice which brought shivers to her spine. "Braden is a genius. Or Ivy's taught me enough so I can finally appreciate a good wine." He grinned. "Todd and I used to sneak into where Mr. Hart concocted the wines. We'd turn the spigot on for different barrels and fill a thermos. Take it down to Lost Creek and fish and talk and get just a little bit drunk. We'd even sing some."

"You sing?"

"Not at all. Croaking frogs sound like angels compared to what comes out of me. I bellow. Off-key. Drunk or sober. That's why I admired Dax so much. Not only does he write amazing songs, but his voice is so rich."

"You have talents of your own," she said.

His brows shot up. "Oh, really?"

Emerson took a big drink of wine, hoping he wouldn't notice the color warming her cheeks. Then she set down her wineglass and removed two plates from the cupboard.

"You smoke amazing meats," she said as she opened the basket and began removing the containers inside.

He shrugged. "That's just cooking. Anyone can learn to cook. Hell, Finley's teaching Holden to cook. He told me he's learned how to make omelets. Spaghetti. Fried chicken. They're going to work on meatloaf next."

"I didn't know Holden was learning to cook," she said, popping the buns into the toaster. "I hope you like a lightly-toasted bun."

"Love it."

He put his wineglass on the counter and started to open the different containers. "Do you want everything I brought? It's the usual stuff."

"Sure. Do you want me to heat the sliced brisket some?"

"I'll do it."

He placed the brisket on one of the empty plates and set it in the microwave. Emerson got two more plates and dipped into the coleslaw, giving them some of it and the potato salad.

"I'm glad you added mac and cheese as a side option," she told him, putting the mac into a bowl and handing it to him to heat.

"Some barbeque joints don't like to mess with it. Dad has always said mac and cheese is more trouble than it's worth, but it's a comfort food for me. I don't know anyone who doesn't like it. That's why I added it, thinking brides and grooms might like it on their special day."

Ry put their sandwiches together, pouring sauce over the meat and adding onions and relish. She topped off their plates with the warmed mac.

"Do you want to eat at the breakfast bar or on the couch?" he asked, holding their plates.

"The couch is more comfy. I'll grab the wine."

They went to her living room and as they ate, they discussed the plot of *Capitol Crimes*.

"Holden told me he did a ton of research for the book," Ry said before biting into his brisket sandwich.

"Yes, he mentioned that he took enough notes for more than one book. I think from what he said that he might be going back to Washington, D.C., for the next book he writes. After his Mr. Hamilton book."

He frowned. "What's that?"

"You'll have to get Holden to tell you about Mr. Hamilton. Just as I had a mentor in Miss Kent, Holden became close with the janitor at his school. Mr. Hamilton was a war vet, a very educated man. He took Holden and several other students under his wing and guided them for years. Holden said Mr. Hamilton made him the man he always wanted to be. His next novel is going to be a love letter written for the custodian."

"That definitely sounds like something I'd like to read. Holden's really talented, writing both novels and now a screenplay."

"I think that's why he and Finley are such a good fit," Emerson said. "Finley is wildly creative. Not only does she photograph people, but she also has started photographing the Hill Country landscape. She and Ivy go out on long drives and take pictures. Ivy then paints different scenes."

"I actually stopped by and saw some of Ivy's paintings the other day. They blew me away. No wonder she's getting a big exhibit showing her work in New York."

They finished their sandwiches, and Emerson asked him if he had room for dessert.

"Only if you've made it. Take that back. You— or the Little Creamery in Brenham."

She laughed, knowing that was the nickname for the makers of Blue Bell Ice Cream.

"No ice cream. Just something new I was playing around with."

"Now I'm really intrigued. Bring it, Frost."

He scooped up their plates and brought them into the kitchen, rinsing them before placing them in the dishwasher. Ry also grabbed the wine bottle, taking it back and refilling their glasses.

"Stay in there," she called. "I'll bring dessert out soon."

When she did and handed him a bowl topped with

whipped cream, his eyes lit up. "I have no idea what this is, but I can't wait to put it in my mouth."

She settled herself on the sofa. "It's a grilled blackberry brioche bread pudding."

"Whoa! Bread pudding is a weakness of mine. This sounds really interesting." He scooped up some and studied it a moment before he bit into it. "Okay. Promise me you'll make this for the next Wednesday dinner. And teach me how to make it."

"You probably feel an affinity for it because I made it on the grill," she revealed.

He took another bite and sighed. "A grilled dessert. Who knew?"

"It's actually fairly easy."

She explained how she whisked milk, eggs, sugar, salt, and vanilla extract together before folding in bread cubes, blackberries, and cream cheese.

"You let the bread soak up everything— about fifteen minutes —and then brush melted butter on foil. I placed the bread mixture in the middle of the foil and folded and sealed it, leaving a little room for steam to form. Then it went on the grill until it was toasty. It's actually better straight off the grill, letting it cool for a few minutes. I didn't have that luxury tonight, though."

Ry took the last bite, obviously savoring it from the contented look on his face. "I'll be your guinea pig anytime, Emerson Frost."

"Do you mean that?" she asked softly, her gaze pinning his. "Because I have another idea."

He placed his bowl on the coffee table. "What are you

thinking about trying out on me?" he asked, his voice growing husky.

Emerson leaned over and kissed him softly. She started to pull away, but his warm hand settled on her nape, and he brought his lips to hers again. The kiss was lingering. Something stirred within her.

Desire?

She was so inexperienced that she didn't know. What she did know was that she wanted to explore these new, fragile feelings with this man. Only him.

Her hands gripped his shoulders, and Emerson kissed Ry with everything she had learned from him previously. The kiss deepened. Heated. Soon, it was as if molten heat ran through her. His hands now roamed her back, moving, stroking, causing chills to rush along her spine. She grew breathless from their kisses, her insides giddy.

Excitedly, she broke the kiss, gazing into his eyes. "I want to have sex with you," she declared.

He frowned. "What? No, Emerson."

Everything inside her came to a screeching halt. The old pattern of rejection reared its ugly head. When she was young, she had tried so hard to be the best little girl she could be for both her mom and dad. She would draw them a picture. Pick a flower. Bring home good grades. Nothing moved her parents, and Emerson quickly retreated within herself. Now, it was happening all over with Ry. She had thought he might be different. That she would have a chance to experience something new with him. To grow and learn a little about herself.

Hot tears spilled down her cheeks as she scrambled from the sofa. Embarrassment filled her.

"You can go," she said dully. "See yourself out."

Retreating from the room, she hurried down the hall, ready to lock herself in the lone bathroom until he was gone. As she reached it, though, Ry's hand clasped her elbow turning her.

"Just go!" she shouted, so tired of being alone and unwanted, knowing she was one of the girls who did the ugly cry and got splotchy cheeks and swollen eyes.

"No," he said firmly.

And then he pulled her into his arms.

Emerson wept, soaking his shirt, clinging to him, humiliated that she did so. Being the nice guy he was, Ry comforted her. Stroked her back and hair. Murmured soft, indiscernible words to her. Everything he did only made her cry harder.

She tried to push away from him, but he held fast.

"Please. Just go. I am already mortified enough as it is."

"Why?" he asked.

Meeting his gaze, she told him, "I knew you were too good for me. That I'm dull and boring and you'd never really be interested in me. I guess I should thank you for at least teaching me how to kiss." She paused, fresh tears coursing down her cheeks. "But rejection hurts, Ry. Asking you to have sex with me was a big deal to me. I get that you don't want to. It still hurts all the same. Please leave. I just want to be alone."

He enveloped her in his arms. Warmth filled her. His clean, masculine scent surrounded her. For a moment, she leaned into him and simply enjoyed the feel of him, knowing it would be the last time she found herself in this position.

Then he lifted her chin, forcing her to look at him.

"I wasn't saying no to *you*, Emerson. I was saying no to sex tonight."

Confusion filled her. "I don't get it."

He smiled gently at her. "I do want to be with you. But I think we need to build up to that. We're getting to know one another. I think we're already building a nice foundation of friendship. I want to expand on that. I don't want to rush things. Especially because it would be the first time for you to take such a big step."

Emerson tried to wrap her head around what he was saying. "So, you aren't turning me down?"

"I am now." He grinned. "But I'm definitely leaving the door open for the future." His palm cradled her cheek. "I don't think you're boring at all. I find you fascinating. I want to get to know you better. I want to be more than friends. And when the time is right, I do want to make love to you. Not have sex."

She really didn't know the difference. All Emerson knew was how she felt being in Ry's arms. How she responded to his kiss. How being in his company made her feel different.

"So, what do you want to do?"

He smiled, a warm smile that felt as if sunshine rained down upon her. "I want to sit on the couch and cuddle with my girlfriend while we watch *Capitol Crimes*."

"Your… girlfriend?"

"Yup. My girlfriend. Are you available for the position, Miss Frost?"

Her heart soared. "Yes, Mr. Blackwood. I believe I am."

Threading his fingers through hers, Ry led her back to the living room. They sat on the couch. He picked up the remote and settled in, his arm going around her shoulders, drawing her into him. Emerson rested her head against him, relaxing.

They watched the movie. At least, Ry did. Her head was spinning the entire time. It felt so right sitting with him. She had never been more content in her life.

Once the movie ended, he turned off the TV. They talked about Wolf's film versus the book. Their conversation was back-and-forth, interesting, with each of them pointing out differences between novel and movie as they discussed the finer points of both.

He gave her a lazy smile. "This was fun."

"Yes," she agreed.

Ry kissed her then, and they continued to kiss for several minutes. Emerson supposed this is what couples did.

And now she was a part of a couple.

She smiled against his mouth.

"What are you smiling about?" he asked.

"Just… being with you. It makes me happy."

He brushed back a lock of hair. "I want to make you happy, Emerson. I'm glad you're willing to give me a chance to do that."

"Are we… do we tell anyone?"

Ry laughed. "I'm ready to shout it from the rooftops. Emerson Frost is my girl."

He kissed her again, long and deep. Then he stood, pulling her to her feet. His arms went about her again, and he kissed her tenderly.

"I'll follow your lead," he said. "You can tell whoever you'd like that we're together. Because we *are* together now, Emerson."

"Okay," she said softly, still trying to adjust the newness of the situation. "I'd like to tell Finley first. We've been friends the longest. Then I'll let the others know."

"I'll wait before I say anything. Guys are worse gossips than girls."

"Really?"

"Really."

Ry kissed her again and took her hand, moving toward the door.

"I'm glad you decided to give me a chance," he said, his voice low and rough.

She framed his face with her hands. "I'm glad you are thoughtful enough not to rush me. And not let me rush us. I don't think many guys would've turned me down when I asked them to have sex with me."

His gaze pinned hers. "When we do come together, I want it to mean something."

She nodded, afraid to speak.

He gave her a light kiss goodbye. "We've got the Bancroft wedding at five tomorrow. Can I see you after that?"

"Yes."

"Goodnight, Emerson."

"Goodnight, Ry."

She let him out the door and locked it behind him, leaning against the door for support because her legs suddenly felt wobbly. She gave into the urge and simply slid her back down the door, plopping on the ground.

Ry Blackwood cared about her. Enough to take things slowly with her. Enough to call her his girlfriend.

Emerson's gut told her she would definitely like being his girlfriend.

She couldn't wait for tomorrow to come.

16

Emerson was still in the habit of waking early and did so today. She decided not only to text Finley but to include Ivy and Harper, as well. She sent a group text to the three women, asking if they might be available to meet at Java Junction this morning for coffee around eight.

Finley responded first, saying that she was already going to be there because she and Holden would be meeting with Wolf at eight to discuss some things about the movie being currently filmed. She thought she would be free by eight-thirty, though. Ivy chimed in and said she could be there at eight-thirty. Harper responded, saying the same.

Glad she had included all three women, Emerson texted the group.

After showering and dressing, she worked on a few designs for cakes and then left for the bakery, speaking briefly with Rhiannon to touch base on how things were going. They decided to meet at the diner again on Monday for breakfast to catch up and talk business.

Frank pulled her aside and said, "Rhiannon was a great hire, Emerson. She doesn't take any crap, but she's also a very understanding person. And she's a terrific baker. Jill and I really like her a lot."

"I'm happy to hear that, Frank. She seems to be thriving in her new role. I'm glad it's working out for everyone."

Going to the front of the bakery, she grabbed a box and collected a few Danishes, along with some kolaches and donut holes. Waving to Jill, she crossed the square to Java Junction and entered. The line was already long for a Saturday morning. Dax was working, along with Scott Bartlett and two teenagers.

She joined the line and spied Finley at a corner table with Holden and Wolf. The director spoke animatedly, gesturing broadly, and Finley seemed just as excited as he was regarding whatever they were discussing.

Then she saw Ivy waving at her from a table in the center of the room. Her friend came over and said, "I've snagged a table for us. Here, let me take the bakery box so you have your hands free."

She handed the box to her friend and after a few minutes, stepped up and gave her order to Dax.

"Coming right up," he said, winking at her.

Emerson couldn't help but wonder about the wink. Had Ry already told Dax about them? She knew they went running together several mornings a week.

She went to where Ivy was seated and asked how her painting was going.

"I'm getting very close to the end. Clive is flying down here in two weeks to look at what I've painted since his last visit. He'll take those paintings back with him. That'll give him the bulk of what will be in the show, and he'll begin working on the layout for the exhibit."

"Ry told me he'd stopped by to see your paintings."

"Yes, he's always been very supportive of my art." Ivy smiled. "He even commissioned me to make a painting for his mom when I was in eighth grade. Shelly still has it hanging in their den."

Finley pulled out a chair and took a seat. "Meeting's over," she said brightly.

"You looked pretty excited as you spoke to Wolf," Emerson observed.

"He was looking at some of the mockups for the ad campaign I've designed. I can't believe I'm involved in marketing a Hollywood movie. Boy, my life sure has changed since Holden came into it."

Emerson couldn't help but feel the same about Ry and said, "I know what you mean."

"Just think, Em. This time last year, we were getting ready to go back to school. Creating lesson plans.

Attending final workshops. Meeting with members of our team. And now look at how crazy different our lives are."

"How are senior portraits coming along?" she asked.

"I'm swamped. I'll still be able to squeeze in Ry in order to get the Blackwood BBQ site updated, especially that catering page. It's starting to look pretty amazing with all the foods he's come up with. Once I took shots of what he'd smoked, he let me take everything home. Holden was in heaven. You'll both need to check out the website and give me some feedback."

"We will," Ivy promised as Dax brought Emerson her latte.

Harper joined them, cup in hand. "Oh, my gosh. Have you told Ivy about last night's debacle?"

"What's going on?" her sister asked. "Did someone get jilted at the altar?"

The other three women laughed, and Harper said, "I can tell you don't get on social media often. We are every-where this morning."

Ivy's nose crinkled. "That sounds bad."

"Actually, Weddings with Hart and the venue come off pretty well," Harper said, sounding relieved. "It's the bride and best man who are getting skewered."

The three of them recounted the events of last night's reception, finishing with how the groom announced he would be seeking an annulment, and the bride fled the room.

"The best man slipped out without a word," Emerson told Ivy.

"Oh, I know all about that," Harper said. "I went to

check on the bride. She was crying a river of tears. Her mom and maid of honor were trying their best to comfort her, but all she wanted was the best man. She kept texting and then calling him, but he wouldn't pick up. It made her cry even harder."

"That was a little cruel of the groom," Ivy said. "Then again, he was betrayed by the two people he loved the most. I guess I can't blame him."

"I felt sorry for him, but I really felt sorry for Mr. Johnson," Harper said. "I even told him I would give him a discount on things."

"That was generous of you," Emerson said.

"He wouldn't' take it."

"Mr. Johnson also spoke to me last night," Finley said. "I'd already taken all the pre-wedding and ceremony photographs. He told me not to bother sticking around for the rest of the reception and guaranteed he'd pay my bill in full. I went ahead and sent him what I'd already photographed. Mr. Johnson told me while he would pay me now in full, his daughter would be reimbursing him. No matter how long it took."

"Same with me," Harper confirmed. "Mr. Johnson apologized for Ashley's atrocious behavior and said he hoped she'd finally learned her lesson. He admitted that he'd spoiled her terribly since she was their only child, but he did not raise her to act so poorly."

"I'd already been paid for both cakes," she said. "I assume Blackwood BBQ was also paid in full before last night."

"Yes, Shy also received payment, but enough of that,"

Harper said. "Let's talk about anything else except weddings."

"I did ask everyone to coffee this morning for a reason," she said, suddenly growing shy about her news. "I have something to share with you."

"Please tell me that you and Ry are finally together," Finley blurted out.

Emerson sucked in a quick breath. "What?"

Ivy placed her hand over Emerson's. "It's obvious to all of us how much he likes you, Em. Do you like him?"

"More than I probably should," she admitted to her friends. "We made it official last night. We are going to be seeing one another."

"Hallelujah!" Harper declared, throwing her arms around Emerson and giving her a big hug. "I told you he was interested in you from the moment he met you."

"He's just... so... so everything," she said, still unsure why Ry was attracted to her. "He's like that guy in the yearbook. You know. The senior superlatives. Most Popular. Most Handsome. Best All-Around. I can't for the life me understand why he's interested in me when he could ask out any woman in Lost Creek."

Ivy clucked her tongue. "How can you say that, Emerson Frost? You're gorgeous and one of the nicest people I've ever known. Why, Ry Blackwood is lucky that he has you."

Finley held up her coffee mug, and the others raised theirs. "To Emerson and Ry."

They clinked their cups together and sipped their coffees. Emerson then opened the box she'd brought from

The Bake House, and everyone began selecting items to eat.

Dax came over and asked, "Any refills needed here?" He leaned over and snagged a kolache from the open box. "I saw you ladies toasting. What are you celebrating?"

Ivy beamed at her husband. "Emerson and Ry are together. Finally."

"Are you kidding? He and I ran together this morning. He didn't say a word to me."

"Don't blame Ry," Emerson said. "He was letting me tell my friends first before he said anything about us to anyone."

Dax placed his hand on her shoulder and squeezed. "Congratulations, Em. I think the two of you'll be great together."

She was happy her friends were so excited for her, but Emerson still worried that she wouldn't be enough for a man like Ry Blackwood.

RY LOADED UP THE VAN WITH ALL THE FOOD FOR TONIGHT'S reception and drove to Lost Creek Winery. He had been on a natural high all day.

Because of Emerson.

It was hard for him to understand how little she seemed to value herself, but he had to remember she had never had anyone in her corner for years. She had grown up with no support system, and it had done a number on her self-esteem. As he built a relationship with her, Ry also wanted to build Emerson's confidence.

He reached the winery and parked behind the event center as Dax pulled up beside him.

"Are the Lone Star Rebels playing tonight?"

"Nope. I'm just going to DJ the reception." His friend offered a hand, and Ry shook it. "I heard you and Emerson finally made it official."

He grinned from ear to ear. "Yes. It took a while to convince her. She's like a scared rabbit, Dax. So beautiful and talented— and yet so unsure of herself."

"If anyone can help Emerson blossom, it's you, buddy."

"Thanks. That means a lot to me, Dax. I'm not just saying that. I'm a little like Emerson in that I closed myself off from the world after Todd's death. I never grew close to any of my fellow soldiers. Yes, I had their six— and would've taken a bullet for them —but I never really made friends with them either."

He paused. "It's been different since I've come home to Lost Creek. From the first night I arrived, you, Braden, and Holden have been so welcoming. I was worried that I'd be like some outsider, and it would take a long time to find my place here again. The friendship you and those guys have offered has meant the world to me."

"I'm glad you came home, Ry," Dax said. "It's been great getting to know you. I hope that our friendship will be one of many decades."

He laughed. "So, you think we'll still be doing Wednesday night dinners and come hobbling in on our walkers in our eighties?"

Dax laughed. "That's exactly what I'm thinking. I believe the years will pass quickly. We'll have kids. Grandkids. And one day we'll look up. We'll all have gray in our hair— or maybe we'll be bald —but our friendship of many years will have seen us through the good times and bad."

A lump formed in his throat.

"If I had a beer in my hand, I'd raise it in a toast and say hear, hear," Ry said.

"We'll have to go out for that beer soon," Dax said. "In the meantime, let me help you carry things in."

It didn't take them long since tonight's wedding only had eighty people, including the wedding party and guests.

Finley showed up, taking a few pictures, and then pulling him aside, showing Ry more photographs she'd like to add to the website's home page and catering tab.

"You make my food look really appetizing, Finley," he praised. "And my mom wanted to thank you for framing those photos of me in my uniforms. She said for you and Holden to stop by the diner anytime and eat for free."

She laughed. "Oh, don't tell my husband that. He'll be there five days a week."

Emerson arrived, causing Ry's heart to skip a beat. He smiled at her, thinking about how everything had seemed right about her from the moment he met her. He wasn't a guy who devoted any time to thinking about love— much less falling in love at first sight —but his feelings were incredibly strong for this woman and had been from the beginning.

Dax helped Emerson set up the two cakes, and then she began helping him with the food prep.

Leaning down, she inhaled deeply. "Ooh. You've never made ribs for a reception I've worked. They smell amazing."

"I was a little surprised that the bride wanted to serve them. They can be pretty messy. Then again, Harper said this bride is pretty country, and most of the guests would be wearing jeans to the wedding. I guess they don't mind a little sauce. I also smoked some sausage and am preparing a chopped brisket sandwich for the plates."

"If you can, save a couple of those ribs for us. I've never tried them at Blackwood BBQ before."

"Oh, I planned to. I've got a whole picnic for us," he shared.

"You do?" she said.

He could hear both the eagerness and wistfulness in her tone and stopped what he was doing, going to her and slipping his arms around her.

"I plan to do all kind of special things for you, Emerson Frost," he promised. "Because you're worth it."

Ry kissed her tenderly, hoping his embrace and kiss conveyed to Emerson just how wonderful she was. He knew he was in uncharted territory with her. She'd never dated. Never had a guy do anything unique for her. It was if she'd been alone on an uncharted island her whole life, watching ships pass her by without offering rescue.

He aimed to change that.

17

Though a few weddings at the winery's event center were held in the early afternoon on weekends, most brides accepted the five o'clock slot offered by Harper. She told brides if they were being married at the winery, they needed to take advantage of the vineyards themselves as a backdrop. Weddings held at night wouldn't show the vineyard to full advantage.

As Emerson now left Lost Creek Winery and followed Ry's catering truck back to town, she was grateful for Harper's policy. With weddings starting at five, they usually ran for half an hour or so, followed by pictures. That meant guests were ready to be seated for dinner at the reception by six or a little after. Once she and Ry plated the food, Harper's assistants took over, serving the meals. It allowed her and Ry to do a bit of cleanup before returning the food bins to the catering van and leaving, while the Weddings with Hart assistants cleared the tables and saw to washing the dishes. It was now six-thirty, which left them the rest of the evening for themselves.

Emerson was trying to get used to being part of a couple, something she had never experienced before. She had no idea what Ry had in mind tonight other than they would be going on a picnic. It didn't matter what they did. She was merely happy to be spending more time with him.

They arrived at Blackwood BBQ, and she helped him bring in the empty food bins to the kitchen, where Carlos was at work, along with a couple of teenagers who served as busboys and dishwashers.

"How did the wedding go?" Carlos asked.

"Everything went like clockwork," Ry told him. "And we have no wedding to cater tomorrow. A blessed day off."

Carlos helped them bring in the rest of the empties, and they bid him goodnight.

As they were leaving the kitchen, Shy Blackwood came through. "Well, hello there, Emerson. I hear you're keeping company with my son these days."

A hot blush spilled across her cheeks. "Yes. I am. And I'm keeping him in line, Sir."

Shy burst out laughing. He glanced to his son. "You have to watch the quiet ones, Ry. I think you've got yourself a real pistol here."

Ry turned to Emerson, his eyes shining with something she couldn't pinpoint. "I definitely have someone special here, Dad." He linked his fingers through hers. "We're off now."

They went to his truck, and Ry helped her inside. She noticed a picnic basket and blanket on the back seat.

When he slipped behind the wheel, she asked, "Where are we going?"

"To Lost Creek Lake. When's the last time you went on a picnic?"

"Never," she replied honestly.

He brought her hand up and kissed her fingers "Things are going to change now for you, Emerson. I'm going to spoil you the way you should've been spoiled all these years."

Leaning in, he gave her a soft kiss. It may have lacked the intense passion of previous kisses, but coupled with his words, it meant everything to her. No one had ever spoiled her. She didn't even know what that might consist of, only that she was putty in this man's hands.

Ry drove the ten minutes outside of town and turned in. Emerson had never been to Lost Creek Lake though it was a popular spot with locals. Especially during the summer.

"Did you know Finley's brother and sister-in-law run Hill Country Sports?" she asked.

"No. Do they sponsor sports teams or rent equipment?"

Emerson said, "They rent things for water sports. Jet skis. Kayaks. Paddleboats."

"We'll have to go kayaking sometime then. I love to do that and haven't been in ages. Have you ever tried it before?"

"No. I don't even know how to swim, Ry," she admitted.

"Then that's something I'll teach you. Everyone should know how to swim."

They drove to an area where few cars were parked and got out, Ry claiming the basket and blanket. She saw a few people out on the lake in small rowboats and some who were swimming.

"Don't worry," he said. "We're going somewhere private."

They hiked up a trail for fifteen minutes, not seeing anyone along the way, and came to an open area with a great view of the water.

"Todd and I used to come here all the time. We'd ride our bikes. Our moms would make sandwiches for us, and we'd fish and roam the lake all day. My cousin Tucker joined us in the summer."

He spread the blanket on the ground and told her to sit. Emerson started to open the basket, but he told her no.

"You just sit and relax. I'll do everything for you tonight."

"You make me feel like a queen, Ry."

"Good. That's the plan."

He lifted out sandwiches and unwrapped them, along with two ribs each, and handed her napkins and a couple of packets with wet wipes in them.

"Because I know we'll get messy."

He uncorked a bottle of wine and poured some into plastic cups for them. "Nothing fancy, but it'll do."

As they ate, she asked, "Did your cousin visit Lost Creek often?"

"Tucker spent every summer here. Being an only child, it was like having a brother every summer. He lost his mom when he was only five years old. His dad was a manager for various country acts and on the road a lot, especially summers. Uncle Travis would drop Tuck off and be gone a solid three months."

"Do you still your cousin or uncle?" watching his face as his eyes got a faraway look in them.

"I haven't seen Tuck in years, not since I left for the army. We stayed in touch as best we could, but he was in a pretty serious car accident a couple of years ago. His wife was killed. I tried everything. Calling. Texting. Even wrote him a few letters. It's as if he dropped off the face of the earth. One of my goals now that I'm back in Texas is to locate him and get in touch with him again."

"That must have been terrible, losing his wife."

"It was even rougher because she was expecting their first child," Ry revealed. "Not only that, but Uncle Travis had passed away about two months before the accident occurred."

"I'll do what I can to help you find him," she said, covering his hand with hers.

"Thank you," he said softly. "It would mean a lot to me to have your help."

They finished their pulled pork sandwiches, and then Emerson tackled the ribs. The meat was tender and juicy, practically falling off the bone.

He opened a wipe and brushed it against her mouth,

cleaning it and then her hands. His touch was light and gentle, but it still shot tingles through her.

"I know you're the dessert girl, but I actually tried making something sweet myself. I got Mom to give me my grandmother's banana pudding recipe."

Ry passed her a sealed container, and she opened the lid. "Looks delicious." After she took one bite, Emerson groaned. "Oh, this is so rich and decadent. Why doesn't Blackwood BBQ serve this?"

"Dad is really set in his ways," he said, his own jaw setting. "He doesn't serve or do anything that his dad and granddad didn't do. I think this banana pudding should be on the menu at the restaurant. I wish some of the dishes I'm coming up with could also be served to our customers, but I can tell now that Dad would never consider changing the menu."

"Have you gotten him to at least taste some of your creations? They would sell themselves, Ry."

"No. Because he'd shut me down flat."

"That has to be frustrating," she said sympathetically. "At least you're able to offer some new entrées to Harper's clients."

"Yes. Next Saturday will be the first time a bride has chosen some of my new menu items. I'm really excited to smoke them and add my own flair to the dishes. Even if Dad would disapprove."

"He doesn't know you've expanded the catering menu?" she asked.

"No," he said flatly. "And I'm not going to be sharing that with him."

"Ry, I do think you should let him know what's going on," Emerson cautioned. "If he finds out otherwise, he could be really angry. You should sit him down and have a talk about the direction you see Blackwood BBQ going, especially since it will be yours to run one day."

A stubborn look came into his eyes. "I appreciate your advice, Emerson, but that's never going to happen. Dad's handed over the catering to me, and he won't ask what I'm doing. No changes will ever be made at Blackwood BBQ until he retires and I step up."

Emerson thought this was a recipe for disaster. She believed at some point, Shy Blackwood would discover that Ry was stepping off the menu and bringing his own signature to dishes. Ry didn't seem to be in a mood, however, to discuss it further. She would table it for another time.

After they finished their banana pudding, he set all their dishes and utensils in the basket and took it back to the truck. Then Ry had her stand and moved the blanket closer to the trees surrounding the clearing. He sat, his back leaning against a tree trunk, and motioned for her to join him. She nestled between his legs, her back against his solid chest, his arms wrapped around her. Emerson had never felt safe in her life.

Until this moment.

With Ry's arms secure about her, she felt the burdens of the world melt away. She relaxed completely for the first time ever.

They talked a long time about their pasts. Ry told her

about the sports he had played, starting in elementary school.

"Flag football was big, and I played it for one season, but I was really into baseball. That meant I played fall ball each year when school started and again in the spring. In-between times, I played basketball for the Y and sometimes soccer. Then in middle and high school, I continued playing sports. Lost Creek is a small place, and so it allowed me to dip my toe into any sport I wanted to try."

"I don't think I would've played sports. Even if I would've been given the chance. I'm not very coordinated. I might have liked to have done something creative during my school years, though. Maybe act in a play."

"It's not too late to try that," he encouraged her. "There's community theater."

She stroked his forearm. "When would I have time to do that? With The Bake House. Weddings with Hart. And now I'm helping you cater weddings on weekends. It doesn't leave me with much free time."

"I can always find someone else to help me if you really want to devote your time to it, Emerson."

"No," she said softly. "I like being able to spend the time with you."

They sat in companionable silence after that, watching the sun dip below the horizon and the moon rise. She could hear the cicadas singing now and thought she had never been more content in her life.

"Where do you see yourself in five years?" he asked out the blue.

Emerson thought a moment. "I guess I've never really

been someone to look too far ahead and make plans. Life was so precarious when I was growing up. Spending time in the foster system, when you could be removed from a home and placed in another without any warning, had me living in the moment. I never really thought beyond the next test coming up at school. The next week at work.

"Then when I came to teach in Lost Creek, I settled into the cycle of the school year. I did my best to help the students given to me each year to not only learn academically, but to become the best people they could be. Then a new group came in, and I started the process all over."

"You're a business owner now," he said. "You should be thinking ahead and formulating a plan for each season. Each year. What you wish to accomplish." He hesitated. "And not just professionally, Emerson. But personally—what goals you might have."

Again, he asked, "Where do you see yourself in five years?"

Her mouth grew dry. "I would hope I'd still own The Bake House," she began. "That it was profitable. That I would still be baking cakes for Weddings with Hart." Swallowing, she added, "But I would like to have children. Maybe even adopt a child from foster care. If I could just rescue one soul and give him or her all the love I have in my heart, it would be worth it."

Ry tiled her face until their gazes met. "You didn't mention anything about marriage."

Keeping a light tone, she said, "Since I've only had a couple of dates, for the first time in almost thirty years, I didn't want to put the cart before the horse. Where do you see yourself in five years, Ry?"

"As a husband and father," he replied. "Anything beyond that is icing on the cake. I came home to Lost Creek with a desire to plant deep roots and become a part of this community. I see how happy my parents have been in their marriage, and I see our friends also happy in theirs. I want kids, Emerson. Plural. You know how being an only child can be lonely. I want to fill a house with kids — and a lot a love."

Ry brushed his lips softly against hers. Emerson knew he wasn't making any promises to her, just letting her know what he wanted out of life. While she had longings to be a mother, she didn't know if she would make for a good wife. She'd witnessed a lousy example of marriage with her own parents and wasn't sure if it was for her.

Emerson abandoned those thoughts— and lived in the moment as she always had —kissing Ry with everything she had.

18

The past three weeks had proven the happiest of Emerson's life.

Because she had spent every day with Ry.

He had taken her to Lost Creek Lake again on two occasions, teaching her the basics of swimming. She'd never even owned a swimsuit and had to borrow one from Finley. She found swimming to be liberating and caught on quickly. Although she would need more practice, Emerson knew if she ever accidentally fell in the water, she could prevent herself from drowning now.

Another thing Ry had taught her was how to country and western dance. He enjoyed music, and Dax had suggested a double date to the Renegade Roadhouse, a dance hall north of Boerne. When she admitted to Ry that she didn't know how to dance, he'd given her a lesson before their night out so she'd be comfortable when they took to the dance floor. While Emerson had always thought herself to be clumsy, Ry steered her about the dance floor with ease, and she felt as if she danced on air when in his arms.

Ivy had taught Dax how to dance, and they both praised her for how quickly she'd caught on.

The best times, though, had been spent together in the event center's large kitchen. Ry was eager to combine his smoked meats with her breads, and the two of them, blending their knowledge and skills, concocted some delicious dishes. They specifically worked on appetizers and came up with several they thought would be good to serve wedding guests, along with three entrees which would help round out the main course offerings.

They had asked their friends to come to the event center for Wednesday night dinner, where they had everyone sample all their new creations. The group had been astonished at the blending of their specialties, and Harper was eager to add all the apps to the catering menu available to brides.

Ry had also made a huge decision, which had streamlined everything. The additional two smokers Shy had bought when Harper had opened Weddings with Hart had been located at Blackwood BBQ. Ry had told his father with the large volume of business they were doing, it didn't make sense to leave the smokers at the restaurant and transport the smoked meats each time. He'd gotten permission from Harper to locate the smokers at the rear of the event center and convinced Shy to move them to the winery.

At first, Shy had protested, but Ry was a persuasive

man. Once the smokers had been relocated, he invited his father to work the next wedding at the winery, and Shy couldn't believe how easily the night unfolded. Ry still transported the sides from the restaurant, but he had told Emerson he felt comfortable making those himself and would most likely take that over, too, doing those on site in the event center's kitchen. The wrap party for Wolf and Ana's new film was tomorrow night, where many of their new apps and dishes would be served. She knew the party would go off without a hitch because of Ry's new setup.

Not only had she and Ry grown closer since they were a couple, but Emerson believed it was time to take their relationship to the next step physically. She was going to hit Ry up with that today and hoped he would agree.

She arrived at Lost Creek Vineyards and received a text from Harper, asking if she could stop by the kitchen and finalize plans for tomorrow night's party. Emerson texted back that Ry would be here any minute, so Harper could come at her convenience. Harper said she would be there in a few minutes.

Once all three of them were there, they went over the plan.

"I'm glad we decided to go with stations," Harper said. "Ana was pleased with that suggestion. She said it would give the party a more festive atmosphere if people could move freely around the space. Since no wedding will occur until Friday, I'm having my staff strike the area where ceremonies take place. That'll be opened up for dancing. I plan to have Dax move his band to that side of the hall."

They looked at Harper's diagram for where each food station would be located, as well as the bars which would be set up at three different spots, identifying what would be served at each place.

"I think we've covered everything," Harper told them. "It will just be getting the food out. I've hired some extra help to man all the stations available."

Ry spoke up. "We can help work those if you need us to."

"No, you're catering the entire event, and Wolf and Ana want you to come and enjoy the party once you have all the food out. Thanks for the offer, though, Ry."

Harper left, and Ry helped Emerson with two of the desserts she would be serving for the party, a strawberry cheesecake bite and tiny blueberry chiffon pies.

"Are you just helping me because you want to sample everything?" she teasingly called over her shoulder.

He came behind her and slipped his arms around her waist, nibbling on her neck. "Well, it is an advantage to having a girlfriend who's a baker. I'm going to have to get Dax to start running farther each morning to make sure I keep off any extra weight."

"You look as if you're hewn from stone, Ry Blackwood," she responded. "I don't think a cheesecake bite or two is going to make a difference."

He turned her in his arms, kissing her deeply.

"So, you like my body?"

"I love your body— and would like to see more of it," she said, flirting with him.

A slow smile spread across his handsome face. "Then I think it's about time you did."

Her heart sped up. "Are you saying what I think you're saying?"

He kissed her again, hard and fast. Breaking the kiss, his gaze met hers.

"I'm dying to make love to you, Emerson Frost."

Her cheeks warmed. "I'm ready for that to happen, Ry Blackwood."

"Then let's finish up all we need to here," he said huskily. "Then we can decide your place— or mine."

Last week, Ry had moved into the apartment above Java Junction, where Dax had lived before he and Ivy got married and moved into a house they'd purchased. The space had been empty, and Ry had told Dax he was ready to move out from his parents' house and into it. Shelly Blackwood had protested, but her son had held firm, saying he would stop by the diner frequently, as well as expect weekly dinner invitations from her.

They finished up with the pies and bites and worked on the chocolate tacos after that. All those items would be kept cold in the massive refrigerator. She would bake the honeybee cupcakes tomorrow and ice them so those would be fresh. Ry had gone in and out, putting items on the smoker and nursing things along.

By now, it was three in the afternoon. He said, "Would you like to go to your house or my apartment?"

"Mine," Emerson told him, thinking she might be more comfortable in familiar surroundings.

"Then I'll meet you there in an hour," he said, walking her to her car and kissing her goodbye.

Emerson had no idea what he would be doing during the next hour, and she certainly had no idea what she should do. She a mix of anticipation and nerves. More than anything, she wanted to be with this man.

And not disappoint him.

That was her greatest fear. She would never ask Ry about any of his previous partners, but she knew a man with his looks and body had plenty of experience. She wanted to satisfy him but figured it would be inevitable when she didn't. Still, Emerson had proven to be a fast learner and hoped she would learn how to please him quickly.

Reaching home, she didn't know whether to turn down the bed or not and finally decided she would. She paced the house anxiously, thinking about movies she had watched where couples made love. One that came to mind was *Pretty Woman,* where Richard Gere played the piano and had his way with Julia Roberts atop the instrument. She might not have a piano, but she was ready to be open to whatever Ry suggested.

He arrived bearing two large canvas bags, saying as he walked to the kitchen, "I stopped by the diner to get us something to eat because all we've done is sample bits and pieces of sweets all day."

His gaze pinned hers. "But dinner is for later. I'm hungry for *you* now."

He placed the bags down, pulling Emerson into his arms for a delicious kiss that made her toes curl.

Ry released her and emptied the first bag, placing the containers into the fridge. From the other bag, he pulled a bottle of wine and a bouquet of flowers.

Handing them to her, he said, "I haven't really given you anything, but you're going to start receiving flowers from me every week," he promised. "You're the kind of women who would appreciate flowers."

Emerson's eyes misted with tears. "No one has ever given me flowers, Ry. Thank you."

She found a flower vase Finley had left behind and filled it with water, trimming the stems and placing the flowers into the vase, imitating what her former roommate had done whenever she had received flowers from a guy.

Ry laced his fingers through hers and led her to her bedroom.

He looked deeply into her eyes. "I know you must be feeling a myriad of emotions. I know I am." He framed her face with his long fingers and kissed her softly. "We're going to take our time, okay?"

"I don't want to disappoint you," she said, her voice breaking, sharing her biggest fear with him.

"I don't want to disappoint *you*."

Emerson thought that was impossible. Then she decided she was in expert hands and would simply follow Ry's lead.

His hands pushed into her hair, his mouth covering hers, causing immediate tingles to rush through her. She gripped his shoulders and kissed him, their tongues warring with one another. That passion she always felt when he kissed her was set ablaze, and her heart slammed against her ribs.

They kissed for several minutes, though, truthfully, Emerson lost track of time. All she knew was that she wanted to be close to Ry. His clean, masculine scent invaded her senses, causing her head to spin. He broke the kiss, both of them struggling to breathe, as his lips trailed along her jaw. Then he moved to where her pulse pounded and nipped at her throat.

Hot desire shot through her.

"Don't think," he said, nuzzling her throat. "Just feel."

Ry's fingers felt hot against her skin as he undid the first button of her blouse. They slid slightly lower, and a second button came undone. Her skin heated as his lips followed his fingers, kissing their way down her front. He spread the shirt open, slipping it from her shoulders, dropping it to the floor as his lips moved along the slope of her shoulder, scalding it.

Then his palm went flat against her back, pressing her to him, as his other hand unclasped her bra. She felt it loosen as his teeth grazed her shoulder, pulling down first one strap and then the other. He removed it, and the bra joined her shirt on the floor.

His blues eyes darkened as he moved his hands to cup her full breasts. "I love your curves."

Slowly, his thumbs brushed back and forth against her nipples, which stood erect, calling out for his attention. A very good kind of chill rippled through her, and her lower body began throbbing in need.

Ry caressed her breasts, his fingers like flames that

licked at them. Then his mouth was on one, taking it in, sucking hard, causing her to whimper. He laved and sucked, his tongue teasing the nipple until Emerson thought she might go mad. Then he moved to the other breast, repeating the same actions. She thought she might go up in flames.

His hands slipped to her bottom, squeezing it, stroking it, making the fire within her burn brighter. His mouth covered hers, greedy in need, taking and taking and taking as she gave everything she had. Boldly, she began unbuttoning his shirt, the backs of her fingers slipping down his rock-hard chest. When she reached the end, she parted his shirt and placed her palms flat against his abs, moving them along the hard planes. She played with his nipples, causing him to suck in a quick breath, hearing his growl, feeling her feminine power for the first time.

And liking it.

She had enjoyed his mouth on her breasts and thought it might be the same for him, so Emerson licked the tip of her tongue against his nipple. Again, another groan— and another smile from her. She circled it with her tongue, teasing him, knowing his heart raced as quickly as hers did.

Ry's fingers made quick work of her capris, peeling them from her. He dipped his fingers into the top of her panties, pulling them down slowly, helping her to step from them.

"Beautiful," he murmured, urging her back a few steps.

Her legs touched the bed, and he maneuvered her until she sat. He moved between her legs, his eyes now almost black. Placing his palm against her belly, he nudged her until she fell back onto the bed. Then he took her knees and moved them further apart. She had no idea what was coming, only that the blood pounded so loudly in her ears that she didn't know if she would hear him if he spoke.

He dragged the pad of his thumb slowly down her slit. Desire enveloped her in a hot rush. He slid it back the other way.

She raised her head. "I might faint," she told him.

"No, you won't," he growled. "You're going to enjoy every minute of this."

He pushed a finger inside her, and she nearly came off the bed.

"Easy," he said, placing one palm against her belly, gently holding her in place.

Then he began caressing her with that finger, bringing sweet sensations. A second finger joined the first as he stroked her deeply. She began writhing on the bed, her breath coming in short spurts as she whimpered with each touch.

"Oh, you're slick now," he said. "So sensitive."

She swallowed. "I feel... like something is starting to build inside me."

"That's good," he said, and she heard the smile in his voice. "Whatever you feel, just go with. Let it unfold naturally."

"Okay," she said, unsure of everything— but him.

His fingers continued working their magic, and then he pulled them from her. Emerson started to protest.

Until he moved even closer. She knew what he did next was going to spark the orgasm rising inside her.

When he slipped his tongue inside her, she gasped aloud. "What are you doing, Ry Blackwood?"

He stopped and raised his head. "I'm making you mine," he said fiercely.

His tongue went inside her again, and it was moving as his fingers had, the strokes long and deep. The urgency within her caught fire and then exploded. She came in a violent rush, crying out his name. Moving. Crying. The waves of pleasure nearly drowned her. Then it slowed. Finally ceased.

Ry moved up until he lay atop her, kissing her deeply. He tasted different, and she realized he tasted of her. The thought was erotic.

He pushed away from the bed and sat on it, removing his boots and socks. She sat up, wrapping her arms around his waist, resting her cheek against his back, breathing him in.

"Gotta stand," he told her, and she let her arms fall away as he undid his jeans and undressed the rest of the way.

Her eyes widened as she looked at him. Broad shoulders. Narrow hips. Flat belly. And a glorious eight-pack that called out to her. Emerson's fingers reached out, dancing lightly, watching with fascination as the muscles bunched and moved.

He drew in a quick breath. "You're playing with fire, Miss Frost," he warned teasingly.

"Something tells me that I'm going to like being

burned, Mr. Blackwood."

Roaring with laughter, he fell onto the mattress, gathering her in his arms, kissing the life out of her. His hands roamed her body, and she returned the favor. His tongue explored her, even as she had her taste of him. Limbs and tongues tangled. Time ceased to exist.

Then he pulled away, leaning down and grasping his jeans, returning with a small foil packet. He tore it open, sheathing himself. He hovered over her, looking like a Greek god, and Emerson eagerly anticipated this final stage of lovemaking.

His fingers slipped inside her, stroking her. "You're definitely ready for me. At least your body is." He hesitated. "Is the rest of you?"

She nodded, holding out her arms.

He came to her, his mouth covering hers even as his body did the same. She felt him against her, and then he pushed inside in one, quick movement.

"Just get used to me a moment," he whispered against her ear.

She felt the fullness of him— and the sudden urge to move. She gave in to it.

"Ah. Are you ready to rock and roll?" he teased.

"Only with you," she said honestly.

Ry withdrew and pushed into her again. Just like when he taught her to dance, Emerson caught his rhythm, and soon they were engrossed in the dance of love. She felt that same quickening inside her again as his fingers came between them and teased the nub inside her. She grew breathless. Lightheaded. Then the orgasm enveloped her again as he cried out, pumping into her. She called his name and hung on for dear life as the bed moved.

They both stilled, Ry collapsing atop her a moment. She clung to him, never wanting to let go. He rolled to his side, bringing her along, and she snuggled against him, their bodies still intimately joined.

Grinning at her, he said, "I think you're better at this than dancing. And you're a helluva dancer," he added huskily.

"That was incredible," she said, on a natural high. "No wonder people want to do this all the time."

"We'll have to make it a regular part of our routine."

Emerson bit her lip. "Was I… was it… okay for you?"

His sunny smiled warmed her. "It was amazing. *You* are amazing. I know this isn't exactly what you want to hear, but I've done this more than a few times." Ry paused. "And this is the best that it's ever been for me."

Doubt filled her. "You're just saying that to be nice."

"No," he said firmly. "I'm not. I've never really taken the time to get to know other lovers the way I have you, Emerson. Knowing you— having the feelings I do for you —that's what made the difference."

She was afraid to ask what those feelings might be because she was finally admitting to herself what she'd known for a while now.

She was in love with Ry Blackwood.

19

$\mathcal{R}$y awoke in Emerson's bed, her body snug against his. He heard her soft breathing and remained still.

They had made love three times. A thorough exploration late yesterday afternoon. A frenetic, passion-crazed time again after dinner, which had exhausted them both. They'd lain in bed afterward, talking for hours, and then he'd convinced her to shower together. She'd had no idea you could make love in the shower, but his girl was a quick study.

That's what he liked about her. Emerson went all-in, no matter what she was doing. Baking a wedding cake. Being loyal to a friend.

And loving him.

He'd always enjoyed sex and had taken pride in making sure it was always good for his partner. Ry had never been long-term with anyone. His time in the army hadn't been conducive for a semi-permanent relationship. He'd used sex as a way to blow off steam. Scratch an itch. Escape from the drudgery— and danger —of the battlefield.

His time with Emerson yesterday had been different from anything he'd experienced. He had never even thought to look for love, despite the fact in coming home to Lost Creek, he'd known he wanted to put down roots. Find a wife. Start a family. Now, he realized that love had found him.

The only problem now was when he should tell Emerson that he loved her.

She'd come a long way from the scared rabbit he'd met. He decided he'd actually read her wrong. She was extremely shy and did lack confidence about things she'd never experienced before. But she was a strong, proud woman. Talented. Smart. Beautiful. And very giving of herself to others. She would make the ideal partner for what Ry wanted in life. A home. His own business. And lots of kids.

He'd taken things slowly with her up until now, but he loved her— and needed her to know that.

Absently, he stroked her forearm as he thought of the best way to share his feelings for her. Then he felt her stir in his arms and realized he'd probably awakened her.

"Sorry," he said, brushing a kiss against her hair. "I didn't mean to mess with your sleep."

She turned so she faced him. "I'm an early bird. You know that. I may not go into The Bake House at three every morning these days, but old habits die hard. Are you going to run with Dax this morning?"

"Not if I can make love to you instead." He hesitated. "Are you too sore?"

"Not a bit," she assured him, pulling him down to her and kissing him. Then she broke the kiss, panic written on her face. "Oh, no. I'm so sorry."

"For what?"

She smiled ruefully. "Morning breath."

"I will take that morning breath and raise it." He kissed her. "See? We both have it. I'm not going to let it stop me from having my wicked way with you."

Emerson laughed as his lips glided along her bare shoulder. "Wicked? Is that what we did? If so, then something wicked this way comes."

Her arms went around him, and she threw one leg over his. They kissed, desire flickering in them both, and Ry lifted her so she straddled him.

She giggled. "Another wicked position?"

"One of the best. Ride me," he urged, knowing he was already hard as stone.

Frowning, she said, "Help me figure this out."

Lifting her, Ry eased her down on his shaft. Understanding lit her eyes. "My, this feels awfully good, Mr. Blackwood." She wriggled her bottom and sucked in a quick breath. "*Very* good."

Soon, the dance of love was in full swing as Emerson figured things out. She rocked against him, leaning over, her full breasts tempting him. He palmed them, squeezing gently, then brought her close enough so he had a mouthful of delectable goodness. The action heated up, and she rode him with enthusiasm, joy on her face. His climax was the strongest of his life, and he realized too late that he hadn't slipped on a condom.

She collapsed against him, breathing hard, her cheek resting against his beating heart.

"That was *way* wicked," she said, laughing. "I think you're going to teach me a lot, Ry Blackwood."

"Can I do that as your husband?" he countered.

Emerson froze. "What?" She looked down at him, their eyes meeting.

"I love you," he said.

She shook her head. "It's the sex talking," she said, denying him. "Men think with their penis at times like this."

"Nope. Not this guy," he protested. "I love you, Emerson. It's a feeling that's gradually happened. I can't pinpoint when I first felt it. It's… just there. I love you. I want a life with you. I want kids with you. Maybe a dog and cat and guinea pig."

"Guinea pig?" she asked, laughter bubbling up from her.

"Well, I'm sure one of our kids is going to be a little out of the mainstream. He— or she —will be the one that wants a guinea pig. They won't have chocolate or vanilla as their favorite ice cream and like something like pistachio instead. But we'll love this kid as much as we love the other ones."

She studied him a long moment. "You really mean it, don't you?"

"If you mean that I love you and want a life with you, then the answer is absolutely yes."

"What if something's wrong with me, and I can't have kids?"

He shrugged. "We'll adopt all of them then. You've already said you want to adopt. Maybe we can go half and half. Have a couple. Adopt a couple."

Tears brimmed in her eyes. "You would do that? Adopt?"

"You bet," he said enthusiastically. "After all, you were in the system. There are all kinds of kids in foster care, waiting for their mom and dad. We are going to make fantastic parents, whether it's kids that have our DNA or kids we choose to be mom and dad to."

Emerson covered his face with kisses. "You are the best, Ry."

"Hey, wait a minute."

She paused. "What?"

"You haven't told me how you feel about me?"

But her gray eyes gave him the answer before she spoke. "I love you, Ry. I thought I was crazy to fall in love with you because guys like you don't give girls like me the time of day. But you've changed my mind. And my heart. I cannot imagine living a single day without you. I need you like fish need water. Like the grass needs rain. Like—"

Ry cut her off, kissing her with everything he had.

Emerson broke the kiss, though. "Let's keep this to ourselves for a while. Not tell anyone." She paused and then quietly said. "Just in case you change your mind."

"I won't ever change my mind, but we can wait a little

bit before we share our good news with family and friends."

As he kissed her again, Ry knew everything was going to be fine.

Because he would spend the rest of his life with the most amazing woman on the planet.

Ry was glad he had decided to move the smokers to the event center. It had made a huge difference in getting out food for the wrap party. Ana had wanted everything to be finger foods, so neither Emerson's desserts nor the food they had combined their efforts on needed any silverware. He had enjoyed combining his smoking skills with her baking ones and concocting several new apps for the party.

From the sound of it, things were in full swing outside the kitchen. Dax and his Lone Star Rebels were playing an eclectic group of songs, which the crowd seemed to appreciate enthusiastically from their hoots and hollers and applause that occurred at the beginning and end of each song.

Ana entered the kitchen as Emerson pulled out a fresh tray of the brisket puff pastries and Ry put together one of his pork sliders.

"You two are doing a fabulous job with the food," she praised. "The cast and crew are having such a wonderful time. I know a wrap party is held at the end of productions, but sometimes people seem too tired to actually celebrate. With your food— and the band —we have a real party atmosphere going."

"I'm glad your guests are enjoying what we're providing," he said.

"This is the last of the food going out," Emerson said. "I hope everyone's enjoying the chocolate tacos you requested."

"They are superb, Emerson," Ana exclaimed. "I'm hoping you'll come to the ranch and teach me how to make them because Eva and Bear have gone wild for them. Once you've finished here, please come join the party. You deserve to kick up your heels after all the hard work you've put in tonight."

"We'll do it," Ry promised, topping the last of the sliders with their buns and signaling to Harper's staff members gathered to begin sending out the last trays to the various stations.

After Ana left, someone new appeared in the kitchen. He recognized Jack Calder from his day on the set. The leading man was the only big name in the *Hill Country Homicide* cast, and Ry had been impressed with Jack's acting skills. He had a woman and two small children with him.

"Hope it's okay to invade the kitchen," the actor said, giving them an easy smile, one which charmed his fans.

"You're welcome to be here," he told Jack. "Is this your family?"

Jack Calder beamed with pride, slipping an arm about his wife's waist. "This is my wife, Sandra, and our kids, Hannah and Billy. We just wanted to come back and thank you for all the fabulous food you've provided tonight. Filming in Texas and working with Wolf and Ana has been a dream. In fact, Sandra and I like Texas so much, we've decided to buy a place here. More and more movies are being shot in Texas. We're thinking it would be great to use Texas as our home base to raise the kids."

"You can't go wrong bringing up your kids in Texas," Ry told him. "Especially a place such as Lost Creek."

"We think we'll buy a ranch similar in size to what Wolf and Ana have," Jack continued. "I'd like the kids to grow up with some animals and have some responsibility. I'm a Midwestern boy with those solid Midwestern values. I don't want Billy and Hannah to become entitled Hollywood brats."

He looked at the two kids, Sandra holding baby Billy, while Jack held Hannah, who looked about three, in his arms.

"We enjoyed all the barbeque," Sandra said. "Especially when combined with the different breads and pastries."

"I like the cheesecake," Hannah piped up, causing them all to laugh.

"It looks as if you've sent all the food out," Jack continued. "Please, come join the party now. Your mom is really making her mark on the dance floor."

Ry chuckled. "Mom loves to dance. And Dad can't stand to. Fortunately, he's a good sport about letting her have as many partners as she chooses."

He looked to Emerson. "Want to go take a turn on the dance floor with me?"

She began untying her apron. "I think that sounds like a wonderful way to end the evening."

Removing his apron, he took Emerson's hand, leading her from the kitchen. The music was loud and the crowd lively. He spied his mom on the dance floor, and she waved to him.

He and Emerson blended into the crowd, and he thought of all the happy times to come in their future.

"I can't believe how much fun dancing is," she said, laughing. "You're introducing me to so many wonderful activities, Ry."

He brought his lips to her ear. "Maybe we can engage in one of those so-called wonderful activities when we get home tonight," he said, causing her to laugh even harder.

The song ended, and he said, "Let's get something to drink. We've earned it."

They headed to one of the three bars, where he asked for a Shiner Bock and Emerson got a glass of sangria. Holden waved to them, and they headed his and Finley's way.

Thrusting out a hand, Ry said, "Congratulations, my friend. Your first filmed screenplay is done."

"There's still a lot of work to come on it," Holden shared. "I've watched a lot of the daily rushes— what was filmed each day —and Wolf will now head into the editing room to tighten it up. Pacing is critical, especially in a murder mystery. Then it'll need a score added."

"It'll premier at a film festival in Austin," Finley added. "You'll be invited as VIP guests, of course." She grinned. "And you won't have to cater a thing."

"It'll be nice to have a night off," he joked.

His mom joined them. "Aren't these movie people just the nicest folks?" Shelly Blackwood asked. "They were so sweet when they filmed scenes in the diner. I was thrilled they invited us to this party as a thank you for using the diner."

"Is Dad here?" Ry asked. "I haven't seen him."

"You know him. He's working at the restaurant tonight. He did say he'd come over after closing." Her eyes skimmed the room. "Wait. There he is. Talk to you soon."

Harper and Braden came up, Harper glowing. She was about six months along now and as busy as ever. If anyone could have a baby and keep a business running smoothly, it would be Harper Hart Clark.

Ivy joined them. "Isn't this a great party? It's nice to have a night out, even if I can't dance with my husband. I've been working non-stop, wanting to finish up the last two paintings which will be in my show in September."

"Would you like to dance, Ivy?" Ry asked. "After all, I have to take care of my little sister."

She looked to Emerson. "Would you mind, Em?"

"Not a bit. Dance as much as you want with him."

They hit the dance floor, and Ivy told him, "I wanted to let you know that Dax and I are going to have a baby."

His feet stopped moving, and he wrapped her in a bear hug. "I can't believe both you and Harper will have kids so close together. That's awesome. Congratulations."

"We'll tell everyone at our friends' dinner tomorrow night, but I wanted you to know before we announced it."

They began moving again, and Ry said, "I'm honored

you shared the news with me, Ivy. I've always thought of you as family. It'll be fun being an uncle to your kids."

Her eyes gleamed at him. "Speaking of family, how are things going with Emerson? Am I going to see a ring on her finger anytime soon?"

"Absolutely," he declared. "She knows that's the end goal. It's been a pretty whirlwind romance, but when you find the one you're meant to be with? You just know."

"That's how it was with Dax," Ivy revealed. "I can't imagine my life without him. He's so loving and supportive of me. And changing subjects, your food tonight was incredible. I want to be invited to every wedding at the winery just so I can keep eating all the wonderful things you and Emerson are creating."

"It's my turn to cook dinner tomorrow night," he told her. "Emerson and I are teaming up together to make something really special for the gang."

"Then I look forward to it."

The song ended, and Ry kissed Ivy's cheek, leading her back to where Emerson and their friends were talking.

Wolf Ramirez tapped him on the shoulder. "Gotta tell you, Ry, this has been the best wrap party I've ever been a part of. You and Emerson have done a fantastic job on the food, and Dax's Lone Star Rebels have really brought the house down."

The director laughed. "I should've started my own production company years, ago, just so all my wrap parties could be held at Lost Creek Vineyards." He looked to Emerson. "Ana and I are really taken with your chocolate tacos? She told me she's talked you into coming to the ranch and showing us how to make them. We'll even feed you dinner in return."

"I'd be happy to come over and do so, Wolf."

Ry started to ask Emerson to dance again when he caught sight of his dad weaving his way through the crowd, heading toward them.

And from the look on Shy Blackwood's reddened face, things were not going to go well.

He had known his dad would be scrutinizing all the food served. Many of the apps included the fusion of Asian cuisine with barbeque. Ry thought he'd prepared himself for the inevitable confrontation, but he saw now that his dad was ready to explode.

Unfortunately, the band finished playing their song just as Shy Blackwood reached them, allowing everyone present to hear him confront Ry.

In a loud voice, Shy demanded, "What the hell are you doing, son? You're ruining the Blackwood name!"

20

Calmly, Ry said, "You don't want to ruin Wolf and Ana's party and embarrass Harper, Dad. Let's take this outside."

Shy Blackwood stormed off without a backward glance as party guests watched him head to the doors and slam one open.

Emerson caught his wrist, worry etched across her face. "Should I—"

"No, babe. I've known this showdown was coming for a long time. This is between Dad and me. I'll deal with him."

He brushed the back of his fingers against her cheek and kissed her softly. "Try not to worry."

"Fat chance," she murmured.

Ry glanced across the room to Dax, who also looked concerned. He mouthed, "Play."

Immediately, Dax launched into another song with a

pounding beat. The crowd responded, and guests began dancing and talking again as Ry crossed the room and exited the event center. He saw his father pacing about fifty yards away and steeled himself, walking toward him.

The minute his dad spotted him, he marched toward Ry, thrusting his cell phone in Ry's face.

"What is this crap all on our website? You've got a lot of explaining to do, Ryland William Blackwood."

He tried not to wince. The last time his dad had used his full birth name was when he confronted Ry about coming home drunk after homecoming.

That was fifteen years ago.

"It's not crap," he said, deliberately keeping his tone even. "I learned a lot when I was cooking in the army, Dad. Asian people really enjoy barbeque. I—"

"Hell could freeze over— and I wouldn't serve anything that ain't pure Texas barbeque in my restaurant. The Blackwood name stands for something, Ry. Something good and pure. Texas and barbeque go hand-in-hand. I learned how to smoke from my daddy and granddaddy, and I'm not gonna change and frou-frou it up."

He jabbed his finger at the cell phone, and Ry could see that the catering page was on the screen.

"I'm pissed you went behind my back and slapped all this on the website. A website I never even wanted. And you're serving this stuff at wedding receptions? And tonight?"

"Because people enjoy it, Dad," he said firmly. "Yes, traditional Blackwood barbeque is magical, and people enjoy eating it. I still provide plenty of that to Harper's wedding guests. But times change, Dad. People look for new things, especially brides and grooms who are trying to make their wedding day special. Yes, Harper and I offer them everything Blackwood BBQ makes. Brisket. Pork. Sausage. Chicken. You name it, I smoke it the way you taught me, and I'm damn good at it.

"But while I was in the military, I played around with merging the barbeque I knew and loved with the Asian flavors I was discovering, both from being stationed in South Korea and on my travels. Soldiers liked it, Dad. Really liked it. I knew one day, when I came home to Lost Creek, I would want to incorporate that into the meats I smoked."

"You should've never come home then, Ry," his father said, bitterness spilling from him. "What you've done ain't right. You've ruined my good name and all the work I've put into Blackwood BBQ all these years."

"No, I haven't," he protested loudly, his temper now flaring. "I'm giving people a choice. And they're enjoying both, Dad. The Texan and the fusion barbeque. Go inside and taste a few things. Ask around and see what everyone thought about the food. Wolf and Ana handpicked every item served at the various stations tonight. Harper's thrilled that my new menu offerings are bringing in even more clients. Even Jack Calder came back to tell me how much he was enjoying what we served tonight."

His father gave him a withering look. "I don't care what they think. It's wrong on every stinkin' level, Ry. You've tarnished the Blackwood name and our legacy in the barbeque world. I want you to get that crap off the website. Better yet, shut the damn thing down. And you tell Harper that the catering goes back to basics, starting tomorrow. I won't allow you to serve—"

"You won't *allow* me?" he asked, his anger full-blown now. "I'm a grown man, Dad. Not the kid who graduated from high school and took off to see the world a dozen years ago. You don't tell me what to do. I make my own decisions."

Shy Blackwood let out a string of curses. "You're done. I don't want you at the restaurant ever again. I'll take over the catering from now on and if Harper and her brides don't like it, they can all go to hell! By God, it's going to be Blackwood BBQ— or nothing at all."

Ry stood firm, even though his heart was breaking at their fallout.

"You're welcome to it," he said. "But you're going to lose a lot of business, you pig-headed old man."

Shy narrowed his eyes, glaring at Ry. "I'd rather lose business than serve what you make. And I'll burn down the entire damn place before I ever think of leaving it to you."

A lump formed in his throat. He loved his dad, but sixty-year-old Shy Blackwood was old school all the way. And Ry wasn't going to compromise.

Even if it cost him his relationship with the man he'd worshiped since the time he could walk.

"I don't want the family business," he said.

"Good. Because you ain't family no more."

With that, his father strode away.

Ry watched him retreat, the ache heavy in his heart,

like a physical pain which might never heal. Turning, he slowly made his way back to the event center, opening the door, hearing Dax singing The Eagles' *Already Gone.* Partiers were on their feet, dancing, singing along, celebrating the end of making their movie.

He owed it to Harper to find her and let her know what was up, but first, he searched for Emerson, who was huddled with Ivy. When she saw him, she threw her arms around him.

"It's okay," he said, trying to comfort her.

"You look upset. How did it go?" she asked.

"He was exactly the Shy Blackwood I know. Obstinate. Inflexible. Not willing to compromise on a single thing." He hesitated. "I'm out."

Emerson frowned. "What do you mean, out?"

"I don't work for Blackwood BBQ anymore. Dad is taking over the catering."

"He can't do that," she protested.

"He can do whatever he wants. He's the owner."

Ry looked to Ivy. "You better take down the website. Dad is livid about the additions I've made on the catering menu. He wants it scuttled."

Ivy eyed him with sympathy. "I'm so sorry, Ry. I'll do it immediately. What I can do is make it inactive for now. Just in case he changes his mind. That way, we wouldn't have to build all the pages again."

"You do whatever you need to do, Ivy. He's furious with me. I don't want you to get caught up in the crossfire." He sighed. "I need to talk to Harper."

"I'll go with you," Emerson offered, taking his hand.

They found Harper and pulled her aside.

"Thank you for not letting Shy make a scene in front of everyone, Ry," Harper said. "I appreciated you stepping in as you did."

"I need to give you a heads up, Harper. Dad will be handling the catering for you in the future."

"What?" Harper rarely became flustered, but her face grew red now. "Is this over the new items?"

"Exactly. You know Dad. He's a charter member of the nothing needs to change school of thought. He'll give your brides the traditional choices currently on the Blackwood BBQ menu, but he refuses to serve anything that I've come up with. In fact, I just told Ivy to take down the website. He wants it gone."

Harper frowned. "That means back to limited choices. Plated dinners. No stations." Her eyes welled with tears. "Oh, Ry, what am I going to do? Several of the upcoming weddings want your menu items. Those brides and grooms have specifically wanted *your* spin on barbeque. Those couples could walk now. Even sue me."

Braden had joined them. "You don't need this kind of stress. It's not good for the baby." He slipped his arm about his wife's shoulders. "All I heard is Shy is going back to catering receptions. But if he can't fulfill the contracts, then Ry should take over those."

Steal his dad's business?

He would say that would have him disbarred from the family— but it already looked as if Shy had booted his only child out the door.

"Hell. Why not?" he ventured.

Emerson asked, "Does this mean you'll open your own business? Compete with Blackwood BBQ?"

"I don't want to," he admitted. "In fact, it's the last thing I want. Mom in the middle. Open warfare declared. But I made a commitment to Harper's clients. If my dad isn't willing to give them what they're asking for, I refuse to allow them to walk away and cost Harper business."

He drew in a long breath, letting it out slowly. "I'll need to look into buying a smoker because Dad'll clear out the ones behind the event center quicker than I can spit." His gaze met Harper's. "Contact your clients and give them the opportunity to go with a traditional menu if they've selected something different. If they still want what I have to offer, then I'll make certain they get what they want. Just share those dates with me."

"Thank you, Ry," Harper said, squeezing his arm. "I can't imagine how rough this is on you." She paused. "Shy'll come around. Give him time."

But he knew his dad. Shy Blackwood was a good soul, the kind of man who was loyal and kind and would give a down-and-out man his last dollar. What Shy wasn't was the kind of guy who changed his mind or got out of his comfort zone. This rift between them was likely to widen instead of shrink. Ry had done the unthinkable.

Messed with Texas barbeque.

And Shy Blackwood would never forgive him for such a cardinal sin.

"I'll call every bride who's booked items from your catering menu tomorrow, Ry," Harper continued. "By the end of the day, I should know which ones will allow

Blackwood BBQ to cater their receptions— and which ones prefer to go with you. Do you have a name you could use for your business?"

Ry thought a moment. "Smokin' Sweethearts."

"I like it," Braden said. "It's catchy. Alliterative."

He turned to Emerson. "Are you ready to go home?"

She nodded. They said goodnight and drove back to her house, shedding their clothes and crawling into bed together. He held her in his arms, glad for her love and warmth.

Then Ry made love to her tenderly. Even so, they climaxed together in a shattering moment of emotions. He couldn't help it, suddenly overcome by the consequences of tonight's argument. He cried for all that he had lost, Emerson comforting him.

As they spooned together, he knew how lucky he was to have this woman by his side.

And he needed to make it official.

"Emerson?" he asked softly.

"Mmm?"

No. She was too sleepy now. Worn out from the long, hard day. When he asked her to formerly marry him, he needed it to be special. Just as she was.

"I love you," he told her, his arms tightening about her.

"I love you, too," she replied, her breathing quickly evening out as she fell asleep.

Ry might have lost his job and his relationship with his dad.

But he had the love of a good woman. One he planned to marry as soon as possible.

21

In the ten days since Shy Blackwood had booted Ry from the family business— and the family —his life had changed exponentially. Ry needed an immediate source of income. Barbequing was in his blood, so he sat down with Emerson, who was eager to assist him in creating a solid plan utilizing his background and skills.

The top priority was purchasing a first-class smoker if he were going to produce quality meats. The gold standard for commercial smokers was Lang, located in Nahunta, Georgia. Ry wouldn't consider any other brand. To get the nine-foot smoker he wanted, along with the trailer hitch swivel front for easier transportation and a fold-down prep area, it would set him back almost eighteen thousand dollars. Fortunately, he had banked almost everything he had earned during his military career, and he was able to pay for his order in cash.

To expedite things and save on the freight shipping charges, which were high, Ry had driven his truck to Georgia in order to pick up the smoker and bring it back to Texas. While he was on the road headed for home, he had arranged a meeting with Jay Warner, the president of Lost Creek's only bank and its chief loan officer.

Ry's idea was to buy a food truck. He couldn't exist off the earnings from the weekend receptions he did for Weddings with Hart. Not every bride would choose him to cater their receptions. Some would still use Blackwood BBQ, while a few others contracted with other local restaurants Harper worked with. Because of that, he wanted to add a new layer to his small business and invest in a food truck.

He went to city hall and looked into permits in the town and places he could park the truck for sales. He thought he could do a decent lunch business, as well as bringing the truck to local events, including games and tournaments. Texans were wild about their sports, and the fever caught on early. Most kids were involved in playing one or more sport, everything from football to soccer to baseball and beyond. He could bring the truck to the city park, where the playing fields were located, and he believed he could do a steady business at that.

Today was his meeting with Jay Warner, and Emerson would be accompanying him to it. She was standing by him during this life crisis, and he loved her all the more for it.

They entered the bank and told the receptionist they had an appointment with Jay. She had them take a seat, and they waited about ten minutes before being ushered into the bank president's large office.

"Thank you for submitting your loan application online before our meeting so I could look over things before we met," Jay said, being friendlier than Ry had expected.

Jay had them take a seat and added, "I've been in touch with the Veterans Bureau and, in turn, the Small Business Administration. Together, they are willing to help you obtain a loan for up to seventy-five thousand dollars to help in creating your business. I have all the necessary paperwork here for you to fill out."

"I'd like to take out a personal loan on top of that, Jay," he said. "The food trucks and kitchens I'm looking at are going to cost more than that seventy-five thousand. I've already paid fully for my smoker."

The bank executive frowned. "I can't thank you enough for your service to our country, Ry. We need more young men making that kind of commitment to our citizens. I think you are doing a disservice to your father, however, by pursuing this idea."

His heart sank. This was more what he had expected.

"You would be competing directly with Shy. That's not good for Lost Creek— or your family. Besides," Jay said almost apologetically, "you have no collateral to back up a personal loan. You're paying a healthy amount each month on your truck, a payment only recently begun. You rent instead of owning your own housing. You have nothing of value the bank could go after if you defaulted on your loan from us. Frankly, I think you should pursue a different direction, Ry. The SBA has programs available specifically for veterans, as well as guidance on how to start up and be successful in a personal business. I'm sure you can find something of value to do now that you're home again. Other than barbeque."

Before he could reply, Jay smiled and said, "I know you and Shy have had words. Harsh ones. I think you should suck it up and apologize to your dad."

He reined in the anger rising within him, knowing it wouldn't do any good to explode.

"I'll take you up on facilitating the military loan. I'll find another avenue to raise the additional funds I need. Let's go ahead and sign whatever paperwork is necessary, Mr. Warner," he said formally. "And I'd like to also open a business checking and credit card account if you can help me with those, as well."

With obvious reluctance, the bank president opened the manila folder in front of him and walked Ry through the documents. He signed them, securing the loan for seventy-five thousand, which he then had placed in his new business account. If he had another choice, he would've taken his business elsewhere, but he didn't want to be petty, much less inconvenience himself. Besides, he should've known what he would be up against, going against his dad in the small town Shy Blackwood had been born and bred in.

The older generation in Lost Creek— if pressed to take sides —would come down in favor of Shy. Ry would have to count on the younger people in town, those in their twenties and thirties, raising families and looking for convenience in picking up a decent meal of barbeque, whether for lunch, dinner, or at a ballgame.

As they got into the truck, Emerson said, "I'm sorry that didn't go better."

"It went exactly as I expected. I've just got to figure out now what I'm going to do. How I'm going to raise the money to see this dream become a reality."

He dropped her at her house so that she could drive her own car to the winery. They made plans to meet at Harper and Braden's at five-thirty for their weekly Wednesday dinner.

Ry spent hours online that afternoon, looking at different food trucks and kitchens, as well as hunting for ways to finance them. Whatever he did, he needed to stay in Lost Creek, though. This was where Emerson had planted her own roots, and he intended for them to build a life together here. He wouldn't let his feud with his father chase him away from the town— and woman —he loved.

He drove to the Clarks and was surprised to see how many cars were already there, thinking he might have gotten the time wrong.

Ringing the doorbell, he was soon greeted by Harper. "Come in, Ry. We need to talk to you."

Puzzled, he followed her into the large den, where he found everyone already seated. Even Wolf and Ana Ramirez were on hand. Sitting, he realized he was the center of attention.

"What's going on?" he asked. "I feel as if I'm coming in

on the middle of a movie and haven't a clue what's been happening."

Dax spoke up. "We've been meeting for the last hour, Ry. Emerson texted everyone to let us know what Jay Warner said at the bank today. We want you to know you have our full support." He paused. "Not just emotionally. Financially, too."

"I don't understand."

Holden cleared his throat. "We want to invest in your food truck. It's as simple as that. We know being turned down at the bank had to be disheartening, but we want you to go for your dream. We think you owning a food truck is a viable business and that with your spin on barbeque, you will make a success of things. We're ready to invest in your business. In *you*."

Tears stung his eyes. "I can't ask for my friends to bankroll this," he protested.

"You didn't ask us," Ivy said. "We want to do this, Ry. You're as much family as you are a friend to each of us. We believe in you. In your vision."

"Some of us can kick in more than others," Finley told him. "We've been blessed to find success professionally in our own lives. While we're having dinner this evening, we want you to share with us what you're interested in investing in and how much you'll need. Then we can figure out our contributions to the operation."

His throat grew thick with emotion. "I'm honored to call each of you my friend. Your belief in me and your support will help me get on my feet. I promise that I'll pay you back as soon as possible."

"Come into the kitchen," Braden said. "I've done a taco bar, so you can assemble your tacos with whatever you want on them."

It took everyone a few minutes to fill their plates, and then the group gathered around the dining room table.

Once everyone was settled, Ry said, "There are three ways to invest in a food truck. Each of them has their pros and cons. If I'm going to do it right, however, I want a new truck, along with a new kitchen."

As they ate, he explained his reasoning. "Food trucks can run anywhere from fifty up to two hundred thousand dollars. With used ones, you run the risk of hidden costs since you don't know how hard the truck was used. Or abused. If you have to replace an engine after you've already purchased it, the costs could soar. Plus, the quality of the kitchen won't suit my needs in that fifty-thousand-dollar price range."

"Is it possible to buy a new truck and an existing kitchen?" Ana asked. "Or could you evaluate a truck to see if it's in good condition and place a new kitchen in it? I don't know if that would be possible, but it's a thought."

"I could get a brand-new kitchen on a used truck chassis for a little over a hundred thousand. Again, with a used truck, I could have a mechanic inspect it, but no one's going to admit they were hard on their vehicle when they go to sell it. I just don't want to open the can of worms mechanical problems could bring to the operation, draining money before or soon after I started up."

"To me, it seems comparable to buying a new home," Wolf said. "Yes, new is more expensive, but you inherit no problems, plus you can design your home to suit your needs."

"That's a good analogy," he said, nodding. "With a new truck, I'd have a warranty. From my research, most come with a five-year warranty or up to two hundred and fifty thousand miles, depending on the model I selected. Even doing proper maintenance, that warranty could be solid gold if I had problem with something, such as a chassis. New also equals reliable. Reliability will help me create a solid customer base, which is vital in this kind of business. I can build a kitchen to my specifications on a new truck, with everything also under warranty."

"I've been helping Ry research things," Emerson said. "The newer trucks hold up to regulations not just in Lost Creek, but for other places in Texas and the U.S. That means he would have the ability to operate his truck anywhere he needed to go for years to come. If Texas landed the Super Bowl or World Series, he could travel to those venues and make a killing. And if for any reason he decided not to stay in this business, new would mean a higher resale value for him."

"There is an option of leasing to own," Ry shared. "It's an alternative worth looking into. It costs a little less than four thousand a month to do so. It's a route I'm willing to take."

"No," Harper said firmly. "Leasing would be the same as buying used. You don't know how many others have leased the truck before you. They could have screwed something up with the truck or the kitchen. I say we're in — and that means we're all in with the best choice."

He concluded with, "You're right. That's why I prefer going new. That way, I'll know I won't have any kind of engine problems or need to replace anything on the truck or in the kitchen. I'll also be able to design the kitchen exactly the way I want it. But that comes with a hefty price tag."

"What are we talking then, Ry?" Wolf asked. "Bottom line it for us."

"It could cost anywhere between a hundred and fifty to two hundred thousand dollars. I've been online, and I think I've found the one I want. It's one seventy-five and has the kitchen layout that would be perfect for my needs."

"Is this the one you really want?" Braden asked.

"I'll need to see it in person, but I think it is. It's got everything I could ask for in the kitchen. It's in San Antonio, at one of the few food truck dealerships in the state, so I can run over there and view it before making a decision." He hesitated. "With my SBA loan of seventy-five thousand, that would mean a hundred thousand is what I need to raise."

"Done," Holden and Dax said in unison, and Dax added, "We can work out the details after dinner, but we want you to get what suits your needs. I'm a former accountant, and I began investing years ago. I've stockpiled a decent amount of money. I can fund the entire loan myself, but I know the others want to chip in, as well."

"I've done really well with the sales of my first two books," Holden added. "I'm happy to kick in a healthy amount so Dax doesn't have to shoulder too big a burden."

The others all chimed in, with Emerson finishing the conversation, saying, "I have some money left to me by Ethel. What's mine is yours, Ry. No loan is necessary."

Tears spilled down his cheeks, and he was man enough to own them.

"When I lost Todd, I lost my best friend and the brother of my heart. Little did I know I would return to Lost Creek years later and find friends just as loyal to me as Todd."

"He's here with you in spirit," Ivy said, smiling gently at him. "Todd would have been the first to tell you to believe in yourself. Think of him as the angel on your shoulder, watching over you now."

Ry shook his head. "You people are incredible. I'm touched beyond words."

Emerson took his hand and squeezed it, her love for him shining in her eyes. Then she gazed out at those seated around the table

"Who's ready for dessert?"

As they all got up to take their plates into the kitchen, a peace settled over him. This next chapter in his life would undoubtedly hold some bumps, but with Emerson, his work ethic, and a group of trusted friends, Ry knew he would make something of himself.

2 2

$\mathcal{E}$merson bustled around the kitchen, washing and drying the last of the equipment she had used this morning. Ry wanted her to accompany him into San Antonio in order to purchase the food truck. They were leaving at nine this morning, and so she had gone into the winery extra early, keeping more to her former baker's hours. She had baked the cakes for Saturday's wedding, and while they baked and cooled, she had iced and decorated the cakes for tomorrow night's wedding. The bride was a second-timer, a widow who had two young children. She had not wanted the fuss of a wedding, but her groom had talked her into holding one at the event center. He had also insisted on both children having a part in the ceremony, making Emerson like him quite a bit as she watched him interact with his soon-to-be stepchildren. The groom had even asked that she bake two small cakes, one for each child, and he'd encouraged them to tell Emerson how they wanted them decorated.

Drying the last of the bowls, she put them aside, returning to her new car. She had finally purchased a new vehicle in Boerne last week at Ry's suggestion, buying a small SUV. Emerson really liked how she sat up a little higher in it and could see everything better, plus it had plenty of space in the rear if she needed to transport anything.

She drove home now, eager to time spend with Ry. He was so excited about his new business venture, as well as the support from his friends in helping to get it off the ground, but Emerson was still concerned about the rift between him and his father.

Shelly Blackwood had come undone upon hearing what had gone down between her husband and son. She had begged Ry to mend the fences between them, but he had told his mother he had nothing to apologize for. That he would continue to see her away from the house but that he couldn't in good conscience give into his father. Shelly had even contacted Emerson regarding the issue, hoping she could somehow bring the two men together. Emerson had said the issue was between Ry and Shy, and they would have to work it out themselves. Still, if she could think of a way to facilitate a reunion between the pair, she would do so.

When she arrived home, Ry's truck already sat in front of her house. He got out of it as she pulled into the driveway, coming to greet her with a kiss.

"How did everything go at the bank?" she asked. "Did

the funds transfer and get credited into your business account?"

Once dinner ended last night, their friends had generously used technology to transfer money from themselves to Ry. He had wanted something in writing about these loans, but Braden had insisted that a handshake between friends was good enough.

"All done," he assured her. "I asked to meet with Jay Warner, so he could verify the transfers. Since all but Wolf had an account at the bank, the money from everyone else was already credited to me this morning from their Lost Creek accounts.

"Because I really want to buy the food truck today and pay cash, I called Dax. He came over right away and also gave me the amount Wolf was in for. I texted Wolf to cancel his transaction if he could from his end. He can settle up with Dax later. That way, I will now have the full amount available to me ASAP. So, we're set to go."

In the car, he asked, "Do you have time for us to grab lunch or do a little sightseeing after we buy the truck?"

"I'd like that. I've never been to San Antonio," she admitted.

"It's only an hour or less from Lost Creek. I can't believe you haven't been. It's got some of the best food in Texas." Then he paused. "I'm sorry, Emerson. I know you haven't had much free time, working two jobs while you've been living in Lost Creek."

"I finished the cakes for tomorrow's wedding, and I baked the two for Saturday's wedding," she told him.

"That means I have the rest of today free. We can do whatever you want in San Antonio."

"I'm happy to play tour guide for you."

On the way, they talked about the food he would offer the food truck's clients.

"I don't want to overextend myself," he said. "I think limiting the menu to a few items will not only streamline things for me, but it'll be less confusing for people when they step up to order. And again, I have to thank you for letting me keep my new smoker in your back yard."

With Ry living above Java Junction, he had nowhere to put his smoker and nurse his meats. Harper had said he could keep it at the winery, especially since Shy had already removed the Blackwood BBQ smoker Ry had used for catering receptions. He was still considering Harper's offer, but for now, the smoker would remain at Emerson's house. She was only a few blocks off the square, and having a central location such as that would really benefit him, especially since he planned to take the food truck out every weekday.

They reached the San Antonio city limits and pulled up to their destination fifteen minutes later. Ry had made an appointment and was greeted by name by a salesman. He introduced Emerson, and the three of them went to look at the exact food truck Ry was interested in purchasing.

The salesman gave them all the specifications regarding the truck, and she and Ry climbed into it, looking over the interior and dashboard and what it had to offer. Then the salesman took them inside the food truck and pointed out the various features the kitchen had to offer.

"It's a little crowded with three of us in here, but it easily fits two workers. I'll give you some time to explore it." He gave Ry the key fob. "Take it out and see what you think. I'll be in office when you finish."

The salesman left, and they spent the next quarter-hour going over the kitchen with a fine-toothed comb. Ry pointed out several things to Emerson and explained why he liked them or where they were located. He walked her through how he would put together the limited dishes they had discussed. While he could cook in the kitchen, most of his menu offerings would already be barbequed for hours on the smoker and would simply be kept warm for the time being. Down the road, he would hire help and begin utilizing the kitchen's features more, considering making some things fresh, such as frying up French fries.

"I think it's the perfect layout," she said encouragingly. "If you're happy, I'm happy."

He slipped his arms around her, drawing her in for a lingering kiss. "I thought that was my line," he said huskily, gazing deeply into her eyes. "I'm doing this for us. I want to make a success of this, Emerson, and I want you to be proud of me."

"I am proud of you. I'll always be proud of you, Ry."

"I love you," he said, kissing her again. "Let's take it for a quick test drive and then go talk numbers."

She knew what was coming because Ry had done the same thing when she'd bought her new car. Emerson had sat back and let him iron out the details with the salesman, helping her walk away with a final price below what she had anticipated paying for the SUV.

Now, the process was repeated again with the food truck's negotiations. It took a good hour to come to an agreement, with Ry insisting he should receive a better deal because he was offering cash for the food truck.

Twice, the salesman checked with his boss, returning with the general manager the second time. The three men sealed the deal, and they spoke to the bank in Lost Creek. Jay Warner assured the general manager that Ry had the necessary funds to make the full payment for the truck, and Ry would be allowed to take the truck with him in a couple of hours after he signed a ream of papers.

"We'll go grab some lunch," he told the pair. "We'll be back around three-thirty."

"Your food truck will be waiting for you, all detailed and ready to roll, including the deed, Mr. Blackwood," the manager assured them.

As they went to his truck, he said, "I hope you don't mind driving my truck back to Lost Creek for me."

"Where are you going to keep the food truck?" Emerson asked. "Is there room in the alley behind Java Junction? I know you park your personal truck there."

Ry cursed under his breath. "I hadn't even thought about that."

"It can stay at my place with the smoker," she told him. "I don't mind. Especially if I can collect any leftovers at the end of the day."

"That would be wonderful. You're wonderful." He leaned in and kissed her cheek. "Let's go down to the

River Walk," he said, helping her into the passenger seat. "It's not far from here."

She had heard of the famed River Walk running through downtown, and as they strolled alongside the river, she felt the serenity of the place.

They stopped at a Mexican food restaurant, which Ry claimed was his favorite on the river, ordering a plate of brisket nachos as an appetizer and then chicken enchiladas for their main course.

When the server asked if they wished to see the dessert menu, Emerson shook her head.

"I can't put another bite in my mouth, but everything was delicious."

They paid the check and Ry said, "We still have a little time to kill. I'd like to take you to El Mercado. We'll save the Alamo for another time when we can stay longer."

They went to the marketplace, moving leisurely by its many booths. He bought her a handmade leather purse she admired and then said they had to stop in Mi Tierra before they left.

"It's a café, but it's also a bakery. I thought you'd enjoy seeing it and sampling some of its goods."

They entered Mi Tierra, and her eyes widened at the incredibly long glass display case.

"This is a baker's paradise!" Emerson exclaimed.

"Let's get a little of a lot of different things," he suggested. "I'll text everyone and see if we can meet at Harper's tonight. I want them to see the food truck in person, and we can celebrate with baked goods."

While she went through the line, picking out everything from fruit turnovers and scones to pecan pralines, sweetbreads, and empanadas, Ry texted Harper first, asking if they could invite everyone to her house to stop by to see the food truck and chow down on things from Mi Tierra. Harper replied immediately, saying they were welcomed to come. She then she sent out a group text to everyone, inviting them to come over at five to see the food truck.

Ry responded first, telling everyone he would not only have the food truck but would be bringing boxes of sweets from Mi Tierra, which was met with enthusiasm. Dax offered to bring the coffee, and Ivy said she would be coming from Lost Creek Winery and would bring a few bottles of wine, as well.

They carried three large bags of bakery goods back to the truck and then returned to the dealership, where the food truck awaited them.

"I'm going to drive straight to Harper and Braden's," Ry said. "I'll have to go a little more slowly than you. I'll meet you there."

"I am truly proud of you, Ry," Emerson said. "I think you'll be very successful as a small business owner. People will line up to eat your barbeque."

He captured her hands in his. "I wouldn't be who I am today without you, Emerson. I want you in every tomorrow of mine."

Her heart began racing. "I feel the same, Ry," she said, feeling lightheaded.

He brought their joined hands up, kissing her knuckles tenderly. "I want to make it official. I hope you're ready to hear this and give me an answer. I want to marry you, Emerson Frost. I want us to spend forever together. Will you marry me?"

Joy rippled through her. She had never been happier than in this moment.

"Yes!" she exclaimed. "Yes, a thousand times."

Ry embraced her, giving her a deep, beautiful kiss.

"Then not only will we be showing off our food truck, we'll also share with the gang that we're engaged. If that's okay with you."

"It's more than okay," she assured him. "I want to shout it from every rooftop."

"Maybe you could settle for standing in the middle of the town square and hollering the news from the gazebo," he teased.

Laughing, he kissed her again.

Emerson couldn't believe she had found someone she loved. Someone who loved her in return. That lost, lonely foster kid was now a business owner and soon-to-be wife.

She knew life would get better every single day with Ry Blackwood as her husband.

23

*E*merson finished decorating the groom's cake for tomorrow night's wedding. She had completed the wedding cake earlier, a dark, dramatic cake with a flora-painted tier, accented with several beautiful white sugar blossoms. She'd texted a picture to the bride, who had immediately replied, immensely pleased with Emerson's work. The bride said that her grandparents sixtieth wedding anniversary was coming up in a few months, and she would be booking the event center for a party honoring them. She told Emerson to be thinking of cake ideas and asked if they could meet once she returned from her honeymoon in Turks and Caicos.

Looking at her calendar, Emerson texted a few available dates, and they settled on a day and time to meet. The bride thanked her again for her creativity, which made Emerson smile. This was what baking cakes for weddings was all about. Making the bride and groom's dreams come true, and she was happy to be a small part of that special day.

Her own special day with Ry would take place the last week in September. They would marry on a Wednesday, with Braden and Finley providing the meal and Rhiannon baking the wedding and groom's cakes. It would be a small affair, with their close friends attending, along with Finley's parents, The Bake House staff, and her former principal and her husband. Ry had invited his mother but said the invitation didn't extend to his father.

Emerson was determined to see the two men settle their differences because if they didn't, she knew Ry would always regret his father not being at the wedding.

His food truck business had been in operation for three weeks, and already he had several loyal regulars. Ry offered an abbreviated menu. He admired Raising Cane's, the popular fast-casual chicken restaurant which gave customers choices of different combinations of chicken fingers or a chicken sandwich. Period. Raising Cane's did offer sides of coleslaw, fries, and Texas toast. Ry believed keeping his menu lean and mean would keep him organized in the kitchen and able to do more business than if he had a dozen or more main offerings.

The Bake House was providing all the buns for the food truck's sandwiches, baked fresh by Frank each morning. Ry offered a traditional sliced brisket or pulled pork sandwich. He had also tinkered with his family's barbeque sauce and come up with one which was tangier and a tad sweeter. He didn't want his father accusing him of stealing anything from the family business.

Two Asian-inspired items were also on the menu, both coming with a separate sauce from the brisket and pork. One was a spicy pork loin sandwich, marinated in a combination of rice wine vinegar, soy sauce, hot pepper paste, garlic, ginger, and red pepper flakes. The second was a pork kebab on a stick, marinaded in peanut butter, making it tender, juicy, and flavorful.

The food truck did a great lunch business during the week, parked every Monday, Wednesday, and Friday on the square. Tuesdays and Thursdays Ry drove it a few blocks away to a parking lot across the street from the town center, which housed the city offices, as well as the police and fire stations. He had taken it to the city ball fields on Saturdays, where youth soccer, flag football, and baseball games were held. The truck was at the park from ten until five, doing a steady business during those hours.

Tonight, Ry would take the truck to the parking lot of the first home game at the high school's football stadium. He would arrive two hours before kickoff, hoping to catch hungry fans before they entered the stadium for all the pregame activities. The concession stands inside the stadium only offered popcorn and nachos to eat, and Ry believed some parents came straight from work to see their children on the field, whether they were playing the game, in the band, cheering, or dancing on the drill team. He had high hopes for this evening.

Harper breezed in. "Status report?"

"Right on schedule," Emerson told her friend. "I just finished with Saturday's cakes. Texted the bride, and she'll be getting with you about scheduling a date at the center for her grandparents' anniversary in a few months."

Harper smiled. "I've really liked working with her. I'll be happy to have her back for a family party."

"Tonight's cakes are done. Stored in the usual place. I'll be back to get them placed."

"That's what I wanted to talk to you about, Em. I think it's a waste of your time to come to the winery and merely roll a couple of cakes out and fuss over their placement. It's something my assistants can easily do." She grinned. "And I hear a certain food truck owner will be at tonight's home game, hawking his barbeque. I know you will be assisting him."

"It would save time, but I'm used to getting the cakes ready for receptions."

"You said it yourself. Both Friday and Saturday night are taken care of. You know I have trustworthy employees. They'll handle it for you."

Emerson hugged Harper. "It really would help. We just don't know what the turnout will be like tonight. I want to be there to pitch in."

"Maybe we should've done another practice session," Harper joked. "We could've gotten in line again and again and seen how fast Ry could get food out."

They had spent a Wednesday dinner doing that very thing after Ry had bought the truck so that he could practice filling orders.

"He's got things down, but I do want to be there backing him up."

"Well, I know of a few customers who'll be there.

Braden and Holden are going to the game together, and Ana told me she and Wolf are also bringing the kids. They've never been to a high school game before, and she thinks Bear will enjoy the game and Eva all the dancing and cheering. They'll all stop by for sandwiches when they get there."

"I'll let Ry know," she said. "I guess I'm off then."

She removed her apron and hung it on a peg in her office off the kitchen. As she went to her car, she thought about Tucker Young. Ever since Ry had shared how he wanted to find his cousin, Emerson had been scouring the Internet. Unfortunately, Tucker had no social media accounts. She did find a Wikipedia article about him and several mentions of him on country music websites. Tucker had been a songwriter before his accident and had contributed songs to a few big-name country artists, though most of his songs had been bought by lesser-known acts.

It had been hard to read the articles about the car crash which severely injured him and took the life of his wife Josie, who was six months pregnant. Efforts had been made to save the baby's life, but those had failed. Since Tucker wasn't a celebrity, what had happened to him after the car crash had not been reported on, and she had hit a dead end trying to locate where he might now be.

As she reached her car, a sudden thought occurred to her. She had spent all her time searching for Tucker, but what if Josie Young had been active on social media? If she had, maybe Emerson could track Tucker down from something Josie had posted or at least allow her to get in touch with someone from Josie's family or a close friend if those accounts hadn't been shut down.

Emerson slid behind the wheel, tapping quickly on her phone.

"Yes!" she said, hitting pay dirt.

After digging a little deeper, she discovered Josie Young still had a Facebook and Instagram account online. She scrolled through Facebook first, seeing the last post was the day before the car accident. The couple had looked so happy and in love. Josie hadn't posted to Facebook often, though. On Instagram, however, she saw a plethora of pictures of vacations the two had taken together. Ones of special meals they'd shared. And a golden retriever who liked to photobomb.

Excitedly, she sent a DM via Instagram, hoping Tucker might still come to this account and would eventually see it.

> Tucker—I'm Emerson Frost, your cousin, Ry's, fiancée. Ry is stateside again and desperate to connect with you. He's already lost Todd Hart. Don't let him lose you, too.

Praying for a good outcome, she sent the message.

It was the day before her wedding, and Emerson had decided to take the bull by the horns.

Time to have it out with Shy Blackwood today.

She smiled at the bride sitting across from her, thanking her for coming in to discuss the designs for the wedding and groom's cakes. They set a time next week for her to return with her groom in order to sample the selections and make their choices.

This was the only appointment Emerson had today. She had nothing to do for the wedding since Harper and all her friends had everything under control. Braden and Finley had taken over preparing the meal for the guests. Dax had the music ready, asking Ry and her what some of their favorite songs were, saying to leave the rest to him. Ivy, freshly home from her triumphant art exhibit in New

York, was seeing to the flowers. Ana and Finley had taken her dress shopping, and Emerson had purchased a tea-length cream-colored dress that she hoped she would be able to wear in the future.

She left the winery and drove back into Lost Creek, heading to where Ry's food truck was located today. A longer than usual line surprised her, and she thought maybe it was because customers knew he wouldn't be open tomorrow for lunch since it was his wedding day. Though the ceremony wasn't starting until five o'clock, Emerson had told Ry he better not be anywhere near smoked meats for the entire day because she wanted her groom smelling like anything but barbeque.

They would take a delayed honeymoon next week to the Texas coast, where the Gulf of Mexico's water was still warm and the beaches would be fairly empty since school was already in session. It would be a long weekend, Thursday through Sunday, since Ry had no catering obligations on his calendar. Rhiannon had agreed to bake the cakes for Emerson's weddings that weekend.

For now, *Operation Heal the Rift* was about to commence.

Joining the line, she chatted with Cyndi Johnson, who was a realtor in town, and Jean Bradley, who owned a local B&B where Holden had stayed when he came to Lost Creek.

Emerson finally reached the front of the line, receiving a warm smile from her handsome fiancé.

"And what might I get you, beautiful?" Ry asked. "I

should've told you that you can always cut to the front of the line."

"Maybe once I'm Mrs. Ry Blackwood, I'll flex a little muscle and do just that. In the meantime, I thought I would take lunch to The Bake House staff."

He wouldn't be suspicious because she'd done this before. Emerson gave her order to Ry.

"Coming right up."

Quickly, he put the order together, grinning at her. "No charge for the bride-to-be."

"I'll see you later then," she said breezily, flashing him a smile.

Returning to her car, Emerson drove straight to Blackwood BBQ. Inside, she went to Jose, who manned the cashier stand.

"I need to speak with Shy. Where is he?"

"In his office, Miss Emerson," the young man told her, eyeing her with curiosity.

"Thank you," she said, glad she would be able to catch Ry's father away from others.

She went down the hall, turning right to where the owner's office was located. The door was open, and she knocked on it.

"We need to talk," she said.

Shy looked up, pulling off his readers, letting them dangle in his fingers.

"I have no quarrel with you, Emerson. I don't see how we have anything to talk about, though."

Boldly, she stepped into his office and closed the door.

"We most certainly have something to discuss, Shy Black-wood. Mainly about what a jerk you're being."

The older man's eyebrows shot up. He glared at her, all previous signs of friendliness gone.

Before he could speak, she marched to the desk and said, "No, you don't get to say anything. I'm the one here doing the talking— and you're going to listen."

She tempered her tone. "Ry is your only child, Shy. He's worshipped the ground you trod upon ever since he could walk. He misses you terribly."

His jaw set stubbornly. "That boy knows where I am. If he wants to come and apologize, he can do so."

"You're a stubborn old goat, Shy," Emerson chastised. "You need to get past it. You may agree to disagree when it comes to barbeque, but you have to make amends and restore your relationship. Do you really think kicking your son out of your family, simply because he added a new dimension to Blackwood BBQ, was the smart thing to do? This isn't about who's right or wrong." She paused. "This is about family."

"The old ways are the best ways," Shy said doggedly. "Ry's tried to change that."

"Ry is still smoking traditional barbeque," Emerson pointed out. "He's also bringing a new aspect to it. One you are too pigheaded to even sample."

Going out on a limb now, because she didn't know if it were true or not, she asked, "How many people have come into Blackwood BBQ and wanted one of Ry's new creations?"

Shy's face grew red. "Some," he admitted grudgingly.

Emerson nodded knowingly. "I'll bet it's been more than some. Ry learned so much during his army days as a cook in South Korea. He visited several countries, observing their traditions and cuisine. He thoughtfully incorporated those into Texas barbeque. He was never trying to throw out your menu, Shy. That's Blackwood history, and Ry has a great respect for it. Your family's barbeque is legendary in the Hill Country. What Ry was trying to do, though, was bring a new layer to what already existed.

She took a deep breath and continued. "There are always going to be people who want their barbeque the tried-and-true way. But in our culture today, especially here in Texas, we're seeing a blending of different cuisines. We have more immigrants in our country than ever before. People want to try new, different things. You've cut off your nose to spite your face. You've lost contact with a beloved son over a very small issue."

When he didn't respond, she added, "It's time to reconnect with your son, Shy. Restore your relationship. Don't think about who's right or wrong— because that's not important. And you need to do this now, before you drift even further apart. Not coming to our wedding tomorrow is simply ridiculous. I'm telling you, hardheadedness is not a reason to stay away. I'm here to ask you to be the man Ry believes you to be, Shy. Offer one another an olive branch. "

Emerson held up the sack she had brought. "I've come

bearing gifts," she announced. "I want you to taste Ry's food and see what he's doing."

When he looked startled, she wasn't above begging. "Please. As a favor to me. After all, I'm an orphan. My dad died in prison on a murder charge. My mom gave up her parental rights and placed me in foster care. She died from a drug overdose. I have no family, Shy. I was hoping by marrying Ry, I would finally belong to one."

She saw Shy considering her request and held her breath.

"All right."

"Thank you," she said sincerely.

She took out the plates Ry had slipped into the bag for her and then placed a brisket sandwich and a container of sauce on it.

"Try this first," she said.

He opened the foil wrapping and lifted the bun, studying the meat inside the sandwich before pouring sauce over it. He replaced the bun and took a bite, chewing thoughtfully. After swallowing, he dipped his finger into the container, tasting the barbeque sauce again.

"The brisket is exactly how I taught him to make it," he conceded. "The sauce is new, though."

"He tinkered with the family recipe," she admitted. "Ry didn't want you to accuse him of stealing it."

Next, she had Shy try the pulled pork. Again, he nodded, proclaiming it to be top-notch quality.

"I have two of the Asian-influenced items I want you to try now. *With* an open mind," she emphasized.

Emerson watched his face carefully as he sampled both the sandwich and kebab. Shy wiped his mouth with a napkin, and their gazes met.

"Pretty damn good."

"It's terrific," she agreed. "So many of the new dishes Ry has created have become a hit. As I said, Shy, he hasn't abandoned his roots. He still knows how to smoke a flavorful meat. He's simply adding to his repertoire. I'm doing the same with my bakery. The Bake House will always offer the items people adore, those tried-and-true sweets, but as I learn new techniques and grow as a baker, I'll incorporate different pies and cookies or ways to decorate my cakes. The brides I bake cakes for will always have the chance to go with a very traditional wedding cake. But as I investigate new methods and stretch creatively, I'm happy to offer new and exciting choices for those who are a little more adventurous or want something a bit more specialized."

She gazed at him steadily. "Ry doesn't want to compete with you. He loves you. He came home, wanting to be a part of Blackwood BBQ. To bring his experiences from his military days and seeing the world to this little part of the Texas Hill Country. You rejected him outright, without tasting a bite of what he'd smoked. Be the man Ry believes you are, Shy. Heal the breach between the two of you."

Fat tears began to run down his face, and Shy pushed to his feet, coming to Emerson and wrapping her in a tight bear hug.

"Thank you," he whispered. "I've been a total moron about this disagreement."

She looked him in the eye. "Then you'll come to the wedding?" she asked hopefully.

"Hell, honey. I might even dance with my wife."

They laughed and hugged again, relief pouring through her.

Then an idea hit her. "Shy? Could I ask a favor of you?"

"You bet. What can I do for you, Emerson?"

"It would mean a lot to me— and Ry —if you agreed to walk me down the aisle."

RY HAD GOTTEN DRESSED FOR THE WEDDING AT HIS apartment, the one he would now be giving up. He was moving in with Emerson at her rental house. He hoped one day they would be able to buy a house of their own. For now, though, he needed to get on his feet financially before they could consider that.

Business was good. The lunch trade proved steady, and he'd built a loyal clientele, repeat customers coming more than once a week. Because of that, he kept the brisket and pulled pork sandwiches as a constant, while changing the fusion dishes every week. It kept the menu fresh for those willing to try new foods, but it also satisfied the regulars who showed up and expected good old Texas barbeque. He'd even added his grandmother's banana pudding to the catering truck's offerings. It was the only dessert offered, very simple to make, and he served it in a small cup with a plastic spoon. Customers couldn't seem to get enough of it.

He was also catering his fair share of weddings at Lost Creek Vineyards. While he hated that it was costing Blackwood BBQ business, Harper had told Ry it couldn't be helped. Brides were willing to step outside the box and excited to have their guests try a new spin on a traditional Texas favorite. Still, he knew his dad must be hurt.

Dax entered the groom's room, smiling at him. "Any nerves, Ry?"

"None," he confirmed. "Marrying Emerson is exactly what I am meant to do."

"I put together the songs you requested and added some fun dance numbers. We can put the mix on after we eat. That way, I can dance the night away with my wife."

Ivy was now starting to show, and Ry couldn't help but think what great parents she and Dax would be.

Braden joined them. "Finley and I have the food under control," he said. "Everything's done and in warming trays. I hope you'll like what we made."

Ry laughed. "The fact that I'm not having to cater my own wedding reception is a true gift, Braden. I can't thank you and Finley enough for handling that for us."

"We're glad to do so. Finley even has Holden acting as our sous chef."

"Maybe if he keeps learning more about how to cook, we should work him into the Wednesday night rotation," Dax suggested. "He keeps telling me he's nailed omelets. If he can conquer pancakes or biscuits, we could do a breakfast supper."

Harper's belly— and then Harper —appeared in the doorway. "It's almost time," she told them. "Ry, you need to come to the front."

"Yes, ma'am," he said, saluting and then following her to the large, open space.

He and Dax, who was serving as his best man, moved toward the glass wall where Judge Grady, who was tonight's officiant stood. Ry greeted the judge and then gazed out over the vineyards, thinking about what a beautiful venue this was for a wedding. Usually, he was stuck in the kitchen, getting plates of food ready to come out, and he'd never really had an opportunity to appreciate the beauty of the setting.

Glancing across the small crowd gathered, he felt the lump forming in his throat. In a short time, he had made life-long friends in Lost Creek, a place he knew he would live for the remainder of his life. He couldn't ask for a better group of friends, which had become family to him.

Instrumental music began playing, and he watched as Holden escorted Ry's mom down the aisle, seating her on the front row. Alone. His chest grew tight, wishing his dad had come today. He began second-guessing himself, thinking he should've reached out. Gone to see his father. If he had, though, it probably would have resulted in a bitter fight, and the gulf between them would have grown even wider. He didn't need that kind of toxicity in his life.

Ry cleared his thoughts, trying to calm himself, as his watched Finley breeze down the aisle. As Emerson's best friend, Finley was acting as maid of honor.

She smiled at him and then winked saucily as she took her spot.

Then the music changed. He eagerly awaited his first glimpse of his bride. She appeared —and Ry's heart stopped.

She came down the aisle on Shy Blackwood's arm.

His throat grew thick with emotion. Ry couldn't look at his dad. Instead, his gaze connected with Emerson, who beamed at him. Then he worked up his courage and glanced his father's way, seeing tears glimmering in Shy's eyes, matching his own.

They reached the front, and Judge Grady asked, "Who gives this woman in marriage?"

Solemnly, his dad said, "Emerson doesn't need to be given to anyone. She's a determined woman who stands on her own two feet. I'm happy, though, to welcome her into the Blackwood family— and hand her off to my son."

Shy brushed a kissed against Emerson's cheek.

Ry moved to his dad, enveloping him, whispering into his ear. "Thank you. I love you, Dad."

His father smiled through his tears. "I love you, son. I'm so proud of you. I'm sorry I've been a stubborn old goat." He glanced to Emerson. "At least that's what the bride called me."

He started laughing. "She did?"

"Emerson is a very smart woman, Ry. You've definitely chosen the right person to marry. Now, go do it."

He hugged his dad again before turning to his bride.

Taking her hands in his, he said, "Thank you. You've done the impossible."

"Shy needed to be here. For you—and for him."

They turned back to Judge Grady, who grinned at them and asked, "Are we ready to have a wedding now?"

"Yes, sir," Ry said.

The weight which had been pressing upon him floated away. He glanced over his shoulder, seeing his parents sitting together. His mom and dad held hands. They looked at him, their eyes shining with love.

He looked back at the judge, who began with, "Dearly beloved, we are gathered here today to join this man and this woman in holy matrimony."

As Ry listed to the words which would bind him to Emerson forever, he knew their love would stand the test of time.

Twenty minutes later, they swept down the aisle together, now united as man and wife, their guests cheering for them. The Italian feast Braden and Finley had prepared was delicious. Rhiannon's cakes were spot on. Everyone danced for several hours.

And happiness shone on his bride's face.

When an Ed Sheeran ballad came on, Ry pulled Emerson close, whispering in her ear, "Are you ready to leave after this song?"

She smiled. "If you're telling me you're itching to start the wedding night, I'll tell you I was ready to leave an hour ago."

"Then let's go." He grabbed her hand and raised it. "Bye, everyone! Thanks for everything! Goodnight!"

Before anyone could stop them, Ry had pushed open the doors, tugging his new wife along with him. They laughed the entire way to his truck. When they reached it, he gave her a slow, deep kiss.

"I love you, Mrs. Blackwood," he said huskily.

"I love you ten times more, Mr. Blackwood," she teased, pulling him down for another kiss.

They finally got into the truck and drove the short way home. Ry carried his bride over the threshold.

"I can't believe we're finally married," Emerson said.

A cell chimed. He saw her phone sitting on the counter and said, "Don't look at it."

She wriggled from his arms. "It might be important."

He caught her wrist, bringing her back to him, kissing her. The minute he broke the kiss, she skittered away, claiming her phone. Ry watched her face as she read the text, not able to discern the emotions which flitted across her face.

Bringing the phone to him, Emerson handed it over. "Read this."

Ry frowned, glancing at the screen.

> It's Tucker Young. I got your message. I'm ready to talk to Ry. Have him call me at this number. 555-234-5858

Stunned, he met her gaze.

"I wasn't sure if Tucker would get my message, much less respond," Emerson said. "I didn't want to raise your hopes in case he didn't reply."

"You are a miracle worker, Emerson Blackwood," Ry proclaimed. He hesitated. "Do you think we can call him now?"

"I'm glad you want to," she responded. "Let's FaceTime him."

They settled on the sofa, and he dialed the number, his hand shaking. Suddenly, Tucker's face was on the screen.

"Hey, Ry," his cousin said.

Ry swallowed, full of emotion, and managed to respond. "Hey, Tuck. I just got married tonight. I want you to meet my wife. This is Emerson."

EPILOGUE

THREE YEARS LATER...

*E*merson gave Hayley and Mark their mini-pancakes spread with peanut butter, while Ry sliced bananas and strawberries for the twins. She went to Michael's highchair and cooed to the seven-month-old, "Who's going to get an official mommy and daddy today?"

"Michael!" Hayley exclaimed.

Her gaze met her husband's, and Ry beamed at her. Emerson knew she was the luckiest woman in the world. They had been married a little over three years, and their twins had been the light of their lives, healthy and happy. Ry had been insistent, though, that they follow through with Emerson's dream of adopting children, so they had gone through a nineteen-hour program with the National Training and Development Curriculum as part of their required foster parent training. The program gave them specialized knowledge on how to care for children in the child welfare system, including discipline and behavior intervention, the effects of abuse and neglect, and how trauma can affect children.

Once they'd earned their certification in foster care, they were expecting an older child to be placed with them, especially since those children were harder to find homes for and they were willing to take on such a child. Instead, however, a little over seven months ago, Michael had come into their lives. His father had been a firefighter killed in the line of duty. His mother had gone into labor at her husband's funeral. She was rushed to the hospital, where she had given birth to her first child after seventeen hours. Unfortunately, she had suffered an aneurysm and died less than twenty-four hours after Michael was born.

Donna Winters, the Department of Family Protective Services case worker they had been assigned to, had contacted them immediately. Little Michael had no relatives to take him and would leave the hospital and be immediately placed into foster care. Donna, knowing the Blackwoods were eager to adopt a child they fostered, suggested them to her supervisor.

And so, Michael had come home, straight into their loving arms.

The last several months had been hectic, with Emerson and Ry balancing their jobs, two toddlers, and a newborn —but Emerson wouldn't have had it any other way.

Michael had turned out to be an easy baby, much more so than Mark or Hayley. He ate and napped well, and he was hitting all his milestones on time. The twins adored their new little brother and were constantly patting him on the head or kissing him, offering the baby one of their toys. Emerson was glad she had detected no jealousy on their part toward the infant.

Michael had been given a bottle upon awakening. Now, she fed the baby a pouch of zucchini and apple, along with a bowl of oatmeal. Michael had begun on solid foods a month ago, and the only thing he had rejected so far was carrots.

Looking to Ry, Emerson asked, "Are you on twin or baby duty now?"

"Definitely baby," he said, wetting a washcloth and wiping the twins' mouths and hands. "Hayley and Mark are becoming too particular when they pick out their outfits for the day. You're welcome to deal with that drama."

The twins had turned two a few days ago, and so far, they showed no signs of being terrible. Just opinionated. They were vocal when it came to what they ate and wore, especially what color of shoes they donned. Mark insisted on wearing mostly Superman or Iron Man shirts, while Hayley bounced between characters from *Frozen* and *Encanto*.

"All right, you two. Let's get dressed so we can go see the judge," she said.

She got them dressed, their shoes on, and their hair brushed, even managing to place a bow in Hayley's hair. By that time, Ry appeared with Michael in his arms. The baby wore a new outfit for this special day, blue pants, a white shirt, suspenders, and a bow tie.

Ry glanced at his watch. "I can't believe we've done this

in record time. We might actually make it to the court-house early."

They went to Emerson's SUV, which held three car seats. She thought if they had more kids, it would mean buying a bigger car, but she would be happy to do so. She had taken to motherhood, and Ry was the perfect partner. He was a man who changed diapers, bathed kids, and was always up for playing or reading to them. She wouldn't want to be on this journey with anyone but Ry Blackwood.

The kids were buckled into their car seats, minus pacifiers for the twins. She was trying to wean them away from sucking one, already concerned about future visits to the orthodontist. Michael never seemed to want a paci. He was, however, drooling like a waterfall since he was teething.

They arrived at the courthouse, and Emerson had Ry raised the tailgate. Each kid received a diaper change before they went inside, with Hayley asking if they could start using their potty when they got home. They had bought a potty chair for each twin, and now that they were two, Emerson was ready to begin that process. Her friends had warned her that Hayley would probably take to toilet training more quickly than Mark, so she and Ry were prepared. They had already shopped and stocked up on pull-ups and would be transitioning into those after today's court date. Harper had suggested they also buy underwear with Disney characters or superheroes on them. She had found that Mark was less like to soil his underwear if they bore Superman or Mickey Mouse's picture on them.

Entering the courthouse, they found their designated courtroom, where Dax and Ivy waited outside with Kristina. The two-and-a-half-year-old saw the twins and came running toward the Blackwoods, telling everyone hi.

"Are you ready for the big day?" Dax asked.

"I know people say it's just a piece of paper, but we're really eager to make Michael an official Blackwood," Ry replied.

"He's felt like ours from the day we brought him home," Emerson said. "We've always had the fear, however, of Michael being taken from us. Having the court declare Michael ours will bring peace of mind." She paused. "How are you feeling, Ivy?"

Her friend smiled. "I think yesterday was the turning point as far as morning sickness goes. I felt really good not having to throw up multiple times. Today has been the same. I've kept everything down this morning." She took Emerson's hand. "We just found out that we're having a boy. Kristina is going to be a big sister."

"That's wonderful news," she said, and Ry also congratulated the couple.

Then Mark let out a huge squeal and took off running. Emerson saw Shy and Shelly heading toward them. Hayley yelled, "Grammy!" and toddled after her brother.

Shy caught both of them, swinging them around, and then setting them on their feet. The twins ran back to their parents as Shy and Shelly joined them.

Shelly slipped an arm about Emerson. "I'm so happy

for you and Ry. Michael is already loved by so many. Shy and I are thrilled to be grandparents to three children now."

She appreciated that Shelly wouldn't make a distinction between the twins and Michael.

Donna Winters appeared and said, "It's time to go in." She touched her fingers to Michael's cheek. "You, little one, are so lucky. You're getting the best parents in the world."

The social worker escorted them into the courtroom, where Randy Peterson, their attorney sat at a table. Peterson had been recommended by Donna, and Emerson had liked the lawyer from the moment they had met. She and Ry took a seat at the table, with Emerson holding Michael and the twins perching on Ry's knees.

"Call the next case," Judge Jackson said to her clerk.

Donna presented the court with the completed adoptive placement paperwork. Michael had been required to live with them for six months before Child Protective Services would allow for the adoption to become permanent. Their attorney presented the Petition to Adopt document to the clerk, who passed it to Judge Jackson. She read over it, and Emerson's heart pounded in anticipation.

"Everything looks to be in order," the judge said. She smiled at them. "I see that you already have children."

"Yes, Your Honor," Emerson said. "I was in foster care for many years, though, and my husband and I wanted to add Michael to our family permanently."

Ry spoke up. "We'd like to foster again in the future,

Your Honor. Hopefully, we'll be back in your courtroom and adopt another child who comes our way."

Judge Jackson nodded. "The State of Texas grants Ryland and Emerson Blackwood's request to adopt the infant Michael, and this adoption is irrevocable. Congratulations, Mr. and Mrs. Blackwood. You officially have another son."

Without being prompted, both twins raised their hands and shouted, "Yay!" causing those in the courtroom to chuckle.

Ry shook hands with their attorney, and they both thanked Donna for the role she had played in the fostering and adoption process.

They left the courtroom, the Tennysons and grandparents accompanying them.

"Congratulations, Mom and Dad. Mark, Hayley, and Michael are lucky to have you as parents."

"Will you look to adopt again anytime soon?" Ivy asked.

Ry laughed, holding his new son close to his chest. "I think we have our hands full for the next couple of years. Once we get everyone out of diapers— and maybe the twins in kindergarten —we'll think about fostering again and see where that leads us."

The older children began skipping, each holding one of their grandparents' hands. Emerson slipped her hand through the crook of Ry's arm.

"I couldn't ask for a better man," she told him. "You are a wonderful husband and father, Ry Blackwood."

"I had no idea when I came home to Lost Creek that I

would find the love of my life, Emerson. I give thanks every day for you— and our growing family."

They stopped at the top of the courthouse steps, Ry giving her a tender kiss. Then they both kissed Michael's head, and Emerson said, "Welcome to the Blackwood family, my sweet love."

PREVIEW: WHISPERED MELODIES

Read on for a preview of Whispered Melodies, book 5 in the Lost Creek, Texas Hill Country series.

PROLOGUE

AUSTIN—TWO YEARS AGO…

Tucker Young pulled his wife into his arms and gave her a tender kiss. Then he rested his hand against her protruding belly. Josie was over six months along now, and they would be having a boy right around Christmastime. He only wished his dad could be here to meet the baby and get to know his first grandchild.

But Travis Young had passed away suddenly two months ago from a heart attack. At least his dad had known they were having a boy. The couple hadn't settled on a name at that time, but once Tucker lost his dad, Josie had suggested they name the boy Travis after his father. The suggestion had touched him, and he hoped that a part of his dad would live on in this baby.

"Are you sure you should stay for the show?" he asked. "There'll be a few people smoking I don't like you to be around that. It's bad for the baby."

Josie cupped his face with her hands, kissing him

lightly. "If someone is smoking nearby, I'll simply get up and move, Tucker. I want to be here tonight for you. You're going to be playing your own songs for this crowd. I want to support you in every way I can. Once the baby comes, I won't be able to come out and see your shows."

Tucker was a songwriter. In fact, that's how he had met Josie. Her older brother had gained a small but loyal following in the country music world, but he hadn't had a breakout song.

Until Tucker wrote him one.

He had contributed three songs to Matt's second album, and all three had charted. Two had cracked the Top Ten, while one had gone to Number One for six weeks. Tucker had been writing songs for several years for minor country acts, as well as performing every now and then in small clubs in and around Austin. Josie had encouraged him, though, to strike out on his own as a performer. Tonight, he was playing a small but popular club on the outskirts of Austin, hoping the songs he would perform would have the crowd itching to dance— or cry in their beer.

She smoothed his hair lovingly. "I know you wish Travis were here tonight. But he is here— in spirit." Josie rubbed her belly. "And this Travis is going to start moving and grooving when he hears his daddy playing up there."

He regularly sang to her belly, hoping his son would learn to recognize his dad's voice. Josie had read a lot about that and believed it would be the case. She also knew their baby would know her voice because she talked a lot each day in her job as a Pre-Kindergarten teacher in

Austin. Josie worked with ESL students and loved what she did. She would take her maternity leave after Travis' birth and then return to the classroom.

Tucker wondered whether he really wanted to make it in country music or not. At least as a performer. He had grown up around the industry. His dad had managed several music acts. Travis Young was forever on the road. A manager had to be there with his band, stroking egos, heading off trouble, and making sure all musicians and their equipment made it to the next venue in one piece. It was a life spent on the road, away from home, and Tucker wasn't certain that was what he truly wanted. Maybe he could continue his songwriting and simply play in places in and around Austin. Josie loved her job so much. He couldn't see asking her to leave it. Besides, being on the road was no life for a kid. He knew that better than most.

His mom had died when Tucker was only five years old. She had been a heavy smoker from the time she was fourteen, and it caught up to her. Gloria Young died of lung cancer at only thirty-five, looking like a shell of herself.

That was when he began traveling full-time with his dad. They were gone throughout the school year. His dad supposedly home schooled him, but that was a joke. Fortunately, Tucker was a curious kid about a lot of things. He read widely and was an ace in math. He taught himself Spanish by listening to and then conversing with many of the roadies.

A nice chunk of time, though, had been spent in Lost Creek, Texas. His mom's sister Shelly lived in the small

Hill Country town with her husband Shy. They had one boy, Ry, and his cousin was Tucker's favorite person in the world. They had been more like brothers than cousins, and he looked forward to those summer months each year. Staying in one place. Sleeping in one bed. Having meals at regular times. Just being a typical boy, not one who lived out of a suitcase and had no friends.

Thanks to his outstanding math skills, Tucker won a scholarship to the University of Texas in Austin and earned a business degree. Those four years of college had made him feel like a normal person. When he graduated, he didn't join his dad on the road again. Instead, he worked a day job at a bank and wrote songs at night. Josie was urging him to give up his loan officer job and take the plunge into music full-time because she believed in his talent. He had told her he would consider it. For now, though, he was hanging onto the job to keep his insurance until after the baby was born.

"Go find yourself a seat out front," he urged his wife. "You know I'll be singing every song for you."

"Here's a kiss for luck," she said, pulling his mouth down to hers.

Once Josie left the tiny dressing room, Tucker went over his set list again. He would only be playing seven songs. He was the warmup act for the country rock band which would follow him. The owner had told him if he liked what he heard, he might give Tucker a regular gig at the club.

A knock sounded on the door and it opened, the owner sticking his head in. "You're on."

Picking up his guitar, he moved down the narrow hallway and stood to the side of the stage while the owner introduced him.

"You may know the songs *Another Beer, Dear*" and *"I Lost My Love Today.*" Well, the guy who wrote 'em is here tonight, and he's gonna play you a few songs. Here's Tucker Young!"

He took the stage to a smattering of applause. He wished he had an entire band backing him up, but there was no money for that at this point in his fledging career. He would need to wow the audience with his voice and guitar alone.

Slipping the guitar strap over his head, he clutched the mike. "How's everyone doing tonight?" he called.

A few people answered, but most were chowing down on their burgers and sipping beers, conversing with friends or dates. He knew not to let that affect him.

His gaze connected with Josie's. She nodded encouragingly at him.

Tucker began with an upbeat song, which got the notice of the crowd. By the end of it, many of them were clapping along.

He moved into his second number, another fast song, and by the time the last note sounded, he had the crowd eating out of his hand.

"This next one's a bit slower, but I wrote it for my wife Josie. Here's to you, Honey."

The crowd continued eating, but as he sang and played, looking out over the room, Tucker saw many of them were listening to him. To his lyrics. His music. He felt the power of the connection between him and the people present at the club. Other than Josie, no one had heard this song, and he could see it moved the audience.

Tucker received resounding applause when he finished. He was flush with success now and returned to a fun song with a fast beat about a one-night stand gone wrong. The audience stayed with him for it and the remaining songs.

When he announced his last song, he was pleased to actually hear a few groans. As he finished, the applause was deafening. The sweet rush of adrenaline ran through him as he slipped off the guitar strap, waving to the crowd, saying, "Goodnight!"

The owner was standing just off-stage and gave him a pleased smile. "You're really good, Young," the older man praised. "The crowd responded well to your songs. If you're interested, I think we can talk about booking you long-term as a warmup on weekends. Come in early tomorrow night. We can talk terms then."

"Yes, sir," Tucker said enthusiastically, heading back to the small dressing room.

Josie joined him moments later, throwing her arms around him, squealing. "You were amazing!"

He gave her a deep kiss. "I couldn't have done any of this without your support. Your love and encouragement means the world to me. I love you so much."

Happiness filled her face. "I love you, too, Tucker." She paused. "I'll bet you've worked up a thirst."

"And I'm also starved," he told her. "I was so nervous, I

didn't eat much today. Now, I think I could eat a whole cow."

"Let's get you burger and beer," she said, taking his hand and leading him back to where several people slapped him on the back as he passed, telling him how good he sounded tonight.

"I'd download anything you put up," one guy told him.

They took seats in an empty booth. Tucker rested his guitar next to him. The server came by, and they ordered two cheeseburgers with grilled onions and basket of fries to share. Josie requested water, while he ordered a beer.

After the server left, his wife said, "You really should think about putting up your songs online. Think about acts which got started on social media. Ed Sheeran. Justin Bieber. Shawn Mendes. You don't need a recording contract these days, Tucker. You can make it without the suits."

He had been toying with that very idea. "We'll have to think about that. In the meantime, the owner wants me to come in early tomorrow night. He liked the crowd's response and wants to talk about me playing here regularly."

Her eyes lit up. "That's fantastic! I'm so proud of you."

He downed his beer and signaled the server for another one. He drank a third when their cheeseburgers arrived.

"Good thing you're driving us home tonight," he said.

His car hadn't started before work this morning, and he had it towed to a garage. The mechanic had told him it was a faulty alternator, and they would work on the car today. He'd gotten a message it was ready to be picked up while they were on their way to the venue tonight. He would have Josie drop him off tomorrow since it was Saturday. It was hard to get around anywhere in Texas unless you had a car.

They asked for the check, but the server told them, "The manager said it's on the house tonight."

"Thank him for us," Tucker said, leaving a generous tip for the server.

He had worked his fair share of jobs during college to supplement his scholarship. Waiting tables had been one of them. He always made sure a server was taken care of.

Going to Josie's car, she climbed behind the wheel as he got into the passenger's seat, a nice buzz making him feel a little sleepy now.

His wife said, "I'd like to hope there wouldn't be much traffic on a Friday night at ten o'clock, but it's Austin. There's always traffic."

She maneuvered them through the streets until they hit the two-lane highway leading them back into Austin and headed toward their apartment.

"The girls at school are going to throw me a baby shower next month," she said, happiness radiating from her. "They asked if you wanted to come. I told them I'd check with you to see if you could the time off."

"Just let me know the day and time. I can get someone at the bank to cover for me. My boss likes me. Hell, she likes you more than me, so I'm sure she'll give me a few hours off so I can attend."

Suddenly, glaring lights blinded them. Josie screamed

and tried to turn the wheel, but something slammed into them with such force that Tucker knew they were going to die.

The car spun and then flipped once. Twice. It came to rest upside down in a gulley beside the road.

He could hardly breath. Realized the airbag had exploded, pressing against him. Tucker tried to push it away. Somehow, he reached into his pocket and retrieved the pocketknife he always carried with him. He jammed it into the airbag, and it deflated.

"Josie!" he hollered, seeing her face buried in her own opened airbag.

Panicking, he worried about the force of the bag exploding. If it had affected the baby.

Once more, he rammed his knife, seeing the airbag deflate. Josie blinked a few times and weakly asked, "What happened?"

"Someone hit us. Hard." He ached all over, especially his leg and head. Tucker figured out they were upside down, but he couldn't think clearly enough to figure out how to right them.

Her eyes fluttered a few times a shut.

Tucker grabbed her hand. "Josie? Josie? Wake up!"

He could hear people talking outside the car, and a man appeared next to the window.

"We've called 911," the man yelled. "We'll try to get you out."

Noise surrounded him as he clutched his wife's hand, kissing her fingers, urging her to open her eyes.

Tucker must have passed out because the next thing he

knew, he was out of the car, being pushed along the ground on a stretcher.

"My wife," he croaked, trying to sit up.

An EMT nudged him back. "We've already gotten her out the vehicle, sir. Just take it easy."

The ride in the ambulance was a blur, as was everything that happened in the ER. His leg ached something terrible, and heard a doctor say it was broken. He kept asking about Josie and the baby, and one doctor assured him she was being cared for. That she'd been taken into surgery.

"Put us in a room together," he begged.

That was the last thing he recalled.

When he awoke, he was in a hospital room. Quickly, he glanced over and saw the other bed unoccupied.

Immediately, Tucker yelled at the top of his lungs. "Josie! Josie! I want Josie!"

A nurse rushed in, saying, "You need to calm yourself, Mr. Young. I know you're upset, but getting all excited isn't good for you."

"Where the hell is my wife?" he demanded, his head aching.

One of the doctors from before appeared at his bedside. One look at the man's face, and Tucker knew the worst had happened.

"No," he moaned. "No. No. No. No. No."

"I'm sorry, Mr. Young," the physician said. "We did everything we could to save your wife and the baby. The trauma from the accident was simply too much for either to survive."

"I'll kill the sumbitch who did this," he growled. "I'll kill him."

Tucker tried to climb out of the bed, but the doctor and nurse held him down.

"He did that to himself," the doctor shared. "The other driver was drunk. He's dead, Mr. Young."

Anger swelled within Tucker. He screamed then, the pain of losing his beloved Josie and little Travis more than he could take.

As they gave him an injection, he drifted off to sleep. Tucker wished he would have died with them.

Without Josie and their baby, his life was over.

Get your copy of Whispered Melodies!

LOST CREEK, TEXAS HILL COUNTRY

The Perfect Blend

Painted Melodies

Script of Love

Love in Every Bite

Whispered Melodies

SUGAR SPRINGS

Shadows of the Past

Learning to Trust Again

A Perfect Match

A Fresh Start

Recipe for Love

MAPLE COVE

Another Chance at Love

A New Beginning

Coming Home

The Lyrics of Love

Finding Home

HOLLYWOOD NAME GAME

Hollywood Heartbreaker

Hollywood Flirt

Hollywood Player

Hollywood Double

Hollywood Enigma

LAWMEN OF THE WEST

Runaway Hearts

Blind Faith

Love and the Lawman

Ballad Beauty

SAGEBRUSH BRIDES

A Game of Chance

Written in the Cards

Outlaw Muse

KNIGHTS OF REDEMPTION

A Bit of Heaven on Earth

A Knight for Kallen

SUDDENLY A DUKE

Portrait of the Duke

Music for the Duke

Polishing the Duke

Designs on the Duke

Fashioning the Duke

Love Blooms with the Duke

Training the Duke

Investigating the Duke

<u>SECOND SONS OF LONDON</u>

Educated by the Earl

Debating with the Duke

Empowered by the Earl

Made for the Marquess

Dubious about the Duke

Valued by the Viscount

Meant for the Marquess

<u>DUKES DONE WRONG</u>

Discouraging the Duke

Deflecting the Duke

Disrupting the Duke

Delighting the Duke

Destiny with a Duke

<u>DUKES OF DISTINCTION</u>

Duke of Renown

Duke of Charm

Duke of Disrepute

Duke of Arrogance

Duke of Honor

<u>SOLDIERS AND SOULMATES</u>

To Heal an Earl

To Tame a Rogue

To Trust a Duke

To Save a Love

To Win a Widow

THE ST. CLAIRS

Devoted to the Duke

Midnight with the Marquess

Embracing the Earl

Defending the Duke

Suddenly a St. Clair

STANDALONE ROMANTIC THRILLERS

Leave Yesterday Behind

Illusions of Death

ABOUT THE AUTHOR

USA Today and Amazon Top 100 bestselling author Alexa Aston lives with her husband in a Dallas suburb, where she eats her fair share of dark chocolate and plots out stories while she walks every morning. She enjoys travel, sports, and binge-watching—and never misses an episode of *Survivor*.

Alexa brings her characters to life in steamy historicals, contemporary romances, and romantic suspense novels that resonate with passion, intensity, and heart.

KEEP UP WITH ALEXA
Visit her website
Newsletter Sign-Up

MORE WAYS TO CONNECT WITH ALEXA